LIFE SENTENCE

LIFE SENTENCE

Nigel Gray

FREMANTLE ARTS CENTRE PRESS

First published 1991 by
FREMANTLE ARTS CENTRE PRESS
193 South Terrace (PO Box 320), South Fremantle
Western Australia, 6162.

Consultant Editor B. R. Coffey.
Designed by John Douglass.
Production Manager Helen Idle.

Typeset in 10/12pt Times Roman by Typestyle, East Perth and printed on
90gsm Offset by Vanguard Press, Perth, Western Australia.

National Library of Australia
Cataloguing-in-publication data

Gray, Nigel, 1941-.
  Life sentence.

  ISBN 1 86368 005 5.

  I. Title

823.914

Fremantle Arts Centre Press receives financial assistance from the Western
Australian Department for the Arts.

CONTENTS

PREFACE

A collection of my stories with the title *Life Sentence* was first published in London by Sinclair Brown in 1984. In 1986 the collection was republished in London in hardback by Macdonald and in paperback by Futura. It appears that very few copies found their way to Australia. In 1988 I migrated to Western Australia, and in 1990 became an Australian citizen. By chance my gaining of citizenship was celebrated by an offer from Fremantle Arts Centre Press to publish a new edition of *Life Sentence* which would become my first book for adults to be brought out by an Australian publisher (following hard on the heels of *Anna's Ghost*, a children's picture book illustrated by the Adelaide artist Craig Smith, from Ashton Scholastic in Sydney).

One of the problems an author has to live with is being permanently damned by the shortcomings of his or her published work. Whenever I have need to read something I wrote some years previously I am humbled by shame and overcome by the (usually impossible) desire to rewrite the offending text. I am grateful to Fremantle Arts Centre Press therefore for the opportunity they gave me to produce new versions of the stories in this collection. Two stories from the original book have been omitted, and one ('The Siren', which previously appeared in *Winter's Crimes 21,* published by Macmillan, London, in 1989) has been added. All of the stories have been revised. In some cases this comprised no more than a minor re-polishing, in others, considerable rewriting. However Australians will be pleased to know that this is a superior product to the British editions that preceded it.

The collection originally consisted of fourteen stories, and was dedicated to fourteen friends. I would like to dedicate this thirteen-story Australian edition to some of the new friends of my new country: Bob Graham; Carlisle Sheridan; Donna Rawlins; Iris Jones; Keith Sinclair; Leanne Fleming; Ray Coffey; Rick Christie; and Veronica Brady; as well as to my wife, Yasmin, and the two of my children who are now Aussies, Jo and Sam; and to the memory of Peter Bartlett — to all of these I owe a debt of gratitude for one reason or another.

Nigel Gray, Kalamunda, January 1991.

LIFE SENTENCE

LIFE SENTENCE

'Hands off cocks. On frocks!' The mate banged his fist on the side of my bunk. I heard him go into the galley and pour the tea. 'Come on!' he barked as he made his way back to the bridge. 'All out. We're hauling!'

I turned onto my back and stared at the patterns of dirt on the ceiling twelve inches in front of my nose. I was in a coffin. The sweat was wet on my body and face. My feet were pressed against the bunk end. My head was touching the thin partition separating me from the galley and the back of the oven. I was rocked and rattled against the bunk sides by the violent motion of the boat. I heard Joe get up. I climbed out, feeling with my toes for the side of Bert's bunk beneath mine, and then down on to the floor, relaxing my legs to absorb the incessant rolling.

'Is Bert up?' Joe said, trying to winkle him out with his words.

'Come on, Bert,' I said, giving his berth a thump. 'We're hauling.'

'Err,' he grunted.

'Not sleeping again, is he?' Joe said.

We sat at the table trying to sip wakefulness from our mugs of tea. Faces were pale and crumpled with fatigue, and I could feel that mine was the same. Bert wormed his way out and joined us.

I heard the skipper come out of his cabin and go up to the bridge. The scrunch of the clutch being put in for the winch gave me a sinking feeling in the pit of my stomach. We dragged ourselves to our feet and put on boots, caps, and frocks. Tim, the mate, came down and joined us. 'I hope there's more here than there was last haul,' he said.

'These waters are fished out,' Joe said.

'It's all them bloody foreigners,' Bert said. 'Dutchmen, Frogs, Russians, all sorts.'

We said the same things every haul. Every three and a half hours, day and night, day after day, as we hunted the fish. The fish got scarcer, but their price went up, and we each got six per cent of the total for the catch.

'What a job,' I said.

'And now they want us to pay to do it,' Bert said.

I stumbled out onto the deck. The wind was wickedly cold. Joe went to one of the winch wheels and I manned the other. Bert and Tim tottered to the far end of the deck, one to each bollard, and we began winching in. The doors came up and were disconnected. The warp crackled and snapped discordantly as we fed it onto the main drums. The net began to slither onto the deck. I switched the drive over to the whipping drum. Bert and Tim hooked the gilson wires onto the net and we hoisted it up, watching intently to see how big a bag there would be. Always hoping, like I was always hoping the rows were over, and the good times come at last. But it was as disappointing as usual.

The fish were emptied onto the deck and Tim re-tied the net bottom. We checked the net for damage, and then went through the process in reverse, lowering the net to the sea bed, as the boat forced its way into the first greying of the cold northern dawn. Once the nets were down, and Joe had descended into the fish room, we started gutting. Fish flap-flap-flapped around our feet. Some lay still, gasping, as though they were desperate, like addicts, for more of what was killing them. I sharpened my knife and passed the steel to Bert. The blade slid in through the gill and slit down the belly. The guts were cut out, heart, stomach, liver; I thought about people I wanted to kill. Gulls flew alongside raucously singing for their supper. Sometimes one would snatch the red guts from my hand. As I stooped for a fish a wave broke over the side slapping into my back, followed by two more in quick succession. The combined noise of engine, wind, and sea was too loud for us to be able to hear each other easily. I was grateful to be spared Bert's trivial chatter, glad enough to be isolated with my own thoughts.

I remembered a story Joe had told during an evening meal. 'The maddest bugger I ever sailed with was that Jack what's-his-name. Remember Jack?' he asked Bill, the skipper. 'Used to be a deckie with Aberdeen Jim.'

'Used to sail with my old man, an' all,' Tim put in.

'Yeah. That's him. Well, he got the DTs. Suddenly went berserk. We was gutting, and he starts screaming, *My little girl's out there! I want to go to her!* Then he goes haring up the deck, over the stern and into the sea.'

'He always was a mad sod,' Tim said.

'Yeah. Always was a mad sod. It was dark. He was lucky we found him.'

'Should've left the bugger there.'

'Nearly had to. Couldn't get him aboard. In the end we had to drag the cunt out by the hair. But as soon as we let go of him he's running up the deck again and trying to jump back in.'

'Should've let him go.'

'Yeah. In the end we had to lock him in the shower and lash the door. We turned back and put in. The ambulance men got him out. But you should've seen the shower. Shit everywhere.'

I kept looking south into the darkness over the stern. *My little girl's out there,* I was thinking. *I want to go to her.* I fantasised about dropping the fish and the knife and running off the end of the deck into the sea. I wondered how easy it would be to drown; whether my survival instinct would force me to struggle to stay afloat. I wondered what death under that cold dark swell would be like.

With the last fish gutted, I hosed the offal from the deck and the blood from the front of my frock. I went back down to the cabin, took off my cap, frock, and boots and climbed into the hothouse of my bunk. 'Might as well get in the bloody oven as try to sleep here,' I said.

'Turning in again, Mike?' Bert said.

'There's Joe shivering over the ice room, and me roasting up here. Whoever designed these bloody crates should be forced to sail in one for a few years.'

'Thought you was on watch.'

'Joe is.'

'What do you think to this business of making us pay a percentage of

3

the fuel then, Mike?'

'Rubbish!' Joe called from the galley.

'Making yourself a brew then, Joe?' Bert said.

'It's no different to asking us to take a smaller percentage,' I said. 'Only they know we wouldn't wear that. The only reason I do this fucking job is for the money, and if they cut the money they can find some other bastard to do it.'

'That's right,' Joe grumbled as he passed. 'We earn every bloody penny.'

'All the other crews agreed to it,' Bert said.

'If the other crews agreed to it, Bert, I'll kiss your arse.'

'This I must see,' Joe said, turning back towards us.

'That's what they told us,' Bert said.

'They've probably told the others *we* agreed to it,' I said. 'That's the trouble with this bloody job. We can never all get together.'

'It's like asking us to pay to come to work,' Bert said. 'It's bad enough fourteen days out and only two home, without having to pay to do it.'

I turned on my side with my face to the wall and opened a paperback novel to stop him from talking to me.

'Having a bit of a read?' he said.

Bill came in at that point. 'Anybody got any good books?' he asked. 'I can't get interested in this.'

'What is it?' Bert wanted to know.

'The Six Fingered Stud'.

'What's a six fingered stud?'

'It's this big black bastard with six fingers on one hand.'

'What does he use his sixth finger for?' I mumbled.

'It's the same bloody thing on every page,' he said, ignoring me. 'He just gets another tart in the sack and shafts her. It's boring as hell.'

'Well, here's a good one,' Bert said, rummaging in his locker. 'It's a crime story. About a rapist who hates himself so much for what he does, he always washes hisself in the toilet.'

'That'll save you the bother of reading that one, Bill,' I said, 'now Bert's told you the story.'

'I'll give it a try,' Bill said.

'And he won't sleep in a bed,' Bert went on. 'He sleeps on the floor to punish hisself.'

'If he wants to punish himself,' I said, 'he wants to get a job like this.'

I stared at the pattern of the text of my book for a while. I was remembering the trip before last.

We docked at one-thirty in the desolation of early morning. I'd been drinking heavily on the boat. I'd washed my hands and face, and shaved in cold water just before we got in, to try to freshen up. The pubs were already closed so the taxi got me home before two o'clock. Maureen hadn't got up. The house was in darkness. I should have had a bath, but alcohol and exhaustion made it seem unnecessary. I crept into the bedroom as quietly as I could so as not to disturb the kids.

'That you?' she grunted.

'Yeah.' I got undressed for the first time in fourteen days, aware of the stale sourness of my body, and slid in beside her.

'You're cold,' she complained, and she shifted away. 'And you smell like a piggery.'

'There was a time when you ran a bath ready for me.' I pressed up against her, my fortnight's deprivation engorging me.

'And your breath stinks. You've been on the bottle again.'

'Can,' I said.

'What?'

'Can. Beer comes in cans now.' I pulled her on to her back and tried to kiss her but she kept twisting her face away.

'No,' she kept saying. 'I don't want to.'

'For God's sake, Maureen, I've been away for two sodding weeks.'

'You're drunk,' she hissed. 'You're drunk. Get off me.' She tried to push me away and her elbow caught my nose. Sudden pain surged into anger and I hit her across the face.

'Bitch!' I said. 'Fucking bitch!' She stopped struggling then. Just lay rigid and unresponding as I pounded on top of her. Her tears were wetting my face. I could hear Mathew crying in the next room. I couldn't come. My erection was going soft. I pulled out of her and turned away and fell asleep.

She was up before I woke in the morning. Mathew, the baby, and Siddy, my little girl, came and played on the bed. Maureen brought my breakfast up and a pile of *Daily Mirror*s from the previous couple of weeks. 'The water's hot,' was all she said. Then she plucked Mathew from my stomach, like lifting a heavy, ripe water melon. 'Come on, you two,' she said, taking hold of Siddy's hand. 'Let's get you dressed.'

Later I got up to the luxury of a hot bath and clean clothes. Maureen and the kids were out. Midday I went down the office. The others were already there. I collected my money in cash, less tax and the allowance that was paid directly to Maureen. The thick wad of notes felt good in the tight pocket of my jeans.

We straggled in ones and twos down to the *Wagon and Horses*. 'I'm going to take it easy today,' I said. 'I got in trouble last night.'

'Drink up,' Joe said. 'I'll come home with you. I'll tell her it was my fault.'

'You just want to give her a belt in the ear,' Bert said, 'like I do mine. That'll shut her up.'

'I'll just stay till one o'clock. If I'm late I'll get my dinner on my head again.'

Most of the men who were home used the *Wagon* at lunchtime. Ratty off the *Resourceful* was there. He asked me and Joe if we'd help him get his bobbins off the boat. 'I've got a crane coming down the dock to lift them. The driver'll come in here and give us a call when he's ready,' he said.

The main topics of conversation in the early drinking hours were always the size and nature of the catch, the selling price, and which boat had found what, and where. That day, there was outrage too, about the new move to make us pay part of the fuel bill. 'It's like asking us to pay to go to work,' Bert kept saying.

The crane driver failed to show up. 'He'll be here in a minute,' Ratty said whenever I mentioned it. The rounds grew bigger as more men joined us, and we started mingling shorts with the lager.

'I'm going to be late,' I said.

'Never mind,' Joe said. 'You're stuck on that bleeding floating prison most of your life. Enjoy yourself while you can.'

Old Peter came in wearing a jersey in purple and white horizontal stripes. Everybody cheered. 'You look like a bee with multiple skellyrosis,' Joe shouted.

'What's that?' said Ratty. 'A Mary Cunt latest fashion?'

'Got it from Queen's Park Rangers,' Old Peter said.

'You'd never make a footballer — you haven't got the haircut.'

'Is that what the well-dressed man-about-town's wearing this season?'

'I'm setting a trend. You'll all be wearing these in a couple of months.'

'If I wore one of those the missus wouldn't let me in the house.'

'From what I've heard your missus won't let you in the house anyway.'

'What you all done up for anyway, Peter — you got a date?'

'I'm not telling you if I have.'

'He'll have a bit of crumpet on the end of his toasting fork before the night's out — they won't be able to resist him in that.'

'Rubbish! That's his burglar's outfit. He's just been doing a job.'

'This round's on you then, Peter.'

By that time we were all bellowing with laughter at whatever anybody said, no matter how silly. Later still, we fragmented into smaller groups and became melancholy, talking about women we'd had, or wanted, and who had left who, and was with who else.

Eventually Elsie turned us out at about four o'clock. 'Oh, Jesus,' I said to Joe as we pissed up the wall of the pub, 'I'm going to get my dinner on my head again.'

'Don't worry,' he said. 'I'll speak to her for you.'

'Don't know where that bastard crane driver's got to,' Ratty said.

We meandered back to the dock. There was no sign of the crane anywhere. 'Oh, come on,' Ratty said. 'Let's *carry* the bugger off.'

'We'll never lift it,' I said.

As we clambered aboard, Joe slipped and fell flat on his back. He lay there in his new bionic suit, gazing up into the drizzle, laughing. I gripped his hand to pull him up, but the deck was wet and he was a dead weight and I fell on top of him. Ratty cheered and ran and threw himself on top of me, my back beer-numbed beneath his big-boned knees. We lay in a heap in the fish-stink and oil and laughed some more. The release of laughing felt as if it was saving me from madness or murder.

Ratty is a very powerful man. He took one end of the line of bobbins, with Joe in the middle, and me at the back. My knees buckled. It felt as if a giant press was trying to squeeze me through the deck. 'I'm going to be six inches shorter by the time we've finished with this lot,' I said.

'Don't worry,' Joe said. 'I'll come with you. I'll tell her it was my fault.'

My feet slithered on the wet deck. Ratty might as well have been carrying the bobbins *and* me *and* Joe. He dragged his leaden centipede onto, and along the dock.

It was nearly five when I got home. Joe was asleep in the taxi. Maureen watched me come in the front door, without speaking. 'I had to help Ratty carry some bobbins,' I said.

'Don't make it worse with your pathetic stories,' she said. 'Credit me with some intelligence.'

'S'true. Really.'

'You're drunk. You're stinking rotten drunk again. I only ever see you for two days, and you're drunk from the time you come home till the time you leave.' She went into the kitchen, slamming the door behind her.

'Go and get fucked!' I yelled.

I didn't feel as though I could manage the stairs. Carrying the bobbins had taken all the strength out of my legs. And besides, to get upstairs I would have to walk past Maureen in the kitchen, and going to bed at five in the afternoon would be like admitting I was as drunk as I actually was.

I stood leaning against the living-room wall, just inside the front door. It occurred to me that the last thing I wanted was for her to go and get fucked. I used to torture myself sometimes on the boat, imagining her going with someone else — but I didn't think she ever did.

I sat down on the settee. Then I lay down and dozed off. I had a vague awareness at some time of throwing up on the carpet. And an even vaguer consciousness, or perhaps a dream, of Maureen standing over me calling me a pig.

When I woke up it was after midnight. There was a strong smell of disinfectant. My stomach was a stagnant pond filled with squirming tadpoles. Someone had hammered nails into the sinuses over my eyes. I sat up and massaged the back of my neck. The muscles were like knotted rope. I went out the back to the lavatory, and then into the kitchen. I found half a shepherd's pie in the fridge. I ate it cold from the casserole with a spoon. Then I went up to bed. I curled around Maureen's back. She pretended I hadn't woken her. I didn't fall asleep till dawn.

Maureen was out with the kids when I woke late morning. I got up at lunchtime with a pounding headache. I stayed home from the pub and made myself a cheese sandwich. In the afternoon I watched the horse-racing on television. They came home about tea time. The kids were tired and squabbled among themselves. Maureen wasn't speaking to me. Twice, I asked her if she would come out for a drink once the kids were in bed, but she just shook her head. After we'd eaten, the kids livened up. I piggy-backed them up to their room and read them some stories. Mat cried for his mother and she came up and cuddled him. I gave Siddy a big hug before I went down, and asked her if she was Daddy's girl, and she said yes. Maureen and I sat in front of the television for a couple of hours without speaking.

'Hey, Mo, let's ask Peggy's girl to come in and sit.'

'It's too late.'

'It's only half nine.'

'That's not what I meant.'

'Come on, Mo.'

'No.'

'Why?'

'I don't want to.'

'How about an early night then? Let's go to bed.' I hated the wheedling tone she was forcing me to use.

'You can go to bed whenever you like,' she said.

'Well fuck you then, you bitch!' I shouted. 'I'm going out and don't fucking moan if I come back pissed because it'll be your fault if I do. You're like a bleeding nun!'

I went to the *Plough* because no one drank there who knew me. I drank slowly, alone, till closing time. I didn't feel like going back home so I went to see if Bridget was in. Bridget was a social worker I'd met one night in a pub, and had slept with a couple of times. She'd been with a number of the other guys too.

'Who's there?' she asked, without opening the door.

'It's me, Mike.'

'Mike who?'

'Mike the trawlerman.'

'What do you want?'

'I've come to see you.'

'It's a bit late, isn't it?'

'Aw, come on Bridget. Open the bloody door.'

She let me in and made coffee. I sat watching her move around the kitchen. She was wearing a white towelling dressing gown. I didn't touch my drink. All I could think of was that it was weeks since I'd enjoyed a woman, and in less than six hours I'd be back on the boat. She made small talk until she'd finished her coffee, and then said, 'I want you to go now. I've got work in the morning.'

I stood up and grabbed hold of her then and kissed her. She struggled in my hands like a fish I was about to gut. I twisted her arm up her back and forced her, face-down, across the kitchen table. She'd told me once that the thing she most feared was being buggered, so I kept whispering, 'I'm going to bugger you, Bridget,' in her ear.

'No,' she was whimpering. 'Please don't.'

'What's it to be then?' I asked. 'A fuck or a suck?'

'I don't want to do anything. Why should I have to?'

'Okay, I'll just have to bugger you.'

'You can fuck me,' she said. 'But you won't get the chance again.'

I picked her up and carried her to the bedroom. I was home less than an hour later.

I washed myself in the bathroom before I went in to bed.

The clutch was let in — a loud, shuddering, grinding crunch. Joe shook my arm. 'We're fast,' he said. 'Everybody out!' He hammered on the side of Bert's bunk. 'Come on, Bert. Not sleeping again, are you?'

I squinted at my watch. 'Jesus wept!' I said. 'We've only been turned in half an hour.'

Tim came through to the galley, practically sleep-walking. 'Bleeding fast again!' he grumbled.

'Come on, Bert,' Joe said. 'Get your hands on top of the covers where we can see them.'

We turned out again into the gunmetal morning. The small boat pitched and tossed at the mercy of the sea as we hauled it back to where the nets were held. Once we were over the pinnacle the nets came free. We emptied out the small catch and inspected the damage. The net was bedecked with coral. Bill came down from the bridge. 'There's some mending to do here,' he said. 'And we'll need a whole new side-section on there.'

Bill set the boat heading into the wind and came back to join us. We cut away the damaged areas, replacing and repairing as necessary. Bert threaded the needles. The rest of us cut and sewed and tied. Occasional waves broke over the bridge and showered us. A squall flurried across the deck, dousing us all, and passed quickly on in front of the wind. My hands became numb and mechanical. We put on shorter bridles before lowering away again. Then we gutted the assorted hake, cod, and monkfish that had been in the net, and turned in.

I slept for a couple of hours. When I woke the wind and sea had got up even more. The boat would rise on the swell and then pitch down into a trough. There would be the thud of the prow meeting the sea and the boat would shudder under the impact, and then grind forward again. It was as though the sea was angrily opposed to our intention of taking what we needed from her. It was a bad marriage. The throbbing pulse of the engine was accompanied by a continual clanging of metal from the deck as hardware was swung from side to side by the rolling motion of the boat. I could hear Bert swearing in the kitchen as he prepared breakfast. Pans were sliding around and water hissed angrily as it slopped from the kettle onto the hotplate.

We hauled again and came up with a few dogfish. Most of them were only pups and we threw back more than we kept. At least dogs didn't need gutting, and there was little else. We gutted and hosed, and made our way as erratically as pin-table balls along the deck and down into the breakfast-smelling haven of the cabin.

'There's no marmalade,' I said.

'Bert! You been spooning it again?' Joe said.

'No. Not me.'

'You must've been. Where's it all gone then?'

'I haven't. I haven't touched it.'

'Bert's been spooning it again,' Joe said.

I got my food down quick and climbed up to the bridge. 'Okay Skip. Grub up.' Bill was measuring on a chart with a pair of dividers. 'Are we going to stay here?' I asked. 'Or try somewhere else?'

'We'll have to stay in the lee of the island while this lot keeps up. We'll move on as soon as it dies down a bit. Listen out for the shipping forecast, will you.'

'Okay. There was bugger-all there that time.'

'A few years ago we didn't bother with dogs. Freddy was on the radio this morning. Said they were paying forty pounds a kit for big dogs. I tried to get our kid, to see what luck he was having, but that bloody set's no good. I've told them. The last two trips, I've told them. But they won't do anything about it. As long as we're inside the law and carrying two sets, they don't give a wank if neither of them work properly. It's like that bloody Decca keeps going spare. Look at it now. The radar's the only thing on this damn boat that works. And that includes Bert. He hasn't fixed either of them lights yet, has he?'

'No. But he's been spooning the marmalade again. You'd better get down and get your breakfast quick, or there'll be nothing left.'

'Use the radar. Stay a mile off shore on the way up and two and a half on the way down. We're inside the limit so keep your eyes peeled. But the buggers on them patrol boats'd get seasick if they put out half a mile in a sea like this. I don't suppose we'll see anything of them.'

There were some Scottish fishermen on the radio talking in Gaelic. And some foreigners — Dutch, or something like that. The shipping forecast was for continued gales. Mac, one of the other skippers in our fleet, came on. He was further north, and catching fuck-all as well. He couldn't hear me very well, so we didn't chat for long.

Oban radio called one of our boats with a message for Magee, their chief engineer. The message was: 'Twenty-third today.' I glanced at the calendar. It was the fifteenth. The operator asked Magee to stand by for a phone link-up. First he got a wrong number. 'Sorry to get you out of bed so early,' he said to the lady who answered. He tried again and got the same lady, so he went through another operator. A man's voice answered then. 'Hello?' he said, suspiciously.

The operator confirmed he'd got the right number. Then he asked, 'Does Mrs Magee live there, please?'

'Yes.'

Pause.

'Could I speak to her then?'

'You want me to get her?'

The operator had started out cheerily enough. Now, a note of exasperation was creeping into his voice. 'Yes, please. If you wouldn't mind.'

A drawn-out silence. And then a sleepy woman's voice: 'Hello?'

'Hold the line, please. I've got your call to the *Reliant*.'

'Oh, but I cancelled it.'

Another pause. Shorter this time. 'No one told me. Well, do you want to speak to him? I've got them standing by, now.'

'Well, all right,' she said uncertainly.

'*Reliant, Reliant,* this is Oban radio calling the *Reliant*. Here is your phone call, over.'

Magee came on. 'Hello, love,' he said. 'Is that you?'

'Yes. I cancelled the call and sent you a telegram instead. Did you get it?'

'Yes, I did.'

'What's it like out there?'

'A bit rough. Everything all right at home?'

'Yes.'

There was an awkward pause. Then: 'Did the plumber come?'

'Yes.'

'Good.'

They were both clearly uncomfortable, not knowing what to say.

'Well,' she said, 'it's our twenty-third today.'

'Yes.'

'Well, don't forget, love,' she said. 'I'll always be here.'

I wandered over to the radar. I couldn't see the screen too clearly. There were tears in my eyes. There was something big out there. Maybe a fisheries protection boat. I tried the binoculars but couldn't see anything. It didn't matter too much anyway. Even a really bad catch would be worth more than the hundred pound fine. I switched the Decca off as it was still going haywire. I checked the radar again to make sure we were on course and had a look at the sounder. There seemed to be plenty of feed about, but little sign of fish. I switched the radio off and sat down by the wheel.

I'll always be here, she'd said. After twenty-three years. Maureen and I had made promises.

The last trip I'd got home in the early hours of a Monday morning. We'd had an engine problem and hadn't put in anywhere on the way back, so there'd been no booze on board. Unusually, I was sober. The taxi dropped me outside the door. I put the front room light on. The room was empty. The furniture was there, but it was bare. Un-lived in. It was like a furnished room after one tenant's moved out and before the next has moved in. It was silent and cold. I went into the kitchen. There was a note on the table:

Dear Mike,
I've left. I've got the children with me.
I'll phone you on Tuesday.

Maureen.

I found myself standing in the front room. I sat down. More than anything I wanted a drink, but we never kept drink in the house. Maureen didn't like it. I craved for a cigarette too, although I hadn't smoked for over a year. I couldn't think. I couldn't understand. The note was about as meaningful to me as if I were a dog and it were from a master who'd abandoned me. The chair, enfolding me, was as cold as the north Atlantic. I was treading water. A phrase kept running through my head. *My little girl's out there.*

I went out through the grey, gritty dawn light to buy cigarettes from a machine. I was surprised to notice how cracked and uneven the paving slabs were. Rubbish was being swirled around by the wind. An old fish and chip paper wrapped itself around my leg. The pavement was a minefield of dog shit. I wanted to walk and smoke, but I didn't have any matches so I had to go back home before I could light up.

I sat smoking in the front room. A new phrase came into my head. *I want to go to her.* I wondered if I was drunk, or suffering from the DTs. I went back to the kitchen. The note really was there. *I've left,* it said. *I've got the children with me.* 'But that's my little girl,' I said aloud. 'That's my baby.' It occurred to me that the note was just a threat. I ran up the stairs two at a time. I looked in the beds. In all three beds. I could see that the covers lay smooth and flat but I tore them back anyway to make sure they were not under the blankets.

It was after nine o'clock. I went to the mini-market on the corner and brought back several packs of beer and more cigarettes. The smoke was hurting my throat. As I emptied each beer can I squeezed it out of shape and hurled it at the wall over the fireplace.

During the afternoon the phone rang.

'Hello?'

'Mike?'

'Yeah.'

'It's me.'

I didn't say anything.

'I'm not coming back.'

No words came into my head.

'The children are fine. I don't want you to see them this trip. It would be too difficult for me. You can see them later. When everything's settled.'

'Where are you?'

'I'm not going to tell you. We're happy here. I don't want to see you at the moment. I'm not coming back, Mike.'

'But Maureen...'

'I'm just phoning to tell you it's final. I want you to realise that. And I want to make arrangements about money for the children's maintenance. They *are* your children.'

'I know they're my children. You don't have to worry about money. As long as I'm working, the office'll pay you, same as usual.'

'But you must realise I'm never coming back.'

'Look, money's not a problem. I do that fucking lousy job so I can provide for my kids. I want them to have the best.'

'Well, I have to tell you, Mike, there's someone else.'

'Why are you doing this on the phone! Why don't you come and talk to me?'

'Because I don't trust you.'

'What d'you mean by that?'

'It would help if you weren't drunk.'

15

'What d'you expect when you run out on me, for Chrissake?'

'I'm living with another man, Mike.'

'Already!'

'I've been thinking about this for a long time.'

'Who is it?'

'You don't know him.'

'But you can't do that. What about my kids?'

'He's lovely with the kids, Mike. He really is. He plays with them a lot. He's what they need. They hardly knew you. You were a stranger to them.'

'What d'you mean — a stranger to them?'

'You were hardly ever there, Mike.'

'That's not my flaming fault. I'm working. I mean, I'm working for them. For you.'

'But they need something more, Mike. John spends *time* with us.'

'Oh, John does, does he? What the fuck does John *do* then, that he has all this time to spare?'

There was a pause before she said, 'He's on the dole.'

'ON THE DOLE! Well, that's fucking great, that is. Sure he's got plenty of time to spend on other men's wives and kids, then. I pay thousands a year in tax! I pay more tax than he fucking *gets* on the dole! I mean, I fucking *keep* that cunt!'

'There's no need to shout, Mike.'

'No need to shout? Listen: I'm serving a fucking life sentence out there, doing hard labour to provide for you and the kids and now you tell me I'm paying some fucking pimp to fuck my wife while I'm away.'

'It's no good you being like that. I've made my decision. I don't care what you do. I won't change my mind even if you won't pay a penny towards the children.'

'What are you on about? I've already said I'll pay you same as usual, haven't I.'

'Well, that's all I wanted to sort out with you for now.'

'But just a minute.'

'I'll get in touch next time you're home.'

'But, Maureen...'

'Bye, Mike.'

'Maureen!' But she'd gone. 'YOU FUCKING TWO-TIMING BITCH, YOU! MAUREEN, YOU CUNT! MAUREEN!'

When it was time for the next haul I went down to make the tea and wake everybody up. 'Hands off cocks,' I called. 'Wakey, wakey, rise and shine.'

'Is Bert up?' Joe asked when we were sitting sipping at the scalding tea.

'Come on, Bert,' I snapped. 'Show a leg. We're hauling.'

'Not sleeping again, is he?' Joe said. 'The lazy old git.'

Tim came in from his cabin, and finally Bert joined us at the table. Whenever we first turned out our faces were cadaverous, making us look like animated corpses out of some cheap horror film. There was a sickening scrunch as Bill let the clutch in for the winch and I felt dismay at having to go on functioning. Getting to my feet seemed to demand greater effort than climbing Everest. But it was like pushing a car to get it started: once I was on my feet I began to go through the routine like an automaton, mechanically putting on boots, frock and cap.

'I hope there's more here than there was last haul,' Tim said.

'No fucking fish anywhere anymore,' Joe said.

'They want to do something about all them bloody foreigners', Bert said. 'They want to bring in the bloody gunboats.'

'They use nets with a mesh the size of a pigeon's arsehole', Joe said. 'It's a wonder there's any fish left at all.'

'What a fucking job!' I said.

'And now they want us to pay to do it,' Bert added.

We stumbled out to our stations on deck like the walking dead. The sky was a dark grey. The sea was darker still. It looked more like material than water. I felt an urge to go and lie down on it; to have it wrapped around me and pulled over my head like a stretcher blanket. We began winching in. Joe's face was screwed up against the cold wind, making him look as if he was in as much pain as I was. It occurred to me that for all I knew, he was. He would not have told me, any more than I would tell him. A squall came upon us. Tim and Bert at the stern were being lashed by the rain from above as well as by the sea from below. The deck was awash. The warp crackled and snapped harshly like gunfire as we wound it in, and the drum axles turned cold rain to hissing steam. I switched the drive over to the whipping drum and we hauled the net in. There was a brief moment of hope just before the bag appeared, like when the first few numbers drawn tally with those on your lottery ticket — but it was as disappointing as usual.

Life didn't deliver many full bags. And when it did you took it for granted and started worrying about the next one.

The squall passed.

Bert joined me, bawling some inanity which was carried away by the wind and lost over the immensity of the indifferent ocean. I concentrated on sharpening my knife. Gutting was the only part of the job that gave me pleasure any more. I set to work on the fish. The yellow of my frock was soon patterned crimson with blood.

I threw a string of guts to a gannet. He failed to catch it and, folding his wings across his back, plummeted into the water. He resurfaced a few metres further on while the squabbling gulls landed on the surface where the offal had once been. I stopped work and stood staring at the sea.

'Come on, Mike,' Tim yelled. 'What's the matter?'

'My little girl's out there,' I said.

'What?'

I shook my head and went back to work. 'Come on, John,' I snarled, picking up a fish that was a cross between a cod and a coley. I slid my blade through its belly. 'You bastard!' I said.

'Who's for a sarny?' Bert asked, when we were back in the cabin.

'I'll have one,' Tim said. 'Bring the cheese, will you, Bert.'

'I think I can manage a cheese butty,' I said.

'Turning in already, Joe?' Bert said as he came in from the galley.

Joe leaned out from his bunk holding a *Men Only* open to show a double page spread of a black woman with her legs apart. 'Look at that!' he slavered. 'Looks like someone's been at it with a meat axe.'

'I haven't seen that one,' Tim said. 'After you, Joe.'

'Nice bit of black velvet, that,' Bert said. 'I had a cooness like that out in Mombasa when I was in the Merchant. I used to sail with a bloke called Nick James. Nearly twenty stone he was. This night we got pissed out of our brains. He was rolling around on the floor of this bar yelling, *I'm a barrel, I'm a barrel.*'

'That must have earned the respect of the local people,' I said.

'We were that drunk. Anyway, I went and found this whore. Lovely big black mamma, she was. What a pair of knockers. I can remember trying to tear her jumper off. *Let me get at them,* I was yelling. I wanted to bite her nipples off. I'm a sadistic bugger, me. I can't remember much after that. Next morning I found myself in a ditch. Didn't have a penny. Lost everything. I had to flog my clothes off to buy hooch. Got back to England in February. I came off the dock at Tilbury and all I had on was a pair of shorts and a singlet, and it was snowing, it was brass monkey weather, and I had to go home like that. I'd sold everything else to buy hooch.'

What am I doing here? I asked myself. *Wallowing in this shit? Why aren't I at home with my wife and children?*

When it had been time to return to the boat after the last trip, Joe had come to collect me in the taxi. I was drunk. 'Come on,' he said. 'Time to go. Where's the old lady?'

'Out.'

'Well, come on.'

'I'm not coming.'

'Don't be daft. Miss a trip and them buggers'll suspend you for a year. There's blokes queuing for the jobs now.'

I was still in my dirty clothes and had no clean bedding. I let Joe lead me away as though he was a warder taking me back to the cells after parole. *All right,* I seemed to be saying, *I'll come quietly.* From then on I'd gone through the motions like a zombie — I'd said it and done it all so often before.

'She kept on so much,' Bert was saying, 'that in the end I took all the little bleeders to the pictures. By the time I'd bought sweets and ice creams and everything it set me back nearly a tenner.'

'You spend more than that on a round of drinks,' I snapped.

'That's right,' Joe said. 'You selfish old git.'

The weather stayed bad all trip. On the way home we spent a day drinking in Douglas. We left in the evening just before dark. There was thick fog on the sea, a grey wall towards which we plunged continuously, but as if in a nightmare, without ever reaching it. Everyone on

19

board was paralytic and in their bunks. It was my watch. I sat by the wheel supping lager from cans we'd brought with us. The automatic pilot was steering us at a forty-five degree angle to the gale-force wind. The boat was rolling dangerously, and the prow was lifting so high the deck was awash with water coming over the stern. The boat shuddered with the force of each wave as though it felt it could not go on, but the drive in its guts forced it to lift and plunge forward again into that grey mass that was as empty as my future. I ached to get off the boat, and dreaded going home. The Decca was working, and periodically I checked our course. I glanced continually at the radar to see what else was about. The nearer we got to home the more boats appeared converging towards the same spot. I opened can after can of lager, trying to numb myself against thought and feeling. I began to nod. Periodically I would wake with a start, check the radar and the Decca, sip some beer, and nod off again. Three waves in a row would smack against the bridge window with enough impact to fell a bull. Then there'd be a short respite, and then three more seas would leap and lash the glass. I opened the rear window for a while to try to wake myself with the chill air. But it was too cold and my legs too weak to stand. I sat down at the wheel and drank and jerked awake and dozed off. I noticed something on the radar. And slept again. It was closer. I was dreaming I was in some bleak, rocky place. I was with Maureen. We were searching for the children. There were four men. They were armed with staves. They were suddenly there beating me. Then I was being held so that I couldn't move. Maureen was naked then. Two of the men held her down. A third mounted her. The dot on the radar was larger now — within half a mile of us. It was approaching us at an angle of about thirty degrees. I wasn't being held any more. Neither was Maureen. I was just watching. The man was fucking her. He was naked now too. She was holding onto his hair with one hand and onto his buttocks with the other, pulling him into her. She was coming and let out a moan with her head tipped back, her eyes closed, and her mouth open. A line of spittle reached across her lips. The dot had reached the centre of the radar. The boat plunged down and down and the sea slammed into the prow and leapt, and hurled itself against the bridge and burst, and foam caked the windscreen. It cleared slowly, the froth patterning down the glass, and then my outlook was blanked out again, and then again. Through the sliding pattern of foaming lace, behind the dense grey veil of the fog, I imagined I saw lights a stone's throw in front of me.

And then I was wide awake. A cargo boat was across our bows. I switched off the automatic pilot and spun the wheel. The boat plunged on. The lights of the cargo vessel shone brighter. It seemed we were going to ram it amidships. I thought, *I'm going to die on the floor of this sea, three hours away from the few people I love.* I felt calm and resigned. I imagined a vast, flat, sandy sea bed, and the dark water around and above me like a cathedral. *I'm going to die,* I thought, *in this cold place, and it doesn't matter.* I took no further action. I neither slowed the engines, roused the others, nor moved for the life raft. But the cargo boat wafted like a ghost ship across our bows as we veered to starboard. We passed so close to her stern that a man could have jumped from one deck to the other.

I did nothing for a while. Then I set the automatic pilot on course again, slumped myself down behind the wheel, and opened another can of beer.

SATURDAY NIGHT OUT

My mother started yelling from downstairs. 'Kevin!' I could hear the irritation in her voice. 'Kevin!'

'What?'

'It's on the table!'

I put on my black motorbike jacket. It wasn't real leather — but it looked like it. I'd made a design on the back with brass studs to match my studded leather belt. She forbade me to wear the jacket when I first got it. She said if I was seen going out like that the neighbours would start talking about her. The neighbours already talk about her as a matter of fact — but that's nothing to do with the way I dress.

'Well come on then. It's getting cold!'

I forced a comb through the worst tangles in my shoulder-length hair and looked at myself in the mirror. I'm not much to look at. But then I'm not a hare-lipped hunchback either.

'Kevin!'

I went downstairs. 'All right!'

'It's not all right!'

I sat down at the living-room table. She plonked a plate of food in front of me and sat opposite with hers. 'Fucking fish fingers again!' I said.

'Less of that language in this house. And if you don't like what I cook

22

you can get your own bloody tea.'

I chewed slowly. The food turned to greasy cardboard in my mouth. 'Hurry up!' she said.

If she was in a hurry to give me something to eat, it always meant one thing: not always the same bloke — just the latest. I know I must have had a father because my mother doesn't have much in common with the Virgin Mary, but I don't know anything about him. He didn't stick around. None of them did, and I can't say I blame them. 'What's your hurry tonight then?' I said.

My old girl, flustered by the question, worked herself up into a little paddy. 'I don't come in from work and stand over the stove cooking for you because I've got nothing better to do. And how many times have I told you not to wear them boots in the house.'

'I'm not wearing them in the house. I'm going out, aren't I.'

'What d'you mean, you're not wearing them in the house? I'm eating my tea in the back yard, I suppose.'

'Oh, give over, will yer. You're like a bleeding...'

'No, I will not give over. Who has to clear up round here after you?'

I shovelled sugar into my tea, abandoning the fish fingers and beans on the cold plate. She was only fiddling with her food too. Her cardigan was unbuttoned revealing a grubby white brassiere. I sipped my tea, feeling like a wild animal with its leg in a trap. 'Do your cardigan up!' I said.

But she was like a dog with a bone. 'You don't lift a finger,' she said.

I lifted a finger to her under the table where she wouldn't see. I didn't feel like arguing, and I didn't feel like eating. I herded the fish fingers around the plate with my knife.

'And hurry up and get that et,' she said. 'And what's the matter with you anyway? You look as if you lost a pound and found a penny.'

'Bone got sacked, didn't he.'

'I'm not surprised. It's a wonder they ever gave *him* a job in the first place.'

'You're so big-hearted, aren't yer. If someone was dying for want of breath you wouldn't fart in their face.'

'Don't be so vulgar. What did he get the sack for, anyway?'

'Don't worry about it.'

'I suppose he got his thieving hands on something that didn't belong to him again.'

'Oh, give over. You're not above getting something for nothing when you can.'

'I've never stole, and I've never let you steal, neither.'

'Don't talk wet, woman. You're always coming home with stuff that fell off the back of a van.'

'That's different. And don't call me *woman*. A little bit of respect, if you please. I'm your mother, and don't you forget it. Where are you going tonight, anyway?'

'Out.'

'I didn't think you was going to stay in and clean up the house. Where are you going, I'm asking you.'

'I told you. Out.'

'Well don't be bringing any of them little tarts back here like last week.'

'People who live in glass houses shouldn't throw stones,' I said, with my mouth full of greasy cardboard.

She banged down her knife and fork and strained towards me across the table. 'What did you say!'

It wasn't a question. She was daring me to repeat it. I looked at her with as much scorn as I could register on my face. I leaned towards her, emphasising my words by jabbing my knife in the air between us. 'I said, the old pot's calling the kettle black.'

'Don't you wave that knife at me! This is still my house, and I won't have anybody talk to me like that in my house or out of it.'

I refocussed on my plate. I could feel her eyes, like electro-shock pads, holding my bowed head.

'So I'm not entitled to have any life of my own,' she said. 'I should be stuck here night after night while you're off gallivanting about. Is that it?'

'And I'm not supposed to lead my own life either, am I.'

'What d'you mean? You're out every night.'

'But you don't like it, do yer. You don't like it if I go out with my mates. That's not right. You don't like it if I go out with a bird. That's not right. Well, what do you want?'

There was a long silence. Then she stood up and began to clear the table. She'd hardly touched her own food. She started up again as she went out to the kitchen. 'Well it wouldn't hurt you to give me a hand round here just once in a while. There's all sorts of things need doing when you haven't got a man around the place.'

'Too many bloody men around the place,' I said to the dead fish on my plate.

She came back to take more things from the table. 'I've slogged and slaved for you all these years. I've worked my fingers to the bone, I have. And what thanks do I get?'

'I didn't ask to be bloody well born.'

'Neither did I,' she said. 'Neither did I. You might think about that sometimes. You seem to think that I'm just here to wait on you hand and foot. Well it's not easy to bring up a child when you're a woman on your own. And hurry up and get that et, and get yourself out from under my feet.'

'Bloody hell, woman! One minute you're on at me to stay in, and the next minute you're on at me to get out.' She snatched the bread packet off the table. 'Do you mind!' I objected. 'I haven't finished with that yet.'

'Well hurry up then.'

'What are you planning tonight, then?' I grinned up at her insolently. 'Going out with your fancy man again, are yer? Or staying in with him more like. Who is it this time? Anyone you know? Or haven't you got round to asking his name yet?'

She grabbed the packet of margarine off the table (a missile she'd used before) and I got ready to duck. 'Less of your lip,' she threatened. 'And wipe that smile off your face.' I grinned at her defiantly, my body tensed, ready to spring away. She pointed a shaking finger towards my face. 'I'll make you smile on the other side of your face one of these days, my lad.'

And then there was a knocking on the back door. *Saved by the bell,* I thought. My mother started. She turned to the mirror that hung over the fireplace and fingered her hair, then glanced at her watch. 'That must be someone for you,' she said. She ran to the window and looked out from behind the curtain to see if her bloke's car was in the street. 'And if I've told you once,' she said, 'I've told you a hundred times not to leave that oily heap of old iron in front of my house.' There was more thumping on the door. It sounded more like the police than the vicar. 'Well?' she said. 'Aren't you going to see who's there?'

'Let them knock.'

'Yeah, you would! Well it's a good job some of us have got some manners.'

She went through to the kitchen, and then I heard Bone's voice. 'Is Kev in?'

'He's having his tea.'

'Tell him we'll hang about out here then, will yer?'

'What — and frighten my neighbours to death? You'd better come in. Wait there.'

As she came back into the living room she said, in a hushed voice, 'It's them two again.'

'What two?' I asked innocently.

'You know very well what two. The one who always looks like he's been dragged through a hedge backwards, and that little rat-faced friend of his. And why you want to get mixed up with the likes of them, I don't know. I don't like them coming round here.'

'Well I don't expect they came to see you — despite the rumours.'

'Any more of that and I'll slap you round the face, big as you are.' At that moment Skin and Bone shambled into the room behind her. 'I thought I told you to wait out there!' she snapped.

'There's always a welcome on the mat,' I said. My mother pointedly turned her back on them and peered into the mirror. She began putting on her false eyelashes.

Skin lounged in the doorway. Bone came and joined me at the table. They made a funny looking couple. Bone's over six foot, and heavy built. He reminded me of one of them large dogs, the sort that have big feet and gentle eyes and make friends with burglars and babies without discriminating. His hair was long and dark with grease, and he was dressed much the same as I was. Skin, though, didn't have a motorbike and he always wore a black suit of cheap cloth that was either concertina'd with creases or shiny from having just been pressed. He's eight or nine inches shorter than Bone, and skinny with it. He's got a pointed face with a rodent-sharp nose, and white hair. He's almost albino. Almost a white rat.

My mother turned and glared at Bone's boots. 'Have you wiped your feet?' she demanded.

'Yes, Missus.'

'I bet you have, an' all.'

'Nearly wore the door mat out,' he said, smiling.

Skin began biting his nails and staring at my old lady's tits.

'Want a cup of rosy?' I asked Bone.

'It's hard luck if they do,' my mother said, 'I'm not waiting on *them* hand and foot.'

'It's a good job some of us have got some manners,' I mimicked.

'It's all right, Missus,' Bone said. 'Just had my tea.'

My mother gave me one of her 'looks', and turned away.

'Coming out?' Bone asked me.

'Seeing Sharron up Jim's.'

'Oh.' Bone sniffed. 'Well...' He looked at me and then glanced meaningfully at my mother. She saw him in the mirror. With one lot of eyelashes glued on she was in the process of lighting herself a fag, but stopped, instantly alert.

The silence was awkward. 'You pushing the fags then, Ma?' I said.

'I'm not green even if I'm cabbage-looking.'

'Your only fault,' I said, 'is you're too generous.'

Bone nodded towards the door. 'Coming out, then?'

'What are you up to now?' the old girl said suspiciously.

'Nothing,' Bone said. 'We're just going up Jim's.'

'Hurry up and clear off then,' she said.

'We're just going to sit here and have a fag first,' I said, baiting her.

'Oh, no, you're not,' she yelled. 'Just take your friends and get out of my house. At once!'

'*Your* house?' I said. 'It's my house too, you know. I pay my whack.'

'I'm not arguing with you! I just want you out! This is my house. I worked hard to get it.'

'On your back,' I said.

As she lunged towards me I leapt backwards knocking my chair crashing to the floor. She grabbed the bread board off the table and hurled it like a frisbee at my head. I moved fast towards the door, bent double. The bread board came sailing across the room like a flying-saucer, sliced through the plaster holy family that stood on top of the telly, and knocked all their heads off. 'Now look what you've done!' she screeched. I didn't hang around to argue. I went through the hall like a greyhound out of a trap and out the front door. A battered and mud-spattered red Ford was pulling up in front of the house. I heard my old girl screaming at Skin and Bone to shove off.

'Don't get your knickers in a twist,' I called. 'Your fancy man's here.'

My mother came into the hall to look out. 'Oh, no,' she said. 'And I'm not ready yet.' She looked near to tears. I felt a real shit then.

'Go upstairs and get ready,' I said. 'I'll tell him to wait.'

Skin and Bone sidled out and stood on the dirt near my bike so as to get a good shufti at the visitor. He heaved himself out of the car and came lumbering towards me. His face looked as if the heavyweight champion of the world had been using it for a punch bag. He smelt as though he hadn't washed for a week, and there were bottles bulging from both of his donkey jacket pockets. *Oh, Ma,* I said to myself. *How could you?'*

'Is this twenty-three?' the gorilla asked.

'Yeah,' I said. 'Go in the kitchen and pour yourself a cup of tea. My mother's gone upstairs to get changed. She'll be down in a minute.'

'That's okay.' He pushed past me and started up the stairs.

'Here, mate,' I said, 'this ain't a high rise block. That's the kitchen through there.'

He turned on the stairs and glowered at me through bloodshot eyes. 'Piss off, sonny Jim!' he said, and carried on up. 'Doris! Where are yer?' he called.

'Is that you, Freddy?' I heard my mother say. 'Here. What you doing? Get out. I'm not ready yet.' He closed the bedroom door behind him.

I felt sick. It felt different from when a strong silent type took a woman in the movies. It felt different from when I tried it with a girl myself. Although what the difference was I didn't know. What I did know was that I wanted to go up and drag him off her and kick him out of the house; but I was chicken. The feeling churning in my stomach was a mixture of disgust, fear and shame. Skin was making crude gestures and doubling over with laughter. 'Let's go and listen to the springs squeak,' he suggested.

'Shut up, rat-face,' I said. 'Go and fart in a can and rattle it.'

'She's not a bad bit of crackling, your old lady,' Skin said. 'Might pay her a visit myself one night.'

I shuddered, as though he'd put his hands on me. 'You're not her type,' I said.

Jim's is a workman's cafe during the day, where truck drivers and cabbies go. Evenings it's one of the few joints outsiders and riff-raff are welcome. At most places, teenagers like us who've left school and are either unemployed or in dead-end jobs have the door slammed in our faces. We're called louts, hooligans, yobbos. If we stick up for our rights the cops are down on us like a ton of bricks, and they'll always take Norman Normal's word against ours. In Jim's, though, if you don't have any money you can just sit and rap with your mates. No one hassles you. Jim keeps his eye on everyone, and the pigs stay away.

It's a scruffy place. It looks as though it hasn't seen a lick of paint since before Noah went into the Ark. There's no pictures or decorations of any kind on the walls. Just patterns of dirt from lounging shoulders, and kids' names and swear words scrawled in biro. It's a long thin room, with one-armed bandits standing either side of the door like bouncers, and the counter facing you as you come in, flanked by pin tables. There's a juke-box; and a row of metal tables and chairs down each wall. It's the place we meet our mates to decide where to go and what to do, and the lucky ones meet their birds to decide what to do and where to do it. And it's the place where we hang out when there's nowhere to go and nothing to do.

Saturday night it was crowded and murky with cigarette smoke. The juke-box was blaring and everyone was yelling to make themselves heard above the racket. There was only one empty table. Skin went to sit down to reserve it while me and Bone went to the counter for teas. 'Hi, Jim,' I said. 'You must be coining it tonight. You'll be able to go to Bermuda for your holidays.'

'You've got to be joking,' he said. 'You two are the last of the big spenders.'

'It must be your haute cuisine that attracts everybody,' I said.

'They've heard about your Cordon Blues,' Bone added.

'What do you want?' Jim said. 'I'm busy.'

'Three teas.'

Jim began slopping a murky brown liquid into a fistful of dirty mugs out of the antique chrome steam engine that stood on his counter. 'Got the boot, didn't I,' Bone told him.

'They want a lad down the timber yard.'

'Don't fancy that.'

'You'd get splinters in your arse, skiving,' I said.

'I'll let you know if I hear of anything,' Jim said.

'And a couple of lumps of Betty's bread pudding,' I said. Then added to Bone, 'If Skin wants any he can get it himself.'

'I hope there ain't a nail in it, Jim, like there was last week,' Bone said.

'If there is I won't charge you no extra.'

'A nail, Jim!' I said in mock horror. 'You should cut them in the bathroom, not in the kitchen.'

'Put a sock in it, and give us the money.'

'You can tell Bet it's good pud,' Bone managed to say with his mouth full.

'I'll tell her,' Jim said.

As we sat down at the table, Bone said, 'We've got a little job planned for tonight.'

'Hey! Spit your crumbs down your own bloody jacket, will yer,' I said, not paying attention. I was thinking about that punch bag, Freddy, in my mother's bedroom, and I was wondering where Sharron was.

Janey detached herself from a group of boys and came over. 'Hi, Kev,' she said. 'Any parties going tonight?'

'Not that I've heard of,' I said. 'Or we wouldn't be sitting here. Want a tea?'

'No, thanks.'

'Coffee?'

'No. I'll have a bite of your pudding, though.'

'Any time,' I said.

'Mmm,' she murmured, licking the crumbs from her lips, 'you've got a lovely pudding, Kev.'

'That's what all the girls say.'

'Tell us if you hear of a party,' she said as she drifted away.

'What you sniffing around that scrubber for?' Skin said.

'She's all right.'

'Yeah. The bicycle. Every bloke in this caff's had his leg over her.'

'Every bloke except you.'

'Shut up, you two,' Bone said. 'You're like an old married couple. What about it, Kev?'

'What've you got planned?'

'Are you in, first?' Skin said.

'I don't know, do I, if you don't tell me what it is. You might be planning on nicking your granny's gold teeth, for all I know. You're thick enough.'

'You want your brains looking at,' Skin said.

Bone put his arm around my shoulder and his face close to mine. I could smell his sweat and the cigarette smoke in his hair. 'Skin's got a job in a menswear shop.'

'I know.'

'He's unlatched the bog window and fixed it so the alarm won't go off. You and me can climb in. It's a piece of piss. He's left a little parcel of stuff he wants, and we help ourselves.'

'Self service, like.'

'Yeah. No risk. No problems. What about it?'

'I'm waiting for Sharron.'

'Come on, man. It'll be a laugh.'

'You don't need anyone for that. Do it on your tod.'

'It'll do you a good turn.'

'It'll do me a good turn if I end up in clink!'

'No chance,' he said. 'Anyway, I ain't got the bottle to go in on my own. I want someone with me.'

'Okay,' I said reluctantly. 'But later. I'm seeing Sharron first.'

When Sharron turned up she got herself a cup of coffee and brought it over to our table. She's a pretty girl, small and fair-haired. She'd been going out with Barry, leader of the local bovver boys, but they'd bust up the previous weekend, and this was our first date.

'What're we going to do then?' Bone asked.

I knew what *I* wanted to do.

'Let's go *some*where,' he said.

'Let's go for a burn-up,' I suggested. 'See if we can top the ton between the Spoon and the seafront.'

'Suits me,' said Bone. 'Let's go.'

'There's no hurry,' I said. And then to Sharron, 'Finish your coffee. Listen, I'll have to drop you off early tonight.'

'Why?'

'I've got to give Bone a hand with something.'

Skin stood up and hovered close to Sharron, biting his nails and trying to see down the front of her dress.

'Come on,' Bone said, getting to his feet. 'You coming or not?'

Sharron gathered her skirt in two handfuls and mounted behind me. She had nice legs. 'We're going to break a record,' I shouted above the revving of the motors. 'So hang on tight.'

'Don't copy what that mad git does,' Skin yelled to Bone. 'Let him kill hisself if he wants. You take it easy.'

'You should wear a crash helmet,' Sharron shouted into my ear.

'Stuff that!' I yelled back.

I headed for the Greasy Spoon roundabout, excited by the feel of Sharron pressed up against me on the pillion. The dark, the damp, the cold, somehow all added up to a feeling of freedom. That's what you get from a motorbike: you feel powerful, and you feel free.

When we got to the Spoon I turned inland. I wanted to hit the circle as fast as I dared in order to get the best possible start. Bone must have wondered where I was going but he just sat on my tail. 'Where are you taking me?' Sharron shouted in my ear as I slowed down to make a U-turn.

'To another planet,' I yelled back.

I opened up, praying there'd be nothing on the circle, and I was in luck. I laid the bike so low I felt the footrest graze the road. Sharron was gripping me with her arms and thighs, pressing her body into my back. As I straightened up I wound the throttle right back and crouched low. The air hit me with the cold force of water from a water canon. The wind was that wind you get off the sea in winter, damp and biting cold, but spiced with the smell of seaweed and endless open space. I screwed my face up against the pressure which was forcing its way into my lungs. My eyes were slits and the water running from them dried on the tight skin of my cheeks. My hair streamed out behind me like a white mare's tail when a gale is blowing against the tide. There were only two cars on that short stretch of road. I overtook the first on the outside, the second on the inside. I saw in my mirror that Bone copied my zig-zag, playing follow-my-leader. I could see the yellow seafront lights ahead. I gripped the throttle wide open and watched the needle creeping up: 80... 85... 90... 93... 95... The circle was looming up fast and I willed the bike to pick up those few extra miles an hour. The needle touched 96 — but we were almost there. The force of the wind had defeated us. 'Fuck you, you bastard!' I screamed into the wind, screaming at the bike, and my boss, my mother, Skin, Barry, Freddy, the world. I slammed the throttle closed and braced my arms to stop us from sliding forward onto the petrol tank. I felt the bike beginning to wobble and I thought, *Oh, Jesus, I'm not going to make it.* I started braking as hard as I dared but the back end began to slide so I let the brakes off a little and we were onto the circle so I just had to lay her down and do my best to get round onto the promenade and hope nothing would be coming towards me. Then I saw the police car. 'Fuck *YOU!*' I screamed again. I was verging on tears of fear now. I heaved the bike up and laid her down the other side. As I came round the circle at fifty miles an hour I felt the bike sliding out from under me so I did the only thing you can do in that situation which is to open up and try to pull out of it. And somehow we made it. Instead of gliding down the brightly lit seafront, we hurled ourselves into the blackness of Snakes Lane — a narrow road that squirms and twists away into the marshy countryside. From the waist down I was jelly, trembling and weak. Bone was still behind me. And behind him, with its blue light flashing, siren wailing and tyres squealing, the police car. Motorbikes had the advantage over the car on the twisting and turning succession of double bends, and our pursuers would have lost sight of us for a while. I swung into a right-hand bend, then instead of swinging left with the road I plunged straight ahead up a cart track between two fields. I switched off my lights and Bone, still behind me, doused his, and after a moment's blindness I blessed the moon. I heard the police car roaring aggressively and wailing like a banshee around the bend behind. My main worries were that I'd smash into something in the shadow like an unlit car being used as a knocking shop, or a piece of abandoned farm equipment; or that I'd catch a wheel in one of the tractor ruts that ran either side of the track and spill myself and Sharron into the hedge. I'd had worse tumbles — but it was hardly the way to begin a romance.

The gate at the top of the track was open and we hit the once-ploughed field. I relaxed in the open space and my eyes grew accustomed to the blue-grey light. But furrows don't make for a smooth ride. As we bumped, jarred and jolted along, Bone came alongside. Giving the copper the slip had changed defeat into a victory. 'We made it,' I yelled. 'We shook the bugger off.' Bone was yelling too, but I couldn't hear what he was saying. Skin was clutching on behind, looking like a corpse in the moonlight as he was shaken and rattled over the ruts. I wondered how Sharron was feeling. I put one arm behind and squeezed her against me. 'You still there?' I called.

We doubled back through the gateway and down the track, crossed Snakes Lane, and rode carefully across the marsh grass down to the grotty beach. We dismounted, and I gave Sharron a hug. I could feel her trembling. Then I turned to Bone. We threw our arms around each other, slapped one another on the back and fell about, laughing.

'Thank Christ you made it into the lane,' I said.

'You were the one who had to find the hole in the dark.'

'No trouble.'

'Not with all that power throbbing between your legs.' I was conscious of Sharron's presence and I felt uncomfortable with Bone's banter. 'When you changed direction on the seafront I nearly had my chips,' he went on.

'Had *your* chips! What about me! I'm on this flaming circle doing about eighty miles an hour, and there's this sodding pig wagon coming towards me.'

'I didn't see it,' Bone said. 'I had my eyes glued to your tail light. You were laid down horizontal as it was. I thought we were never going to get round, and then you laid her down the other way and I thought, *Fuck me, he's trying to kill us all. He's a fucking Kamikaze.*'

'But we gave that bluebottle the slip.'

'The poor sod's probably still going round them bends trying...'

'Going round *the* bend, more like.'

'...trying to catch us up.'

'Trying to catch the phantom bikers.'

Fuelled by the left-over adrenalin we bear-hugged each other and danced around with the relief and the delight of it all and, laughing uproariously, fell into a tangled heap on the sand.

Skin was morose. 'Bloody nutters,' he kept muttering.

We disentangled ourselves and got up, brushing the damp sand off our clothes. Sharron was laughing, but she was still shaking with cold and fright. 'You're not dressed for biking,' I said, as I held her against me to warm her.

'I'll wear something more suitable next time,' she said.

'Next time? Is that a promise?' I held her tighter and she snuggled into my arms like a mouse pressing itself into its nest.

'Apart from being frozen to death, I was nearly scared to death.'

'Nothing to be scared of.'

'Not much. You're a loony. When did they let you out?'

'People enjoy being scared, anyway.'

'Don't talk daft.'

'Why do they go to fairs, then — on big wheels and big dippers and that, and to see scary films?'

'Girls do it so they've got an excuse to grab hold of boys.'

'You can grab hold of me any time.'

'When you take me on that thing I don't have much choice, do I.'

'It's good though, i'n'it.'

'My mother said I should keep off motorbikes and now I know why. I nearly had kittens.'

'Funny place to have them.'

Bone interrupted. 'Skin wants to go for a drink.'

'Don't be daft,' I said. 'That cop might be lurking about.'

'That's what I keep telling that creep.'

'It's you who'll get done, Bone, not him.'

'I know. Anyway, I said I'll take him. You coming?'

'We'll hang around here for a bit.'

'It's all right for some,' Bone said, punching my arm.

'See you later.'

'In about an hour. Up Jim's.'

'Stay away from the fuzz,' I yelled as they rode off.

And I was alone with Sharron. I felt very small suddenly. The beach and the sea and the mud flats seemed to stretch endlessly under that vast night sky. But the town, lit up by its decorations to lure the trippers, was only a couple of miles down the estuary. And the island, ablaze with the lights of its four oil refineries, was only three or four miles up river. There was a horseshoe of industrial noise and dirt around us like a prison wall. I stood there with my arms around her for a long time, feeling awkward. 'Shall we sit down?' I managed at last.

We sat on the damp sand and stared at the sea. It was calm, and the three-quarter moon was reflected and broken in it. The sea lapped quietly on the shingle, and the pebbles rumbled against each other as small waves moved them a little, this way and that. 'I like it here,' I said. 'Even if it's only the estuary. It's better than living inland somewhere.' You couldn't see how dirty the water was in the dark. When the tide was out it exposed more than a mile of foul-smelling mud. 'Look at the island,' I said. 'It looks like a gigantic spaceship with all them lights and all them pipes twisting about and all them tanks of different shapes and sizes. You'd think the island would sink under the weight of it all.' I began making patterns with stones in the sand. I couldn't bear the feeling of smallness and aloneness and I felt a compulsion to go on talking even though I knew I was making a fool of myself. 'I like getting away from all the noise. It's nice here, away from everybody. Don't you think so?' She made a small movement; almost a shrug. 'You're very pretty,' I said.

'And you're very sweet.' Something about that word and the way she said it made it sound artificial. In any case I didn't want to be 'sweet'. I couldn't imagine her calling Barry that. If she did he'd probably smack her in the mouth. I didn't say anything for a while.

'What's that?' she asked.

'What's what?'

'What you're making.'

'Oh. It's a maze. But none of the roads leads out. They're all dead ends.'

'You're a funny boy.'

Boy, I thought. *I bet she doesn't call Barry 'boy' either.*

A car wound slowly along the lane behind us towards the town. I wondered if it was the law going back with its tail between its legs. 'Shall I tell you the first thing I noticed about you,' she said. 'Your hands. You've got nice hands.' I was surprised. I'd never thought of hands as things that could be either nice or not nice. A hand was just a useful lump of meat on the end of your arm. 'One evening you were sitting at the next table in Jim's. You were fiddling with a cigarette packet, turning it over and over while you were talking.'

I couldn't think of anything to say. I laid her back on the beach and began kissing her. I had one hand under her head so that her hair didn't get full of sand, and while I was kissing her I used my other hand to open her jacket. I slid my cold hand into the top of her dress. I felt her breast, first on the outside of her bra, and then inside. Her flesh was soft and warm, and her nipple became erect under my cold fingers. She lay under me passively. I became conscious of nothing except *her*; no sounds or sensations other than her smell, her breathing, her mouth and hair and skin, her heartbeat, and her warm breast under my hand. It seemed she would let me do anything. I was going to win the Big Prize. And then she said, 'I don't feel like it tonight, Kev.'

I became a crumpled rag. I still had an erection, but it was numb like a length of metal pipe down my jeans. I kissed her once more and then got to my feet and ambled down to the edge of the water. I knelt on the damp sand like a kid and began ploughing into it with my hands. I started building — I don't know why. I built a wall all round, and a tower in the middle. Sharron came and watched for a while without speaking, and then she said, 'You're not angry, are you?'

'No,' I said. 'It's all right. Maybe next time?'

She ignored the question. 'What's that?' she asked, pointing with her foot.

I squatted there for a while, looking at it, thinking about it. 'I think it's a Safe Place,' I said. 'This wall will keep out unfriendlies, like my mother, and Barry — people like that. And this place in the middle is where I'll stay with my girl.' She didn't respond in any way. I looked up to read her face, but the moon was behind her head so I couldn't see her expression. 'Do you want to share my Safe Place with me?'

She laughed. But didn't reply. I stood up wiping the sand off my hands onto my jeans. 'Let me,' she said. She took a handkerchief from her jacket pocket and wiped my hands with it. It warmed me — being looked after like that.

'Thank you,' I said. As we turned to go back up to the bike she trod on the wall of my Safe Place. I don't think she even noticed.

I took Sharron back to Jim's. Bone was waiting outside. I told her I'd see her later, and she went away from me into the steamy warmth of the cafe.

'Get anything?' Bone asked.

'What do you think?'

'Lucky bastard.'

'Is there any loot in it tonight?'

'Skin says the guv'nor takes the money to a deposit box at the bank. He leaves a bit of small, but that's in a safe about as easy to get into as the Queen Mother's pantyhose. It's not enough to bother about, and anyway, we haven't got the equipment for anything like that.'

'It's not worth it then, is it.'

'Why not? They've got some good gear.'

'I reckon Skin's just using us.'

'Don't be daft. He ain't using *me*.'

'He's keeping well out of it, isn't he.'

'He's got to. Use your loaf.'

'I don't trust him. He wouldn't piss on you if you was on fire.'

'He's all right.'

'What about Benny getting done?'

'Benny's a shithead.'

'That's not the point. Skin'd grass on anyone.'

'Give over. All we've got to do is go in the window and help ourselves to some gear. There's nothing to it.'

'And get a load for Skin.'

'That's fair enough.'

'I suppose so,' I said, grudgingly. 'What did your old girl say about you getting the push?'

'Nothing. She's all right. The old cock had a go at me, though.'

'He's got room to talk.'

'I know. I knocked him down the bloody stairs. He had it coming. He's been getting on my tit for a long time. He came up in my bedroom and started.'

'He ain't done a bloody day's work in ten years.'

'I called him a drunken old git, and he took a swipe at me; so I thumped him out of the room onto the landing. Then he fell down the stairs.'

'Then what?'

'Nothing. He shut hisself in the front room with a bottle of cooking sherry and wouldn't come out. I heard him crying in there,' Bone was trying to sound unconcerned. But his face gave him away.

I tried to think of something to say. 'He's a big bugger', I said.

'He used to be one hell of a tough customer when he was at sea, but he's gone soft as shit now. He's drunk hisself stupid.'

Two girls came clomping up the street in bum-freezer jackets and skintight jeans and high heels. One was good-looking with a mass of dyed black hair. The other was a real scrawny-looking piece with sparse fair hair and no more tit than I had. They were both dressed the same — which was unfortunate for the ugly one. They were giggling and giving us sidelong glances. 'I could do that a favour,' Bone said. 'It ain't going to win any prizes, but I wouldn't kick it out of bed. Shall we fix ourselves up for after?'

'Well, if we do,' I said, 'I don't fancy yours.'

'You don't look at the mantelpiece when you poke the fire. I'll toss you for first choice.'

'I don't fancy any more tonight.'

'Never heard you say no before.'

The girls disappeared into Jim's, wagging their tails behind them. 'I just don't fancy any more, that's all.'

Bone studied me for a moment, and then a grin began to spread over his face. 'You really did get something out of Barry's bird, then.'

'I told yer, didn't I.' I felt annoyed that he'd called her '*Barry's* bird'.

'Well, you want to be careful, mate. Barry'll put the boot in your plums if you don't watch out.'

'What about this piddling little job, then?' I said. 'Let's get this half-baked show on the road.'

We rode up and down the main street twice, looking out for the Old Bill. Some of the shops had their windows lit up, but there were no pedestrians about, and little traffic. Skin's shop was next door to the cinema. I switched off my motor, free-wheeled up the alley and parked round the back by the staff entrance. We stood for a while, listening. All I could hear was the muffled sound track of the film, an occasional car passing along the road, and my heart beating. My insides turned to water. I pissed up against the shop wall. Bone joined me. It sounded like the bath being filled with both taps. 'Let's go,' Bone whispered. I was heartened to hear from the shaky tightness of his voice that he was as nervous as I was.

He lumbered up the drainpipe like an old orang-utan, and I followed more clumsily. I could feel flakes of paint and rust falling into my hair. Bone reached across and got himself upright, with some difficulty, on a narrow window ledge. I was hoping that Skin had forgotten to unfasten the window, or that his boss had closed it again, but when Bone levered the top-light, it opened. He tried to haul himself through, but his shoulder knocked the stay and the window trapped him so that he couldn't move. 'Kev,' he called, hoarsely. 'Hold this up for us, will yer.'

I grabbed hold of his legs and clambered onto the ledge. Then I held the window up while Bone wriggled himself through. I heard him crash, swearing, onto the floor. 'Bloody hell,' he complained. 'They might've put the seat down. I nearly fell down the bog.'

'Mind you don't pull the flush,' I said. 'I might never see you again.'

When he got up he held the window open and helped pull me through. I was dragged into the shop head first, like a difficult birth. I scraped my shins on the window frame, bounced off the toilet seat and fell onto my head on the floor. Bone gave me a hand up and we dusted ourselves down in the dark. 'Bloody Foreskin might've slung a safety net under the window,' I complained.

'What worries me,' said Bone, with rare foresight, 'is how we're going to get out again.'

I held the back of Bone's jacket as we groped our way out to the stairs like a pantomime horse. Bone walked into a wall and I walked into his back. 'Ow,' he said, rubbing his forehead.

'It's dark,' I offered sympathetically.

'Course it's dark.'

'Know what?'

'No. What?'

'We should've brought a torch.'

'What for?'

I thought about it for a moment and realised it wasn't such a good idea. 'We could have flashed an SOS to a passing copper,' I said, 'so he could come and get us out.'

Once in the shop there was enough light from the street through the glass doors for us to be able to find our way around. I was surrounded by the comforting smells of new clothes. 'Here's Skin's parcel,' Bone said.

'What's he got in *there* — the kitchen sink?' I said. 'How are we supposed to get *that* home on our bikes?'

'Dunno.'

'I can't see what colour anything is.'

'Stop moaning. Count your blessings.'

'Not before they're hatched.'

I piled up socks and underwear, T-shirts, jeans, trainers, jumpers and then, lavishly pouring blessings on the heads of Jesus, Mary, Joseph and the Holy Ghost, I found a *real* leather jacket that fitted me.

We were both making up parcels for ourselves, like Skin's (though smaller) when we heard the footsteps. There had of course been the clip clip of feet from time to time going up or down the pavement — but these were definitely *not* going past. I wondered if Skin had set us up. It flashed through my mind that the filth might be letting him off some misdemeanour in exchange for convictions against other young offenders. I thought about Benny getting sent down for possession of the dope he'd bought off Skin. Skin was an apprentice supergrass if ever I saw one. The two sets of footsteps came right into the shop doorway and stopped. I ducked behind a counter, closed my eyes and tried not to breathe. Then I heard the girl's voice. 'Don't,' she whined. 'I don't feel like it tonight.'

'Too bad,' said a male voice. 'I do.'

The girl sounded like Sharron. Maybe she was out there doing it with

41

Barry. And she'd think I was a wimp. When she hadn't wanted me to do it, I'd just stopped. But *he* just went ahead and had her anyway. I felt sick. I felt like sitting on the floor and crying. I felt like throwing myself through the glass door and trying to strangle that big ape with my hands (catching him with his trousers down, so to speak).

Bone was pulling my sleeve. 'Come on,' he said. 'It's only a couple having their oats. Cop hold of this.' He thrust his parcel into my arms. 'You bring our stuff — I'll bring Skin's.'

'If you can lift it,' I said.

We stumbled upstairs like cartoon Christmas shoppers, blinded by the dark and our armfuls of outsize packages. All the windows were barred. It seemed we had to go out the way we came in. 'Oh, shit,' Bone said.

'What's the matter?'

'Can't get the parcels out. Window's too small.'

'Listen. I'll go out. You chuck the gear down, and we'll re-parcel it down there.'

'What if the Old Bill comes while we're at it?'

'I'll tell them we found the stuff lying around. I'll say we're keeping Britain tidy. And I ain't going out there head first, either. Help me get my feet out.' I hooked my heels onto the frame, then twisted over. Bone cradled me in his arms. We must have looked like crazy wrestlers, or weird lovers.

'*There was a young man from Norway,*' Bone recited, '*who hung by his heels from a doorway...*'

When my legs were sticking out of the bog window like a pair of flag poles, I said, 'Bone, I've got cold feet.'

'That's nothing,' he said, 'I'm shitting bricks.'

With his support I managed to writhe painfully through the window and find a footing on the outside ledge. I swung across to the drainpipe and slid down. The feel of firm ground under my feet was as much of a relief as it would have been after a sick month at sea. But even before I reached terra firma our booty started to fly as Bone hurled everything out after me. 'Some bags,' I croaked up at him.

'This is no time to be going after old bags.'

'Get us some bags out of the shop.'

42

The cascade dried up for a while. I went about gathering up the scattered clothing until I was suddenly clouted around the head. I stumbled, looking about me in the darkness to see who the protagonist was. I thought it must either be a copper swatting me with his truncheon, or Barry giving me some finger pie. In fact I'd been hit on the head by a wad of paper bags. 'What did you do that for?' I hissed angrily.

'You said you wanted some bags.'

'Yeah. But I didn't want them round the ear'ole.'

The monsoon of material resumed. Everything was muddled now. But if I got nothing out of it apart from the jacket, I didn't care — and I was wearing that.

After the flurry of cloth had finally ceased, Bone called pathetically, 'Kev. I can't get out.'

'We ought to take this up for a career,' I said.

'Kev. What am I going to do?'

'You could put some of their gear on and stand very still in the window.'

'I'm serious.'

'Well, what goes up must come down.'

'I helped you out. I can't get my feet through.'

I started climbing back up the drainpipe. 'Come out head first.'

'I'll bash my brains out.'

'If we'd got any brains,' I said, 'we wouldn't be here in the first place. Hang about. I'm coming up.'

When my feet were on a level with the sill I reached across with an arm and leg and came the closest I've ever been to a fatal heart attack as the drainpipe parted company with the wall. I felt myself begin to swing gracefully out into space. My impulse was to grip hold of the pipe like a slow loris clinging on to a tree in a typhoon, but despite my panic I managed to lunge for the comparative safety of the window sill. My feet scrabbled ineffectively against the brickwork, but Bone, whose head and shoulders were sticking out of the top-light like a gargoyle on a church wall, grabbed my arm. The drainpipe crashed down into the back yard with a loud enough clamour to wake the shop's owner from his sleep in front of the telly two miles away, never mind the goons down the other end of the Main Street in the police station.

'What did you want to make all that noise for?' Bone complained, as he hauled me up so I could get a foothold on the ledge.

'Why d'you think?' I said. 'I was trying to summon the fire brigade to get us down.'

Bone squirmed out, like a maggot crawling out of an apple. I managed to support him until he too got his feet onto the sill. We stood there then, as nervous as a bride and groom, side by side on the window sill, getting our breath back, gazing at the ground six metres below, wondering how the hell we were going to get down. It looked an awful long drop. 'Do you come here often?' I asked Bone.

'It's somewhere to hang out,' he said.

'Have you got any ideas?'

'If I could hang from your ankles, I could drop from there.'

'Then how am I going to get down?'

'I could break your fall.'

'I could break my neck.'

'Well what are we going to do?'

'There's no alternative,' I said. 'It'll have to be a lovers' leap.'

It was a painful landing. But neither of us broke anything. We gathered all the gear we could find in the dark and, balancing our piles of swag on our petrol tanks, sped away from the shop like bats out of hell, leaving an occasional pair of underpants like a night bird fluttering in our wake.

After we'd dumped everything in Bone's garage, I went back for Sharron. Jim's was empty. Jim came in from the back room. 'You back again? Ain't you got no home to go to?'

'This *is* home,' I said. 'Not doing much business, are yer.'

'The rest of the world's got more sense than to spend the night in here. What d'you want then?'

'Tea. Nice and hot.' I poked my hands into my armpits to warm them. 'Bleeding freezing out there.' Brown liquid came spluttering and splurting out of Jim's shining chrome antique. I examined my distorted reflection in the side of it trying to see how the jacket looked in the light, but I looked like a string bean gone black with blight. 'One of these days, Jim,' I said, 'that thing'll blow up.'

'Don't you believe it. She'll still be making tea after *you*'ve been blown up.'

I warmed my hands round my mug. 'Cor, that's nice. Got anything to eat?'

'You come into money or something?'

'I couldn't afford your prices otherwise.'

'Nothing much left. Couple of pies.'

'Yeah. Piece of apple pie'll go down very nicely.'

'They're pork pies.'

'Oh, well, that'll do. I don't suppose I'll be able to taste the difference. Seen Sharron?'

'She went.'

'She say if she was coming back?'

'Nah. Didn't say nothing.'

'Did she go with anyone?'

'Yeah.'

'Who?'

He hesitated, and then said, 'Barry.'

It was like having a pail of piss chucked in my face. I went down to a table at the far end. I managed to force down half the pie, and drowned myself in my tea. Jim collected dishes, gave the table tops a cursory wipe with a wet rag, and disappeared back into his room. I sat in the empty cafe, brooding. I knew Sharron wouldn't be coming back, but I decided to wait anyway — just in case.

After a while I slotted some coins in the juke-box and had a couple of games on a pin table. I was only two thousand off a bonus game when the cafe door jangled open. Barry came in with four of his boys. The studs and toe-caps of their boots scraped and clicked on the floor like spurs. Barry glanced at me. He looked surprised — probably at finding me there on my own. They ignored me and concentrated on buying coffees at the counter. My next ball went more or less straight for a burton. I stood leaning on the pin table before I played my final ball wondering what I could do. Barry and his lackeys brought their drinks to a table behind me, but none of them sat down. Jim disappeared again, which was like seeing my lifebelt swept out to sea. He was probably watching something on telly with Betty. *Don't go down,* I said to myself.

Stay on your feet whatever you do so they can't put the boot in. And I played my last ball. The lights on the pin table headstone flashed on and off and the counter clunked round as though it was counting up the dead in the next world war. But I finished two hundred short of the total I needed. The pin table held me up. I could feel eyes on my back like poison darts.

'Just take a butcher's at that,' a voice sneered.

'It's just a long streak of gnatspit.'

'What a wanker.'

'He's shitting hisself.'

'Fancies itself with the birds.'

'Put the boot in his fucking face.'

'Mess it up so no bride'll want to look at it again.'

'Put the boot in his fucking cobblers, more like.'

'Yeah. Ruin his fucking chances.'

I gripped the edges of the pin table to try to stop from shaking. I heard the boots, and felt the warm breath on my ear. Barry's voice was soft — as if he was talking to a girl. 'Want to come outside with me, darling?'

I turned to face him, with my back pressed against the pin table so no one could get behind me. I wished the juke-box would shut up so that Jim might hear, but the bass and drums continued to thump, and the guitars cried, and the young man went on wailing his anger and frustration and pain. With an attempt at bravado I stared into Barry's startlingly blue and sneering eyes as scornfully as my fear-taut face muscles allowed.

'What yer screwing, mate?' Barry said, his boys jostling in around us.

I hated talking in clichés. My mother talked in nothing but clichés: small portions of language, pre-packed and poisoned with preservatives. But fear had numbed my brain. 'I don't know,' I said. 'It's not labelled.'

Barry stood squarely in front of me, legs apart, booted feet planted firmly on the cafe floor, thumbs shoved into the top of his belt. 'You hairy cunt,' he sneered.

I realised that if I could provoke a fight without going outside my chances of survival would be increased tenfold. 'If you were a man', I said contemptuously, 'a hairy cunt would turn you on.'

He looked puzzled for a moment. Then, without removing his hands from his belt, launched himself forward and nutted me full in the mouth. The blood, pain and terror tasted like a funny sort of victory. I let out a cry, hopefully loud enough to alert Jim, and Barry nutted me again, this time his forehead cracking against my left eye. 'Keep your filthy paws off my bird, Cunt!' he snarled. The mafia crowded in throwing kicks and punches, mercifully getting in each other's way in their greed to get a piece of the action. I didn't fight back. I was only concerned with shielding myself as far as I could, making as much noise as possible, and trying to stay on my feet till Jim came to get them off.

'Pack it in! I'm not having no fighting in here! I haven't got a licence! Now pack it in when I tell yer!'

Never mind the jokes, I thought. He had to really thump a couple of them. He landed one a right-hander on the ear which sent him crashing into a table and onto his knees.

'Get out!' It was Betty's voice. 'Go on! Out! Come back when you can behave yourselves.'

Jim hustled them towards the door. 'Don't worry,' Barry said. 'We ain't finished with you yet.'

'Come on! Out! The lot of yer!' Jim slammed the door behind them and tucked his shirt back into his trousers. 'You all right, son?'

'Yeah.' I walked my fingers gingerly around my face. My nose was bleeding. I had a split lip which was sore and bloody and puffing up. But most of the pain was located around my eye.

'I'll get a cloth.'

He came back with one of his wet dish rags that didn't smell too good. Betty took it out of his hands. 'Let me,' she said. I was glad of its warmth, but more, I was glad of Betty's mothering attention. 'There,' she said. 'You'll do.'

'I don't know what's the matter with you lads,' Jim said. 'Why you can't get on without fighting each other, I don't know.'

'You were the same,' Betty said.

'I suppose so. Want a cuppa?'

I craved for them to go on fussing over me, but I was also embarrassed by it. 'No, Jim, ta. Think I'll get back.'

'You're going to have a right shiner there tomorrow.'

'Tie a bit of best steak over it,' Betty advised. 'It'll be better in no time.'

'Will a meat and potato pie do?' I asked.

I found my mother slumped asleep in an armchair in front of the telly. There was an old horror movie showing. A man dressed up as an ape had got a woman in a flimsy dress tied, with her arms above her head, to a wooden frame. My mother was sitting with her feet in the fireplace. The fire had burned low. She still had her make-up on. False eyelashes — the lot. But she wasn't wearing her going-out clothes. It was obvious that Guy the Gorilla had got what he'd come for, and cleared off. She looked ugly, with her face twisted in uncomfortable sleep, her mouth hanging open, dribbling a little onto the chair back. The light from fire and telly was unflattering, making her look older than she really was. She seemed pathetic. I despised her for not having more pride, for letting herself be used. And I hated her because I was wallowing in self pity, and wanted someone to comfort me. I dragged a chair out from the table and collapsed onto it, groaning.

'Wh? Wh's'at?'

'Me.'

Her eyes and voice were heavy with sleep. 'Oh, 's you.' She sat up and pulled her jumper down across her stomach. She fingered her hair, and rubbed her eyes, and looked at her watch in the light from the telly. I could see anger simmering in her. 'What's got into you, then? What you doing home this early on a Saturday night?'

'Christ, woman! Every night you're on at me about coming in late, and when I come home early you moan about that.'

She switched the telly off, then squatted and began to poke the fire in order to coax the last heat out of the dying coals. 'I was not moaning,' she said sarcastically in an affected voice. 'I was merely expressing my surprise that you had deigned to come home at a reasonable hour for once in your bleeding life.'

'What've you done with King Kong?'

'Mind your own business.'

'Why d'you let them treat you like this, Ma?'

'It's got nothing to do with you.' She sat down again. 'Put the light on, will yer,' she said in a tired voice. She kicked off her shoes, undid her stockings and began rolling them down her legs. 'I said, would you put the light on. Or is that too much to ask?'

'Put the bloody light on yourself.'

She was on her feet then, like an eager fighter coming out of her corner at the beginning of a round. 'Can't you do one little thing for me?' She stormed across the room to the light switch by the door. 'I work my fingers to the bone, I do, in this house, and what thanks do I get? You sodding men, you're all the same. You take what you can get, and you give nothing. Well I'm fed up with it. Fed up to the back teeth.'

Of course, it didn't help to know that she was shouting at them more than she was shouting at me. I could hear the tears of angry frustration working their way into her voice and recognised that for the danger signal it was. I noticed the holy family had disappeared, exposing a stain on the wallpaper behind the telly like yellow blood, where she'd thrown the margarine at me the day after the room was last redecorated. I couldn't see out of my left eye because the swelling had closed it completely. I could feel dried blood stretching my skin. 'What's the matter with your face?' she asked in a surprised voice.

I looked away. 'You give me the face-ache — that's what's the matter with it'

'Don't you be so bloody cheeky to me or I'll give you another face-ache to go with the one you've got.'

Neither of us spoke for a moment. Ashes fell in the grate. Then she said more quietly, 'What happened to you? I asked.'

'Came off my bike, didn't I.'

She pulled out a chair and sat down at the table. 'Don't come the old soldier with me. What did you fall on — a knuckle sandwich?'

'Told yer. Came off my bike.'

'Well if you did, it serves you bloody well right. It's a death trap, that thing.'

Another brief silence. I could hear shrieking from next door's television: a woman being abused for the entertainment of the masses.

She said impatiently, 'Well, do you want a cup of tea or something?'

'No.'

'Well, what *do* you want then?'

I stared at her with my one good eye, shook my head sadly, and said, 'You wouldn't know, would yer.'

49

I waited, but instead of the reaction I expected, she crumpled. Her lips puckered like a child's, and she began to cry.

THE PARTY

I live with my mum. My mum goes to work. She won't let me play out.
She says the street is dirty. She says the kids are rough. She thinks I'll
get in trouble. When it's holidays, she makes me stay in. I have to stay
in all day. If I get out — she beats me. When she goes to work she locks
the doors.

We live in two rooms. The rooms are upstairs. Miss Bence lives
downstairs. Miss Bence is old. She's so old she just sits by the fire, and
doesn't speak. When I grow up, I'm not going to be old like Miss Bence.
When I grow up, I'm not going to be poor like my mum. When I grow
up, I'm going to be a workman and make lots of money.

This week it's holidays. This week it's Janet Smith's birthday. Janet
Smith is in my class. Her dad's got a shop. He's a greengrocer. *Smith the
Greengrocer,* on the corner. He sells fruit and veg. I go to *Smith*'s on
Saturdays. I go there to buy seven pounds of potatoes, and I smell the
lovely smell of fruit and veg. When I grow up, I think I'll be a
greengrocer like Mr Smith. Then I won't be hungry any more.

Today is Janet Smith's party. She talked about it at school the day we
broke up. She invited all her friends. She didn't invite me. (Even though
I've played with her behind the cycle sheds.)

Today it's raining. My mum went to work and locked the doors. It's
rained all day. This afternoon I sat by the window. I sat staring out. There

51

weren't even any cats about. Too wet for cats. The rain poured down. It bounced on the kitchen roof. It bounced on the toilet roof. It bounced in the back yard and made black puddles by the bin.

It got to three o'clock. I knew Janet Smith was having her party. I knew all the kids were having fun. I opened the window. Rain spat in my face. I climbed over the sill. The rain gave me stinging slaps behind my legs. I lowered myself onto the sloping kitchen roof. It was wet, shining and slippery like a winter playground slide. I crept along the cold roof like a cat. I climbed down onto the toilet roof. I sat on the wet tiles and did a slithery crab-like walk down the roof on my hands and feet and bum.

Then I jumped. I landed in a puddle in the yard. The water splashed up my socks. My legs stung. My feet burned like bonfires. I tried to dry my hands on my shorts, but my shorts were soggy like a sponge. I went out of the yard and down the road.

Janet Smith lives at number three. I slowed down outside her house. I sauntered past. I peeped in the front window. I saw kids sitting at the table. I carried on walking, to the corner. And still the cold rain poured down. I turned round and walked back. The kids were eating tea. They were wearing paper hats. The table was wearing a white cloth. Balloons hung down from the ceiling. I passed on.

And still it rained. I turned round and walked back again. I saw jellies, and sandwiches, and cakes, and ice cream. I wandered up and down the street in the rain. My shirt was like a dishcloth. Rain ran from my hair, dripped down my neck, and dribbled down my back. I put my hands in my pockets to keep them warm. My knees were as cold as icicles. Each time I passed number three, I peered inside. The kids were playing by the fire, laughing, and having fun.

Then the front door opened. Mrs Smith came out. ' Whatever are you doing, child,' she said, 'in the rain without a coat?'

'Nothing,' I said.

'Well you'd better come in,' she said, 'and do nothing in the dry.'

She took my hand. We went inside. I was going to the party after all. The hall was warm, and bright, and dry. I heard chattering and laughter. She led me into the front room. The chatter and laughter stopped. All these kids stared.

No one liked me.

Mrs Smith towelled my hair, and sat me in an armchair. She brought me left-overs from the tea. The cakes clogged up my mouth. The jelly tasted sour. The kids played together. No one spoke to me.

I got down from the chair. 'I've got to go,' I said.

'Stay,' said Mrs Smith. 'Stay and play.'

'My mum says I have to be home by four,' I said.

I could feel the kids throwing faces at my back. I came out into the cold rain that spits and stings and slaps.

The day's gloom will soon deepen into night. I can't get in our house. The door is locked. Miss Bence is deaf.

I'm waiting for my mum.

JAMIE

Mr and Mrs Collins had not been able to have children of their own, so they'd adopted Jamie as a baby. He'd been a great disappointment to them.

Mr Collins was a big man, good at sports, good at his job. Jamie was a runt. He hated sports. He was no good at school. He failed his exams. Mr Collins' hopes turned sour. His dreams changed to contempt. In the end he took as much notice of Jamie as he might of a fly on the wall.

Mrs Collins was less disdainful, but also dissatisfied with her son. The experience had taught her that she liked babies but not children. She tried to do her duty, to provide for him and to protect him from the worst, but only in a half-hearted and loveless sort of way. As Jamie grew older she became more and more involved in committees and voluntary organisations.

At school, Jamie had always been a loner, an outsider, with few friends. This problem was made worse because Mr Collins was ambitious and changed jobs frequently, always pursuing promotion. This meant that Jamie was often the *new boy,* having to make his way in a strange and hostile environment.

At the last school Jamie went to he formed an unusual bond with Jack, a big, tough lad of his own age. Like Jamie, Jack was an under-achiever. They'd slithered down the academic ladder until they'd arrived together at the very bottom.

Jamie was no favourite of the teachers. His written work and concentration were poor, and his attitude was sullen and ungracious. *Insipid* was a word they often used about him. Jack was known to be a mischief-maker, but he had a spark of vitality and resilience about him which made him less unpopular with the teachers; so more often than not it was Jamie who carried the can.

When the lads played football in the dinner break, Jamie, known as Jammy to all at school, often had to be ball-boy. He was frightened to refuse because he knew from experience that Jack enjoyed demonstrating his torture techniques in front of an admiring audience. Sometimes, if someone was needed to make up a team, Jamie would have to play. He was always the last one chosen and Jack made sure, if at all possible, that Jamie wasn't on his side. Nor did he miss any opportunity of making crunching and unfair tackles whenever he got close enough (with boots that cracked on shins like stones).

At least being a friend of Jack's meant that Jamie was saved from a certain amount of bullying he would otherwise have come in for from other boys. They seemed to accept that Jammy was Jack's, and by and large left him alone.

Jamie was not good at fighting or defending himself and while at school only twice ever started a fight. The first occasion left him sick with guilt and shame and feeling that he'd got his just desserts. In Jamie's class there was another natural victim: a boy named Tear. The name itself set the lad up like an Aunt Sally for the bullies and tormentors. One day Tear informed on Jamie when a teacher demanded to know who was the Clever Dick whose watch alarm had gone off. 'Like to get up late, do we?' he'd sneered. 'Then we can stay in late after school.' At break, Jamie, egged on by Jack, challenged Tear to fight. (Tear was the only boy in the year Jamie thought he could beat.) Tear refused. Jamie pursued him around the playground calling him a coward until finally he had him cornered by the cycle sheds. Tear, possibly out of fear, turned on Jamie then and lashed out, causing Jamie's nose to flood with blood. A small crowd had collected to watch the spectacle and at this point began to jeer with dissatisfaction. Jack stepped out from among them and put an arm on Jamie's shoulders. 'The fight isn't over,' he said. 'He's not crying — are you Jammy?' It was this apparent concern rather than the damage he had suffered that made Jamie cry. Jack, showing the same sort of contempt as Jamie's father, took him into the wash room and cleaned him up.

The other fight that Jamie instigated was, strangely, against Cheadle, one of the school's most notorious bullies. Cheadle was already developed like a full-grown man, while Jamie was still a child. Cheadle had the worst acne Jamie had ever seen, although nobody mentioned it for obvious reasons. One bleak and sleeting morning Cheadle had cornered Caplan, a fat Jewish lad whose parents owned the laundrette in town, and was taunting him: 'Yid!' 'Fat maggot!' 'Jewish slime!' and so on. Caplan, afraid and upset, was quickly reduced to tears. Jamie, surprising himself as much as everybody else, stepped between them and even put out an ineffectual hand to push Cheadle away. 'Leave him alone,' he said sulkily.

Cheadle laughed in disbelief. ' Look what's crawled out the cheese,' he jeered.

'Just lay off him,' Jamie mumbled.

Cheadle laughed again more loudly. It was like Charlie Chaplin confronting Charles Atlas. 'What're you going to do about it, you little turd?'

'Just leave him,' Jamie whined, looking down at his feet. What followed could hardly be called a fight. Cheadle thumped Jamie three times and flattened him onto the wet asphalt. 'Get up, Wimp!' Cheadle said. But Jack stepped in and said, 'Leave him, Cheadle. He's had enough.'

Jamie never analysed the strange and special partnership he'd fallen into. Jack was sometimes a good friend to him, though Jamie was never sure why. He was just grateful that he had a friend at all. But Jack's moods changed as quickly and unpredictably as the weather, and Jamie would never know when cordiality would revert to bullying. Jack never thought about it either. He related to Jamie as if the smaller boy were a pet, a dumb creature he could take things out on, and yet still have as a companion, who would do as he was told, and still be there when Jack wanted him. Perhaps Jack was lonelier than he or Jamie realised.

Jamie could remember the beginning of their peculiar relationship.

He'd not long been at the school. It was a time of changing over between classes. They were waiting for the teacher to come. Jamie was singing to himself. 'Here, listen to Jammy!' Jack said. Of course Jamie clammed up but a crowd of boys and girls collected around him. 'Go on then,' Jack said.

'Go on what?'

'Go on singing!'

'I'm not singing.'

'Yes you were. Go on!'

'I don't want to.'

Jack pushed Jamie up against the wall at the back of the classroom. He got hold of one of Jamie's fingers and bent it back, causing intense pain. 'Sing!' he said. 'Sing when I bloody tell yer!'

'All right, all right,' Jamie whimpered. Jack eased his grip and Jamie began to sing in a shaky and tuneless voice, '*Love, love me do. You know I love you.*'

The class, all ears now, erupted into uncontrollable laughter. Jamie ached for a bomb to be dropped on the school, or an earthquake to start, anything that would distract their attention and save him from this ordeal.

About half the boys in Jamie's class had either got girl-friends or had been out with girls. Jamie had never had the opportunity of such an experience. It wasn't that he didn't think about girls. It wasn't that he didn't want to feel their arms, kiss their mouths, and find himself in that secret place he dreamed about like any normal boy. It was on his mind often at school as he caught a glimpse of a girl's thigh, or saw the sun shining through a grimy school window onto silky hair. It was on his mind often at home as he watched the dancers on television programmes or lay in bed holding himself with a hot urgent hand. Sometimes when a group of boys was teasing a girl, perhaps tickling her, pulling her about, he tried to join in, but the girl's giggles soon turned to anger. Slapped or ridiculed, he would slink off, red-faced, to lick his wounds alone.

Jack of course had far more success in arousing the interest of girls but somehow, surprisingly, never had a girl-friend. Jamie sometimes wondered why.

The prettiest girl in their class was Belinda. The two boys sometimes followed Belinda and her friends home from school, with Jack showing off to catch her attention. On one of these occasions a refuse lorry turned into the street just behind them. 'Hey, watch this,' Jack called. He snatched Jamie's cap from his head and threw it into the stinking garbage in the back of the passing lorry.

'Hey!' protested Jamie. 'That's my cap!'

Belinda laughed with cruel amusement, and Jack laughed with self-satisfaction. Jamie trembled impotently, furious about this latest needless humiliation in front of the girls.

A few minutes later a van pulled across the road and stopped beside them, two wheels up on the kerb and the hazard lights flashing. The driver wound down the window and poked out a dirt-smeared face. 'Jack!' he said. Jack looked surprised, then worried. 'Listen, tell your mum I'm going to be late. There's an emergency job come up. It'll take two, three hours. All right? Now don't forget this time or you'll feel the back of my hand round your face.'

'No, Dad,' Jack said.

It was a white van with blue writing on the side which read: *ABC DRAIN CLEARING — DRAIN REPAIR WORK*. Jamie would remember the incident with shame in later years but at that time it seemed that fate had put a weapon into his hands. 'Was that your dad?' he asked.

'Yeah,' Jack admitted, reddening. 'So what?'

'Is that what he does then — clean out drains!'

'What about it?' Jack said aggressively.

'Does he have to clean the shit out of blocked sewers then?'

Jack looked quickly and anxiously towards Belinda whose face, Jamie was delighted to see, wore an expression of disgust. She turned with her friends and sauntered away.

'Watch it, Jammy!' Jack warned.

'Sorry,' Jamie said. 'I only asked.'

One Christmas Jamie's father had bought him a table-tennis table. Although it was a present for Jamie, Mr Collins chose it because it was a game he himself loved to play. It was in fact the only thing that father and son did together, and because Jamie spent so many hours at the table to please his father it had become the one game that he could play well.

One evening after school Jamie asked Jack if he'd like to come home for a game.

'What — you got your own table?' Jack said, incredulously.

'Yes.'

'All right. Have you done your history homework?'

'Yes. I did it last night.'

'Can I borrow it tonight?'

'As long as you don't copy word for word.'

'Don't be daft,' Jack said. 'I'm not stupid.'

As they turned into *The Avenue* Jack looked at the big detached houses with their large and well-stocked gardens. 'You live in one of these?' he sneered. Having expected Jack to be impressed, Jamie was taken aback. He felt apologetic and didn't know how to respond. When they entered the house Jamie was thankful that both parents were out. He knew that Mrs Collins and Jack would have taken an instant and intense dislike to each other.

'What d'you need a bloody great house like this for, for three people?' Jack said accusingly.

'It's just ordinary,' Jamie said.

'Just ordinary! What you on about! I've got three brothers and we could fit our whole house in your front room.'

Jamie was beginning to feel that this had been a mistake. They dropped their coats in the hall and he quickly led the way through to the table-tennis room and picked up a bat. Jack started cockily, knowing that Jamie was hopeless at all sports and expecting to trounce him. In the knock-up Jamie didn't try too hard. He saved his best shots for the actual game. 'Best of five,' he said.

When the match started Jack played confidently but gradually Jamie established his superiority, secretly gloating over every point he won. Here at last was something in which he excelled. He began to show off, putting a lot of spin on the ball, placing shots carefully out of reach so that Jack had to run continually from side to side, once even crashing heavily into the wall in an effort to get to a finely angled ball. Jamie won the first game 21-7 and was leading the second 19-3. Jack, flushed with shame and anger, mis-hit a wildly spinning ball long, and threw his bat at the table, taking off a scrape of green surface. 'Don't do that!' Jamie snapped, afraid of what his father would say.

'Shut your face!' Jack said. 'I've got to go.'

'What — 'cos you're losing?'

'Watch your mouth!' He came towards Jamie belligerently. Jamie didn't do or say anything. If Jack had hit him it wouldn't have mattered. It would just have been a recognition of Jamie's victory, and both boys knew that. Jamie stood his ground and after a moment's threatening glare Jack left the room. As he gathered up his things in the hall he asked gruffly, 'Where's the history?'

Jamie dragged it out of his school bag. Jack snatched it and went to the front door.

'See you tomorrow,' Jamie said.

'Not if I see you first.' Jack went down the path and out of the gate and began to swagger back towards the main road. As Jamie closed the front door his inner glow of satisfaction curdled with the apprehension of losing the only friend he had.

The next morning as they came into the classroom before the first period Jamie asked: 'Did you do the history last night?

'Yeah.'

'Can I have my book then?'

'Lost it.'

'What d'you mean?'

'Lost it, didn't I.'

'How could you have lost it?'

'Dunno.'

'Oh, come on. Don't muck about.'

'I'm not mucking about.'

'Well let's have my book then.'

'I've lost the bloody book, I told yer.'

'Well what am I going to do?'

'*I* don't know. That's your problem.'

'Oh, come on. I lent you my book. I helped you.'

'Well I can't help it. I've lost it, haven't I. I can't give it to you if I haven't got it.'

'Well where have you lost it?'

'I don't know. If I knew that, I wouldn't have lost it, would I.'

Jamie felt sick, less with the fear of the punishment he'd get for not having done his history homework and the misery of having to do it all over again, than with the unforgivable injustice of the betrayal. He believed that Jack had deliberately 'lost' the book, deliberately destroyed it, chucked it in the bin, and it seemed a terrible treachery given that he'd only had the book because of Jamie's generosity.

That sunny, though chilly April evening their strange friendship was finally ended. The two boys usually walked home from school together. There were various routes they could take. The longest detour was the most interesting. A side turning off the High Street led to a footpath along by the allotments. The footpath ended in a large cow-pasture which was divided by a meandering brown river. Across the field was a stile and a lane leading to the older area of the town where Jack lived. It was less than a mile further along the main road to the newer private development where the Collins' house was situated.

That evening as they walked beside the river, Jack unexpectedly shoulder-charged Jamie, as in a football match. Jamie stumbled sideways off the bank, landing in the sludge on the verge of the river. As he pulled a foot out of the slurping mud his shoe stuck and was left behind. He had to bury a hand in the cold mire to steady himself as he balanced on one leg to drag the reluctant shoe out. He then sat on the wet bank to put the mud-filled shoe squelchily back onto his foot. 'What did you do that for?' he said angrily.

'Cos I felt like it, that's why.'

Jamie tied his shoe, smeared the mud from his hands onto his trousers, and stood up. They resumed their walk together, but this time Jamie made sure he was on the side away from the river. As they came towards a cow-pat on the ground Jack suddenly shoulder-charged again. Jamie staggered sideways almost stepping into the cow muck but managing to hop across. Infuriated, he made a clumsy attempt to shoulder-charge Jack. The bigger boy, being prepared, side-stepped nimbly and stuck out a foot. Jamie tripped and went sprawling onto all-fours into the shallow water at the edge of the river. 'That'll teach yer to try and push me in the river,' Jack said.

Jamie stood up but found it difficult to extricate his feet from the clinging ooze in order to climb up onto the bank. 'Give us a hand up,' he demanded resentfully.

Jack looked around, then picked up a stick from the ground. He came back to Jamie, holding the stick suggestively with two hands in front of his fly and said: 'Grab hold of this.'

Jamie did so — then let go with a squeal of disgust. He looked at the cow shit on his hands. Jack dropped the stick and laughed. 'Poor old Jammy,' he said. 'Cor, you don't half pong, Jammy.'

Jamie stood with his feet stuck in the mud under three inches of numbing water and his foul-smelling hands dangling at his sides. He looked up at his friend who was dancing and whooping like a parody of a drunken Red-Indian. *Friend! Is this what it means to have a friend!* he asked himself.

With difficulty he freed his feet from the mud and then turned his back on Jack and began to walk slowly, carefully, feeling his way with his feet, into the river. Jack watched, grinning with satisfaction, expecting to see Jamie bending to wash his hands. But Jamie continued to make his slow, careful way into the water.

'What're you doing?' Jack said. 'Come out of there. Your books're getting all wet. You'll catch bloody pneumonia. You'll kill yourself.'

Jamie said nothing. He gave no indication of having heard. The water rose to his waist, then to his chest, gripping him with its icy scissor-hold, binding his chest so tightly he could hardly catch his breath. He held his arms up like a cowboy at gunpoint but then, becoming more aware of the cow shit on his hands he lowered them. He rubbed his hands together in a washing motion under the water which now rose to his neck in a freezing stranglehold. He began to be afraid. He wasn't sure how deep the water would be — whether he would have to swim, and could he swim dressed in heavy clothing and almost paralysed by the intense cold?

'Come back, you stupid twit. You'll drown. You'll drown in there. Come out of it.'

Jamie ignored the shouts and continued to shuffle along his own, cold, independent, chosen path. He clamped his mouth shut and whimpered as the murky water reached his chin. But with his next step the water and his fear began to recede. Jamie emerged slowly, shivering, body burning with the fire of the cold, like his hands when he'd played too long in the snow, and unspeaking, and without once looking back, made his way to the other side of the river, where he climbed the bank, and walked away.

NOTHING TO DO

Krishna is fifteen. He lives in the New Town. For four years he lived in North London. There, he was crammed with his mother, brothers, and sisters, into two rooms and a kitchen — the bottom half of an old terraced house. Before that he spent his first eleven years in Kenya where his father, a doctor, still lives. Krishna remembers his father as being a severe, unbending man who never played with him. His English mother on the other hand is an easy-going, good natured woman, who wants to make up for lost time and have some fun before she's too old.

In the New Town Krishna's family have a four-bedroomed house. His two older sisters share a bedroom, as do his two younger brothers. Krishna has a room to himself. (During the years they lived in London the three boys had to roll out strips of foam rubber on the living-room floor every night. His mother and sisters slept in the sitting-room so they could watch television after the boys were in bed.) Krishna is delighted with his room, even though it's only sparsely furnished. He likes the house with its central heating and large sitting-room (where nobody sleeps). There's a garden outside, and a garden shed. (If he'd been given the *shed* to himself it would have seemed palatial after the place in London.)

But outside Krishna's back gate he's less happy. He lives on the edge of the New Town, close to fields and a couple of ponds. He doesn't go to the fields or ponds often. There were no fields in Nairobi. Nor were there fields in North London. The closest thing to a field was Finsbury Park, where his mother didn't like him to go. She was afraid of him being interfered with by one of the dirty old men who hang around there. He never was. He *was* sometimes beaten up by gangs of boys. The white boys beat him up because he was black, and the black boys to pinch his pocket money. Anyway, being a stranger to fields, he doesn't know about the abundance of interesting life to be found there. Being a stranger to ponds, he's puzzled and amused by the boys and men who wait for hours to catch small fish which they eventually throw back into the water.

At school, Krishna is like a fish out of water. Of course, it's always hard for a new kid. It's especially hard if you're part Asian. Krishna doesn't *feel* Asian. After all, his mother is English. But he's not allowed to feel English either. He's called a Paki. He's tired of trying to explain that he has no connections with Pakistan. His father's family have lived in Kenya for more than sixty years, and before that came from southern India. But no one listens. He's not popular with the teachers either. They regard him as withdrawn and uncooperative. When a big lad the white kids call 'Smell' shoved him out of the dinner line, Bullivant threatened him with detention. Krishna tried to explain, but the Bull snorted: 'Don't answer back! We can soon send you back where you came from!' Krishna was shocked. On top of that he wondered where the Bull might be referring to. Krishna doesn't feel that there *is* anywhere he comes from.

In London Krishna enjoyed escaping from the grim, city grime to the movies. In the New Town there is no cinema. There is a hall where they show films from time to time, but Krishna isn't sure exactly where it is and has never been there. There's a youth club on the next estate, but he doesn't go there either. For one thing the kids on the next estate are hostile to kids from Krishna's estate, and secondly he's always found youth clubs boring and the adults who run them patronising. Krishna is always saying, *There's nothing to do here.* It's true that he sometimes used to say that even when he lived in London, but now he says it more often.

Although Krishna is pleased to have such a good house to live in, with a room of his own and all, he feels at a loss in the New Town. This is partly because he's left his friends behind and hasn't yet made new ones, but primarily because he's been taken away from the all-consuming passion of his life. Krishna feels like a space-walking astronaut on one end of an umbilical cord whose space module has disintegrated on the other, because there's no football team in the New Town. The team from the nearest big town is in the fourth division, and (not having any feelings of loyalty to the locality) Krishna doesn't consider *that* to be football at all.

Krishna is an Arsenal supporter. In London he never missed a home game. He saw the greatest clubs at Highbury. The greatest players. But it wasn't just the football. It was the *occasion*. Every week had its focal point, its highlight. And more, he was part of a vast mass of people who were all *on the same side*. For Krishna, being an Arsenal supporter was like living in wartime when everyone supported each other. It made him feel good. It made him feel brave, and protected. In the New Town he doesn't feel good. He feels afraid and vulnerable. Krishna carries this feeling on his evening wanderings around the New Town. When he's with his brothers it settles like a blown egg inside him. When he's alone it swells to the size of a cricket ball. He was carrying it the evening he got beaten up in the car park beneath the shopping centre. After that it distended into a football. (It's unpleasant to feel as if you've got a large air-filled ball lodged in your gut.)

You might think that, having been punched and kicked by seven boys (four of whom were older than he was), Krishna would keep as far away from the shopping centre car park as from an unexploded bomb. But then again, an unexploded bomb is as much a magnet for young lads as a flame is to a moth. Perhaps it is because the shopping centre lights are the brightest in the New Town. Perhaps it is because the shopping centre precinct is in the *middle* of the New Town like the hub of a wheel. Perhaps it is because that's where other young people who have nothing to do congregate. (And fighting is better than loneliness.) In any case the fact is that the following evening, after complaining that there is nothing to do, and leaving his mother to cry (unknown to him) over the bruising on his face and legs, Krishna limps off on one of his nocturnal rambles towards the shopping centre.

As he approaches the centre he sees a dented beer can lying in a puddle. With his unhurt leg he dribbles it along the road. In front of the pub is a grey concrete wall. He blasts the can ferociously against the wall three times, practising penalties. The third time he hurts his toe, so he abandons the can and goes to peer in the pub window. The lights inside are dim which makes the window into a mirror. He has to press his face to the glass. There are few people in there. A small group of men and women sit at one table. A couple hold hands at another. Two young men lean against the bar chatting to the barmaid. The bar itself, with its coloured bottles and sparkling glasses, and the juke-box, with its gaudy index, are the only areas of brightness in the room.

With its dimness, and its brightness, the pub seems as if it would be a warm and friendly place to be. But Krishna is fifteen. The law doesn't allow him to find out. One of the two young men changes position and catches sight of Krishna's face pressed to the window. Krishna quickly moves away. Beside the lifts that take the trolleys up to the supermarket there's a soggy cardboard carton. Krishna kicks it so that it slithers across the pavement scattering rubbish. He continues on his way to nowhere in particular. He's in a vast grey cavern. He has a feeling of cold dampness not only inside his coat, but inside his body, and he remembers the white dry heat of Africa.

Krishna shivers. He shivers partly from cold and partly from fear. His football inflates like a Christmas balloon. (The enormous shabby cellar is a scary place even to someone who has not already been attacked there.) Krishna notices the delicate patterns on the grey concrete walls. The patterns are in fact the grain of the shuttering boards which has left its marks like fossils in rock. He notices that dirt and death have collected in the square perspex bowls of the overhead lights, reducing their brightness, and that many are broken with the bowl missing and the unlit neon tubes dangling like teats from cows' udders. A shout echoes around the cavern, making him freeze. It seems to come from every direction at once. He looks around carefully but can't see anyone.

Krishna stops outside the betting shop. (Most of the shops are up in the mall, but a few have been relegated — like fourth division teams.) He stares at the spotlit cut-outs of racehorses, one grey, one brown, with their tight little knots of jockey in red and blue. A notice shouts at him in red print. *NO PERSON UNDER THE AGE OF EIGHTEEN IS*

ALLOWED ON THESE PREMISES. Krishna is pleased to see that lots of maroon tiles have come off the wall leaving dirty white patches of ugliness. Next door is:

BRIAN & MANDY
ladi   g ntleme   air stylis

By climbing onto a narrow ledge on the wall you can swing on the lower letters and break them off. Krishna tries to climb up but his leg hurts too much. He stands back and studies the sign. He decides to come back with his brothers when his leg is better. By standing on their shoulders he'll be able to reach the larger letters at the top. By taking away the **R**, **A**, **&**, and the **DY**, he can alter the sign to read **B I N MAN**. Krishna passes on, pleased with his new-formed plan.

A green litter bin has been broken off its concrete pillar. Krishna picks it up. It is surprisingly heavy. He heaves it into the road and it lands noisily a couple of feet in front of him. He is at the far end of the cavern now and gazes out at two pyramids. One is a pyramid of light — an advert for the shopping centre and for the supermarkets that can be found in it. The other is the dark pyramid of the multi-denominational church. Krishna leaves the pavement and wanders across the undercover car park. He's drawn to the spot where he was beaten up the night before. He stands remembering, searching the asphalt for signs of his blood. He's disappointed that he can't find any.

At the top end of the car park he finds a jumble of supermarket trolleys. He pushes one down the slope. It makes its erratic way some twenty metres until it comes to rest against a pillar. He shoves another one, but its wheels are stiff and it stops a couple of metres away. He tries a third. It runs sedately towards a red Ford Cortina, changing direction slightly this way and that as though unable to make up its mind, then gathers speed, batters into the car's rear bumper, slides around it and scrapes along the side of a blue Hillman Avenger. Krishna is spellbound until it comes quietly to rest against a kerb, but his balloon has been inflated to bursting point. He wants to run, but when he tries his leg hurts too much. He listens and watches, but no one comes.

Krishna limps hurriedly away from the car park. Between the shopping centre and the main road there is a ribbon of earth, sprouting slender trees. The more established trees reach four or five metres into the air. Between them there are saplings no taller than Krishna himself. As he passes under the trees he reaches up and snaps off a small branch. He tries another. It doesn't snap. The living tree resists. Krishna has to twist and tear the slim limb from the trunk. His balloon is gas-filled. It lifts him off his feet as he leaps for higher branches. He then turns his attention to the saplings his own size. He wrestles with one after another. A trail of broken trees marks his progress. He is too preoccupied to hear the police car pull in to the kerb behind him.

LOCKOUT

I'd been out of work ten weeks. I used to go down the *Ship* and make a pint last two hours. If the tide was right I could watch the battered old cockle boats as they meandered gracefully in or out, following the water-hidden course of the creek. I'd tried my hand at that one time. But like everything else that looks easy to the ignorant, there's a skill — a knack I couldn't get the hang of.

The men flicked their short-handled rakes through the mud like chickens scratching for mites. They made mounds of the wet-shining shellfish, then scooped them into wicker baskets. They gathered their harvest bent double for six hours without a break, till the sea reclaimed the sandbanks again. Then they ate, or slept, or sat smoking over fistfuls of grimy cards, till the sea gently lifted them and nudged them in the direction of home, telling them it was time to go.

I lasted one day. I scraped and scrabbled, collecting heaps of wet sand peppered with broken cockle shells. Hardly able to straighten my body, I carried my baskets on the yoke down the springy plank from boat to shore. In the cockle shed I turned out my load only to be told I'd earned nothing. Too many were damaged. I would have thumped the gaffer's sneering face, except my arms were leaden, and my back ached fiercely, and more important, I saw his hands, big hands like joints of meat, red, cut, and swollen, hanging from thick wrists and forearms like ships' hawsers where the knotted veins stood out like a warning.

It was more pleasant sitting by a coal fire in the *Ship* watching the cockle boats out of the window. Elegant as a family of swans, they swam up or down the twisting creek on the tide.

One evening my reverie was interrupted by Terry — a friend I hadn't seen for over a year. We'd both been taken on (or taken in) together as 'trainee managers' at Woolworths. We started in November, worked like slaves through the Christmas rush, and were given our cards on New Year's Eve when the stocktaking was finished. It was Woolworths' way of wishing us a happy New Year. Anyway, there was Terry, large as life, treating me to a couple of pints in the *Ship,* and a piece of promising news into the bargain. He was working as an upholstery tacker in a furniture factory, and they were desperate for a cutter. I'd never done any cutting in my life but Terry said they only made one style of suite so it would be simple enough. I'd just have to bluff my way in.

The next day I went round to the factory first thing. Frank Columbus, the gaffer, was a short heavy character, nearly as wide as he was high. He looked very much like Yogi Bear only he wasn't so good looking. He was having to do the cutting himself and seemed so relieved that I'd materialised in answer to his silent prayers that he just left the scissors half way across a chalk line on the cloth and told me to get on with it. With a little bit of help from my friend I quickly got the hang of it. The patterns were already made, and the art was to get as many suites as possible out of the rolls of cheap Belgian cloth, and the challenge grabbed me. (I've always been one for puzzles and crosswords — as long as they're not too hard.)

Columbus was a self-made man. He'd worked as a tacker in East End sweat shops, and later become a shop steward. He'd made a bit of money and opened up a little one-man factory — which burnt down. He picked up the insurance and started another place with half a dozen employees. By coincidence that burnt down too. (There's a lot of very inflammable material in three-piece suites.) Now he had a much more impressive enterprise: two machinists; two lorry drivers; an old man and a boy to do the odd jobs, like sweeping up; a cutter (that was me); and up to twenty-five tackers. He went out on the road and did the selling himself.

He made only one style of suite per season — something simple with a bed-settee. In the trade there's two peaks a year. He took on unskilled men as business built up, paying them a small basic for a couple of weeks till they went onto piece rates. They were slow at first so they didn't earn much but they got faster as business increased. Soon they'd be speedy enough to earn good money, and there'd be plenty of overtime. Then as trade began to slacken off the overtime dried up. Columbus would cut the rate for the job. There was no union, so when he cut the rate you could take it or leave it. Most of the men took it. They'd go on short time. The rate would be cut again. Then he'd start laying people off. The stroppiest characters went first. Finally he'd just be left with half a dozen compliant ones to tide him over. When trade picked up he took on new men. Put them next to one of the old hands who had to teach the newcomer the job. This meant that the experienced men couldn't get on so fast so that their earnings were reduced, which helped compensate Columbus for the small basic he was paying the new men.

The blokes were a mixed bunch, same as anywhere else. The old guard formed a sort of elite. There was ugly little Ron who had a lovely smile that transformed his face, like a light being switched on in a dark room. He had a baby, and he used to rabbit about it all the time. We knew the day his nipper's first tooth came through; the first time he crawled; and clapped his hands; and the day he climbed to the top of the stairs there was as much talk in the shop as if someone had been up Everest. There was old Henry who wore his trilby all the time. The men said he went to bed in it. He certainly crapped with it on, because Roger the Dodger lay on the floor and looked under the door to find out. One tea break half a dozen blokes got hold of Henry and held him down and took his hat off. He was as bald as a light bulb, and looked thirty years older. Young Roger fancied himself with the 'birds'. He was married but spent most of his evenings out 'sniffing after crumpet'. He had a toddler too, but hardly ever mentioned it. Henry used to say that Rog didn't even know the kid's name. Thick Dick was one of them people who get their words muddled up. He used to talk about old Henry's tilbury hat. About driving down the artillery road instead of the arterial road. About using conundrums when you had a bit of the other. And he claimed to believe in the Immaculate Contraception. Then there was poor Gilbert, who came to work in a suit and tie. Gilbert wasn't his real name, but that's what everybody called him. He was either too stupid to realise when people were taking the piss out of him or too timid to let on he knew.

As the orders flooded in Columbus used to wave handfuls of them under the men's noses as though they were magic fivers that would hypnotise the men into working faster. He prattled on as if we were all riding on a great wave of affluence that would break with its natural undulating pattern and continue to rise for ever. Some of the blokes knew better, and when Columbus was out, made sarcastic comments about the racket he worked. Others didn't want to know. They preferred to dream in a fool's paradise rather than think about the reality of the coming hell of another spell of unemployment. And if they kept their noses clean maybe they'd be among the select few who'd be kept on. But Little John wouldn't leave them to dream in peace. He was like a hungry dog worrying at the bones of their anxieties. He was a big Scot who never indulged in horseplay, or joked, or even spoke more than was absolutely necessary. Some of the lads, like Terry, and Roger, and Ron, used to work in bursts of energetic speed and then lark about or chat while their batteries recharged. But Little John worked slowly and steadily with a scowl of intense concentration, like a death mask, clamped onto his heavy-jowled face, the first to bend to his job and the last to straighten his back at tea break or knocking off. The lads used to laugh about him because he was a member of the Labour Party and went canvassing at election times. John would never have let on but he'd had the misfortune to canvass old Henry at the last election. Henry had still been hovering on his doorstep when John called on the old lady next door.

'I'm canvassing on behalf of the Labour Party.'

'Eh? What?'

'I'm canvassing on behalf of the Labour Party.'

'It's no good. I can't hear you.'

'I'M CANVASSING ON BEHALF OF...'

'It's no good. I'm deaf. I can't hear.' John had given up and stomped back down the path while the old girl scowled from the step. 'And close the gate after you.'

John had mumbled bad-temperedly, only just loud enough for Henry to hear: 'Och, bugger the gate.'

But the old girl let him have it full volume: 'AND BUGGER THE LABOUR PARTY TOO, MATE!'

Henry was fond of telling the story. 'And bugger the Labour Party too, Mate!' became a catchphrase in the shop. John would react to it with his customary scowl and silence, but whenever the topic of Columbus' methods of operation was raised he came out of himself like a second John Knox. He would glower from behind his glasses, waving a finger at us like a mother threatening her wayward children. 'We all know how this place is run. We all know this is a sweat shop. Nothing more. And we're the bloody fools who do the sweating.'

'Aw, come off it. Columbus does his whack. He works like a truncheon.'

'Trojan, Dick, Trojan. He works like a Trojan.'

'Well, what I mean to say, he works like a workhouse.'

'Perhaps he means the Trojan workhouse.'

'Perhaps he means the Athenian clotheshorse.'

'I'll have to ask my friend, Grecian Ern.'

'You'd be better off asking the Indian Hemp.'

Everybody was laughing except Dick, and, of course, John. He put down his staple gun, and perched on the edge of his trestle looking as uncomfortable as a constipated parrot. 'All right. I'll grant ye that. He works. But he works for himself. And he pays himself well enough for it, does he no'? He has a new Jaguar every year. Ron here works hard too. What sort of car have you got, Ron?' Ron looked at his staple gun, twisting it in his hands, embarrassed as a kid picked on by a teacher in school. But John answered the question himself. 'It's a twelve-year-old death trap. It shouldna be allowed on the road.'

'Wer! S'all right.'

Terry laughed. 'Leave off, Ron. It's only held together by the rust.'

John jabbed his finger towards Henry as if he was accusing him of a crime. 'Henry's fifty-five years old, and he has to come to work, rain or shine, on a bicycle.'

'Well that old bike's good enough for me. I wouldn't drive a car if you paid me.'

'Yeah, he gave a good price for that old bone shaker — to the scrap man.'

'*Any old iron, any old iron,*
any, any, any old iron.' A chorus of voices joined in.
'*You look neat, talk about a treat,*
you look dapper from your napper to your feet,
dressed in style, with a brand new tile,
and your father's old green tie on,
I wouldn't give you tuppence for your old push bike,
old iron! old iron!
da diddy da da,
da diddy da da,
da diddy da da,' in a raucus rising crescendo, and everyone found
something to bash for the final: *Bang! Bang!*

When the laughter died down, John got up from his trestle and opened
his mouth, but then checked himself and sat down again before going on.
'How many men here own their own house? Not one. Not a single one.
And you know where he lives. You know the estate he lives on. They're
all big houses up there. He hasna got a bigger family than some of us,
has he? But he's got a bigger house all right. And that house is worth
more than we would earn at our present rate of pay in over twenty years.
So who pays for that? For his house? For his car? For his wife's car?'

'The insurance company.'

Some of the men laughed. John ignored it. 'You do. I do. We're
slaving for his benefit. And when he's used us he'll throw us on the scrap
heap like potato peelings after he's eaten.' The machine-gun fire of the
staple guns and the continual angry snake-hiss of released compressed
air had died away and exposed the generator on its own. 'How many
men have been laid off since you came here, Henry?'

'No good asking him, he can't count.'

'Tell them, Henry.'

'He said it. I went to night school. I can't count in the day.'

'And we'll go too. Ye know that. We'll all go. There's not a man
that's been here two years. The likes of me'll go first, but you'll all go
before long. Because if you stay here you'll know how the place is run.
You'll know things he doesna want the new men to know.'

'Look, there's nothing we can do about that. All you can do is screw
what you can out of it while the going's good.'

74

'Or make it a secure job with fair rates.'

'How?'

'By joining the union.'

'You can stuff the unions.'

'What union?'

'There's a union for workers in the tailoring and upholstery trades.'

'Why ain't you in the union then?'

'Firstly because I was never in this trade before now, and second because if I joined, Columbus would give me the sack, and I've two bairns to feed. You know he won't employ union men. But if we all joined he couldna throw us all out. Not while the orders are flooding in. If I phoned the union today we could have a man down here tomorrow. It wouldna commit us to anything, but at least we'd know what the union could do for us.'

One of the machinists was a timid teenager called Sandra. The other was Edna, a forty-year-old dragon (like a man with drag on — hard-faced and masculine-looking). She had a square face with a big nose and strong jaw. Edna had never married. Her mother had died when Edna was in her teens and Edna had kept house for her old man. He was a seasoned invalid now with one foot in the grave. (The other had been amputated because of gangrene.) She was breadwinner, nurse, and housekeeper. I pitied him.

I gave the cut cloth to Sandra and Edna who machined it before passing it on to the men. The radio above Sandra's head permanently pumped out boring muzak that blended into the drone of the generator. Edna talked incessantly, with a fag hanging from her lipstick-gashed mouth spilling grey ash onto her work, and with her eyes screwed up against the smoke.

One day there was a photograph in the *Daily Mirror* of a black rock singer embracing the blonde model he was living with. Edna couldn't take her eyes off it. 'Look at that! I think it's disgusting. I wouldn't let one near me with a barge pole.'

I laughed. 'That's very Freudian, Edna.'

She twisted her head briefly to glare at me, then turned back to Sandra. 'I don't know who asked him to shove his oar in.'

'There you go again,' I said.

She ignored me. 'Just look at it. Disgusting! They want to get back to the jungle where they came from. I wouldn't stay in the same room as one of them. If there was one come in here now I'd get up and walk out.'

'I'm a spade, Edna.' She jerked round as though she'd just got an electric shock. I grinned. 'Didn't you know?'

'What you talking about?'

'I'm coloured. You can't tell with mixed blood. My mother's English, see. But my old man's as black as the ace of spades. Which is what he is, really. He's ace, my old man. I came out lily-white like my mother while my brother's as black as the black hole of Calcutta like the old man. And if I have kids they're just as like to be black as white. Once you've got a touch of the old tar brush you can never tell.'

They'd both stopped machining and were half turned on their chairs looking at me sceptically. I nodded reassuringly. 'Straight up. I wouldn't lie about a thing like that.'

They turned back to their work, unsure, talking in low tones so it was difficult for me to hear. But I caught one comment of Edna's: 'I always thought there was something shifty about him.' When I saw Edna take a pile of arms down to the tackers I followed and nipped into the bog, leaving the door open, so I could listen. 'Here, do you know what? That bugger up there's a bleeding half-breed!'

The day Little John phoned the union Columbus hadn't come back when we knocked off, but Edna stayed late. The next morning, before anyone else had got cracking, Columbus wandered down the shop and stood watching John who was already bent over a chair firing staples nineteen to the dozen.

'I've got your cards here, Stevenson.'

John straightened up looking more resigned than surprised. 'My cards. Why?'

'Because I don't want you in my factory, that's why.'

John's face flushed and then paled as the adrenalin rushed through his bloodstream. He looked as if he was about to hand the gaffer a bunch of fives, but Columbus was a hard case himself and stood his ground, unflinching. 'So on your bike. And see what the union's got to say about that.'

Most of the men were making some sort of pretence of starting work, but Terry threw down his gun and crossed the floor. 'Hang about. What's he done?'

Columbus was a bit taken aback because he wasn't used to the blokes interfering in his goings on. They were mostly trying to hang on to their own jobs. 'All right, Terry. Get back to your bench.'

'You can't kick somebody out like that.'

'Can't I? I'm the guv'nor here. This is my shop. I can do what I like. He's out. Any more from you and you join him.'

I dropped the chalk and pattern onto the cloth and hurried down the length of the factory. Terry stood, looking as immovable as a sentry on duty in Whitehall, eyeballing Columbus without batting an eyelid. The hands stood watching, nervously, to see what would happen next. John was packing up in slow motion, putting his tools and apron and sandwich box into a canvas bag. Henry saw me coming. 'Look out. Here comes trouble.'

Columbus looked round, startled, taken off guard. 'What d'you think you're doing?'

I stood shoulder to shoulder with Terry who had his hands stuffed into his kangaroo pouch.

'Look at them. The terrible twins.'

'I've warned you already, Terry. Get back to work. Another word you're out too. And you — get back to the cutting!'

We didn't budge. Little John stopped what he was doing, surprise in his eyes and a flush of excitement on his face. 'Why don't we all down tools till lunchtime and see what this union man's got to say for himself. Seeing that he's coming anyway.'

Columbus clenched and unclenched his fists. He was as flushed as a vicar in a strip club. His voice was husky. 'Anyone who's not working within two minutes can collect his cards and get out.' .

John leaned an elbow on the chair that was standing on his trestles, and waved a forefinger in the air. 'We live in a country which is still democratic, after a fashion, and we have the right to...'

'Get out! Get out! You're not making bloody speeches here!' Columbus sprang towards John ready to give him some finger pie but Terry, myself, Ron and Rog crowded him. Some of the blokes called out to let John have his say, and 'Mutiny on the Bounty!' and so on. Columbus looked scared for a moment like an animal trainer when the beasts suddenly turn on him. He sidled out from among us and walked deliberately slowly up the shop. He stopped outside his office and turned towards us. 'I'm closing this factory down as from now. You've got two minutes to get off my property. All of you. Or I'll call the police and have you arrested for trespass. If any of you want a job you can come at eight in the morning. I'll tell you then who I'm prepared to take on. The rest can collect their cards and bugger off.'

The blokes packed up quietly. We all went outside and gathered on the loading bay. It was cold and sunny. A bright blue sky without a cloud. Some of the men were morose but most of us were slightly intoxicated with the events of the day and the unexpected liberation from the prison of work. Columbus locked the place up and gave Edna and Sandra a lift in his bronze Jag. The old man and the boy went home too. The drivers were already out. We had a game of football in the cold sunshine, kicking Columbus' head in each time we booted the ball. Sid Levy, the union man, turned up at midday. He was a big stooped guy in a shabby grey suit, more like a cricket umpire than a rabble-rouser. His tired, mumbled speech made few converts. It was John really who persuaded the doubters. On a show of hands we were unanimous for joining the union.

Next morning we were all given our cards at the door. We started a daily picket outside the factory. Within a few days Columbus had hired a dozen new men. He was paying them a high basic and teaching them himself. He got police protection to take them in and out. He also tried to intimidate some of the pickets, but no actual violence came about — only threats. We realised our picketing was ineffectual. Then Dave, one of the drivers, got laid off and gave us a list of all the shops he could remember delivering to. John got someone he knew to run off a leaflet on a duplicator. Car loads of us swooped on shops, starting locally and then moving further afield. If we found a Columbus suite in a shop we told the manager that if he didn't take it out there and then we'd picket his entrance and turn his customers away. There was hardly a single one where they didn't whip it out at once so we would clear off from in front of their shop. It was fun at first, a crowd of us off together like a works' outing, but the novelty soon wore off. We didn't have the freedom, or the spending money, to enjoy the holiday. We got fed up and our hands were itching to be doing something that felt useful again. But gradually firms were returning and cancelling orders, so after six weeks Columbus sacked all his new men. They were just 'sacrificial lambs on the altar of his expediency' as John put it. (He was getting more like John Knox every day.) Columbus took us all back (except one or two, like Gilbert, who'd got other jobs) and declared it a 100 per cent union shop.

Relations with Columbus were a bit strained, but there was a good feeling among the men. We were back at work one week when Columbus gave Little John a special order to do — a different style of suite with an ordinary settee instead of the usual convertible. John had never tackled anything like it before but he was quite pleased with the change and the challenge, even though it meant his piece-rate would drop. Next morning, Columbus examined the settee John was working on, and fired him for inferior work. It was true that John's craftsmanship wasn't great. He'd never done an apprenticeship. He'd only ever learned how to do the one suite. We demanded to see the union man. Columbus agreed and let us call him on the office phone. We sat around drinking tea and rabbiting till he came. Some of us were feeling pretty bolshie, raring to go again, but most of the blokes were fed up with being out so long. They didn't want any more trouble. Eventually Levy turned up, in the same baggy grey suit with dinner stains down the front. It looked as though he'd once been a bigger man than he now was. (Maybe he'd been better at feeding himself too.) He spent over half an hour in the office with Columbus. We saw Sandra taking them cups of tea. When they came out they walked over to John's trestles. Columbus pointed out faults in the settee. Levy nodded sadly. He looked at us and shrugged. 'Sorry, boys. An employer is within his rights dismissing someone for bad workmanship.'

I got to my feet, hardly able to believe my ears. 'Supposing Columbus switches off the compressor one day and says it's not working. None of these blokes can use a hammer.'

Levy shrugged again. 'What can I do? You're not properly trained men. You haven't got a leg to stand on.'

John and Terry stood up beside me. We looked around at the rest of the men. They were tired and defeated. Columbus had John's cards and pay envelope in his hands. John took them. Terry walked over to his jacket which was hanging behind his bench and got his still-new union card. I took mine out of my back pocket. We went up to Levy who was standing stooped and helpless in the middle of the floor. We ripped our cards into shreds and threw the pieces like confetti into his face.

Levy didn't say anything. He just shrugged again apologetically. Columbus tried not to smile. 'This is a 100 per cent union shop, boys. If you're no longer union members I'm afraid you'll have to go. Otherwise I'll have a strike on my hands. I'll get your cards ready.'

John shook hands with us and went off home for lunch. Terry and I went down the *Ship*. We made our pints last a couple of hours sitting by the warm coal fire watching the cockle boats glide over the brown water like swans. Terry's gloomy face suddenly brightened. 'Hey! Why don't we see if we can get a job on one of them.'

HELLO BAKER

One of my favourite customers was Dolly. When she opened the front door and saw it was me, her eyes would light up. Sometimes she'd have the door open before I'd even got up the path. Dolly was a Tuesday, Thursday, Saturday call.

'Come in, Baker,' she said that Tuesday. 'Help yourself to a fag, mate, the kettle's boiling.'

'That's music to my ears, Dolly.' I followed her up the narrow dark passage into the kitchen. I was still half prepared for Pippy to waddle over and do her fat best to welcome me. She'd died the week before, although her basket was still under the kitchen table and the smell of her was in the room. I tossed onto the table Dolly's loaf and a bag containing two battered custard tarts (which I'd nicked out of the pig waste the previous Saturday evening), and flopped down onto a kitchen chair. The chair wobbled and tried to throw me onto the floor. 'How come I always get the chair with the wonky leg?' I complained, getting to my feet again.

'Trust you to pick that one. Should've been chucked out years ago. And the old man with it.'

I tested another chair for firmness before trusting myself on it. 'Your hubby's not much of a handy man then.' I took two fags from her packet on the table and lit them.

'No, he's not.' She poured steaming water into the teapot. 'If you know of any nice young men who're good with their hands, you send them round here.'

'You told me you weren't interested in men, Doll.' I laid her cigarette on the edge of the dirty ashtray and drew deep on my own.

'But if it was a *young* man, that would be different.'

'Well I'm young. Won't I do?'

'You'll do all right. But I won't say what you'll do for.' She caught her foot in a hole in the worn lino, spilling tea onto the floor.

'Have a good trip?'

'Damn that lino.' She slumped down at the table. 'Oh, Baker, this house gives me the willies. I'd like to stick the whole bloody place in the dustbin.'

'Why don't you do it up, Doll — brighten it up a bit?'

'I haven't the heart, Baker, I really haven't.'

The kitchen looked as if it hadn't been redecorated since the house was built. There were half a dozen faded, greasy-looking stains up the wallpaper as though, long ago, somebody used to periodically throw their dinner up the wall, and had then given up. There was a mountain of dirty clothes by the washing machine, and rubbish overflowed from a plastic bucket and a row of cardboard cartons onto the floor. A wad of yellow newspaper was sellotaped over a crack in the window. Even the *busy lizzy* on the sill over the sink had died from lack of water. 'Them plaster ducks could go for a start,' I said.

'You keep your hands off my ducks. One of these days they'll be antiques — worth a lot of money.'

'That'll be the day. You want to liberate them — right out the window.'

'I'll liberate them at you if you're not careful.'

'What have I done?'

'I wouldn't mind liberating them at my hubby's head. That I *would* like to see.'

She splashed a little milk from a bottle into two chipped mugs. Mine had *Mother* on it. Hers had a picture of the Queen. 'Give us plenty of milk to cool it down,' I said. 'I'm really late today.'

'I noticed. What you been up to?'

'A bit of this, and a bit of that, and a...'

'...bit of the other — I know.' She stirred the tea in the pot and then poured it into the mugs. She shoved mine towards me, slopping a little onto the table top. She got up again and went to the cupboard for a packet of sugar. She was thin, but she heaved herself out of her chair like a very fat person; as though her body weighed too much for her legs. It seemed an effort for her to do the simplest things. It was as though she had almost no life left in her. She stabbed a spoon into the sugar and pushed the bag towards me. 'Help yourself, love.' Her eyes were full of warmth, yet her face was unsmiling. Her mouth was tightly set in a bitter line of resentment. Looking at her, I thought of Jenny, my girlfriend, and wondered what twenty-odd years would do to *her*. The thought depressed me, so I gave myself an extra spoonful of sugar.

'I've brought you a little present, gal,' I said. 'A couple of nice custards.'

'Ow, go on, Baker — you can't afford it.'

'Don't worry about that. I'll add it on some bugger's bill who can.'

'You'll come to a sticky end, you will.'

'I came to a sticky end last night as a matter of fact: I sat in a box of jam tarts.'

'You want to stay away from tarts.'

'That's what my mother always told me.'

She laughed. 'There's no flies on you.'

'There was last night when my end was all splattered with jam.'

'As long as it weren't splattered with anything worse.'

'Now, now, Dolly. Keep it clean.'

'And you keep yo'r'n clean, an' all.'

The washing machine, which had been making gurgling and swishing noises, began to vibrate violently as though it was trying to shake itself to pieces. 'Shake it, baby,' I sang. 'She knows how to shake that thang.'

'Don't worry about that, dearie,' Dolly said. 'It gets like that sometimes.'

I tore open the bag of custard tarts. 'You can have one if you promise not to shove it in my face,' I said. And then, in mock surprise: 'Oh, bugger it.'

'What's the matter? Don't tell me they've gone mouldy already like them apple things you brought me last week.'

'No, Doll. 'Course not. But I'm afraid I must have squashed them a bit getting them out of the van.'

'Trust you,' she said. 'But I won't look a gift horse in the mouth. It makes a change from you trying to sell me a van-full of rubbish.'

'What d'you mean? Don't the old man like those meat pies you get him?'

'They're putrid. That's why I give them to him.'

'You're not being very complimentary about my wares.'

'I'm telling you, if it was anyone else trying to palm that junk off on me, I'd tell them where to put it.'

'I bet you would. But then, I've got the knack.'

'Yes, and I know what you've got the knack for. I suppose that's why you're so late.'

'Well, no, to tell the truth we had a bit of bother down the yard. Trouble at t'mill.'

'And what was that all about?'

'It's this new bloody manager. He's put your bread up threepence a loaf by the way. I forgot to tell you.'

'Thanks very much.'

'I said, to him, I said, *What will Dolly say?* I said. *Get them used to eating shit, and they'll eat shit,* he said.'

'Charming, I'm sure. You want more tea?'

'No, Doll. I'd better get along. I'm all behind like the cow's tail. All the lonely young housewives are waiting for me.' I stubbed out my fag in the ashtray, drained my cup and stood up.

'I bet they are too. Here, let me give you a piece of advice, Baker.'

I shoved a collapsed custard tart in my mouth and licked my fingers. 'Go on then,' I said, with my mouth full. 'I could do with some good advice.'

The washing machine ceased its rowdy dance in the corner and became quiet as if it too was in need of some good advice. Dolly was sitting with her elbows on the table, her greasy hair hanging forward over her face, her fag held limply in one claw-like hand, the smoke rising into her eyes. 'Know what?' she said. 'I couldn't count on my hands how many opportunities I turned down in my life; how many times I said no. When I was a girl I was taught to say no, and I always did — more's the pity. And look where it's got me. I've had no fun in my life, Baker. I mean that. A life without joy in it. A wasted life. Don't waste your life, Baker. You take a tip from me: say yes — to everything.'

I was nonplussed. In the nine months I'd known Dolly, we'd always stuck to light-hearted banter. I stood looking at her, until she seemed to suddenly remember I was still there. She smiled at me a smile that was a mixture of resignation and apology. I said, 'Don't talk as though it's all over, Doll. Start having fun now. It's never too late.'

'Nah...'

'What d'you mean, no? Listen to your own advice. You've got to start saying *yes*.'

'All right, clever clogs. Here, I've got a little present for you.'

I felt embarrassed. 'A pressie?' I said. 'Cor, just like Christmas.'

She produced a green and white striped woollen hat out of a basket of wools and needles by her chair. 'I knitted it meself. It'll keep your brains warm and dry in the winter.'

'That's lovely, Dolly,' I said. 'Thanks very much.' I put it on and ran out to the van. She stood at the door, waving. As soon as I turned the corner I pulled the hat off and threw it in the back.

Late Thursday morning the drizzle started. By early afternoon the rain was heavier, but just before I got to Dolly's it suddenly stopped. Dolly was waiting at the front door. I grabbed the basket out of the back and sprinted up the concrete path. 'Hello, Baker,' she said. 'Got something nice for me today? I need something to cheer me up.'

'What do I come for, Dolly, if it's not to bring a little ray of sunshine on a rainy day?'

'I suppose you want a cup of tea?'

'You know me, Dolly. I'm just a lad who can't say no.'

'A lad after my own heart.' She led the way down the passage, her blotchy legs like pale posts jammed into lemon, fur-lined slippers. 'Bring your basket with you.'

'Nah. I'll leave her outside. You know what they say, Dolly: two's company, three's a crowd.' I blinked as I entered the neon brightness of the kitchen.

'Your bread-basket, I'm talking about.'

'Now, now, Dolly, don't get personal.' The kettle was heating on the gas stove. Another carton of rubbish had joined the queue by the back door. The dog basket lay empty under the kitchen table. 'Gonna get another dog, Doll?'

Dolly shovelled tea into the pot. 'Nah. We only got her for the kids 'cos they were so upset when our Rover got run over. Nearly fourteen, Pippy was.'

I had to stack up dirty dinner and breakfast dishes to make room for my basket on the table. I collapsed onto a chair, then tipped back against the wall stretching my legs out to rest my feet on the dog basket. 'Me dogs is killing me,' I said.

'It was mine kept me alive, mate. Lovely little puppy, she was, when we got her. Never thought she'd grow into that fat, lazy lump.'

'Yeah, well, you know what they say: big oaks from little acorns grow.' I made a hard-on gesture with my right arm and fist.

'Come on, then. Let's see.'

'I told you, Doll: you show me yours and I'll show you mine.'

'And I told you, an' all: I'm past that, dearie.'

'Don't be daft, Dolly. You can't be past it at thirty.'

'Thirty! Coo blimey, wish I was, mate. More like a hundred and thirty.'

'Get out! You're as old as you feel.' She looked old, standing leaning against the sink, staring at nothing.

'That's what I said: a hundred and thirty.'

The kitchen was gradually filling with steam from the boiling kettle. 'Yeah, well, if I want a Turkish bath, Doll, I'll go to Istanbul.'

She jumped. 'Sorry, love. Miles away.' She turned off the gas, picked the kettle up with a folded tea cloth and poured scalding water into the teapot. 'Help yourself to a fag, mate.'

I scooped the cigarette packet and the ashtray towards me like a roulette player pulling in his winnings. The ashtray was overflowing. It left a trail of grey ash across the table top like foam in the wake of a ship. 'Christ, Dolly! Trying to smoke yourself to death?'

'Don't mind if I do, love.'

The answer was ambiguous. I wasn't sure whether she'd heard correctly. I lit up two cigarettes. She plonked the teapot and mugs on the faded blue and white table top. Then the sugar packet and milk bottle. I held a fag out to her and she took it between her lips in a way that would have been a sexual invitation from a younger woman. She ruffled my wet hair with one hand, like a grown up to a child, as if to nullify her action, and began rummaging through my basket with the other. 'Where's your hat?' she said, without looking at me. 'I didn't sit here knitting you a bloody hat for nothing. I try and look after you but you won't look after yourself, will yer.'

'Yeah, well, we didn't have a tea cosy at home, and the green stripes matched the curtains, so my mother purloined it. Don't think I don't appreciate it.' Sensing her hurt, I felt guilty and awkward.

'Haven't got much here, have you.'

'What d'you mean? Nice length of swiss roll there. Try that for size.'

'I want something to eat — not poke the fire with. These yesterday's doughnuts?'

'Dolly! Would I bring you stale cakes? My nuts are as fresh as primroses on the first of May.'

She yanked a packet of cream doughnuts out of the basket along with her large sliced and a meat pie and threw them on the table, then sat down and poured the tea. 'Well it's nice seeing you, even if you haven't got anything worth having.'

'What! They're queuing up to sample my wares. They all want to lick the cream off the end of my doughnut.'

Her eyes seemed to have sunk deep into her head, and the puffy shadows under them looked like bruises. I was suddenly aware, as though getting her into focus for the first time, of just how lined her face was, and how deep the folds of her skin. She'd made up over the top of it all, but without care. The fag hung from her mouth where the lipstick didn't quite match up with her lips. The dead ash was creeping towards her. She said, 'I'll believe yer. Thousands wouldn't.' She stirred the teas sloppily and pushed mine across. Then, turning her nose up at the doughnuts, she ripped open the packet and slid one towards me on a torn-off corner of the paper bag. 'What've you been doing with yourself lately, then?' she asked.

I could see she was in distress. I didn't know how to handle it. I tried to be entertaining. 'I had a terrible time last night.'

'Getaway! You kids don't know you're born.'

'Straight up. I'm waiting for a bus home, right. I'm stood at the bloody bus stop for hours getting soaked through. When a bus finally does turn up, I get on; I sit there till the conductress comes round for my fare. I say, all friendly like, *Cor blimey, darling, I thought you was never going to bloody come.* She goes, *What? What did you say?* I goes, *I thought you was never going to come.* She goes, *No you never. You said a WORD.* So she rings the bell and the bus screeches to a halt. She goes, *Get off my bus!* Then the driver comes round. He's about six foot six and looks as if he might be a champion wrestler in his spare time. He goes, *What's the matter?* She goes, *He used LANGUAGE.* He goes, *LANGUAGE! Right, mate. Orf! Unless you want a clout in the ear!'*

'So what did you do?'

'What d'you think I did. I got off. I had to walk about three bloody mile home in the pissing rain.'

'That'll teach yer.'

'What d'you mean?'

'You need your bleeding mouth washed out with soap and water, you.'

'Hark who's talking.'

We both took a sip of the hot tea, dark brown and bitter. She seemed about to burst into tears. The dam started to crumble. I had a glimpse of the built-up pressure behind, and it was frightening. 'I'm just about at the end of my tether, Baker,' she said, her voice shaking. 'The silence in this house!'

I was at a loss for comforting words. 'What time's your old man get in?'

'The old man?' Scorn turned her words into venom. 'We haven't spoke to each other for years. This house is like a bloody morgue, mate.'

I tried to summon up that scenario, but it was beyond my powers of imagination. 'Don't you talk to each other at all — not even to have a row or anything?'

'Nah.'

'What about when he...you know. Don't he say, *Excuse me*, or something?'

'There's none of that, mate. Had none of that for years.' She was regaining control. Her jaw muscles bulged with the tension of biting it all back. I lowered my eyes and stubbed out my fag in the heaped ashtray, winding the butt round and round, drilling into the ashes.

'Getaway, Doll. He probably does it when you're asleep.'

'Over my dead body! I only married him in the first place because he got me in the club. There was no pill in them days — no safe abortions. That was the end of *my* fun.'

'I thought you told me you always said no.'

'I did say no — but that bugger didn't take any notice. Before we was married he was after it three times a night, and after we married he could hardly manage it three times a year.'

The fridge turned itself off. It was suddenly deathly quiet. I pushed the ashtray towards Dolly. The neon tube was buzzing — I hadn't noticed before. The ashtray rattled on the table as she stubbed out her cigarette. I glanced at my watch. She noticed. 'Ere y'are, love. Have another.' She thrust the open packet towards me like a knife.

'Time's getting on.'

'Come on. One for the road.'

'All right. One more fag before I go. That'll be my famous last words, Doll.'

'One more hole, more like.'

'Yeah. One more go before I fag.'

We each helped ourselves to another cigarette, and I struck a match. 'You know some geezer's famous last words?' I dropped the match into the ashtray and, grabbing my throat with both hands, writhed about on my chair, and croaked in a strangled voice, 'This wallpaper is killing me!' Unsmiling, she glanced up at the birds and marshes on the grubby wallpaper as if seeing them for the first time. I sat looking at her sad old face while time passed in awkward silence. 'Is that straight up?' I asked at last. 'I mean, how do you manage — if you don't speak to each other.'

She topped up the mugs from the pot. 'We know the ropes. I put his dinner on the table when he comes in. He leaves the money on the table Thursday night. He's never left me short of housekeeping, I will say that for him.'

'Do you have separate beds and that?'

'Nah.'

'Sleep in the same bed?'

'Yeah.'

'Never touch?'

'Nah.'

'Well that's a rum do, i'n'it.'

It started raining again, pattering against the kitchen window. I got up and crossed to the sink. I poured half a cup of chocolate-brown tea down the drain and placed the mug gently to rest among the heaped dishes in the red plastic washing up bowl. The dog-end sizzled as I stubbed it into the wet waste in the sink basket. I stared out through a moving raindrop pattern at the neglected back yard and the heavy grey pall of the sky. I didn't feel able to go out and finish the round, as though her company had drained the life out of me. The fridge switched itself back on.

'We only stuck it out because of the kids,' she said. 'The two eldest are married now. All moved away. Youngest is training as a manager in a supermarket.' I knew what 'trainee manager' was a euphemism for — I'd been there, done that: cheap labour in the stock room. 'They're good kids,' she said.

'See them much?'

'Nothing for them here. Best off out of it, aren't they. It's enough to give you the creeps, this house.' I wanted to get away. I went to the table and put a hand on the basket handle. 'I have a laugh with them,' she said. 'But they want to be with youngsters their own age, don't they. Not an old crab like me.'

'Now, come on, Dolly. Give over. I don't come here for the commission on my sales, you know. Got my eye on you, gal.'

She smiled. 'You're twenty years too late, mate.'

'That's the story of my life. Always missing the boat. I was two weeks late being born, and I haven't caught up with myself yet.'

'You don't give up trying, do yer.'

'That's what my teachers used to say, Doll. I was always trying. The most trying kid in the school.'

'You're wasting your talent being a baker, you are. You want to get your finger out and get on in the world.'

'Nah. Let the greedy buggers get the ulcers, Doll. My talent lies in other fields. The field I had a bit of talent in last night had thistles — but she didn't see the point.'

I lifted the basket, sliding my arm under the handle. I held it in the crook of my elbow, making a hard-on gesture with my forearm and fist, and winked at her. She got to her feet, pushing the chair away with the backs of her legs, holding on to the table with both hands. She looked wide-eyed, frightened. 'Not going yet, are yer?' There was panic in her voice.

'Well, Doll...' I glanced at my watch, but didn't register the time. 'It's getting on. All them loafers waiting for their crumpet, and all that crumpet waiting for a loaf. I'll never get done.'

'You're not the only one,' she said, her voice full now of regrets, and she smiled at her joke. I laughed with relief and turned towards the door. I pushed the cover flap down to keep the merchandise dry. Neither of us had touched the doughnuts.

I stopped in the passage doorway and stood looking back at her. 'Why don't you leave, Doll? I mean, why do you stay now — now the kids are gone?'

'Where would I go? Who wants an old bag like me? It's too late now.'

'I'll tell you what. One of these nights I'll come for you, ay? In the dead of night. Listen for the tapping on the pane.'

Her jaw was clenched, the jaw muscles bulging and moving. Her eyes were dull as she looked into mine, nodding. I wondered whether she'd been pretty when she was young. I went back to her, put my free arm around her shoulders and kissed her on the cheek. Her eyes were like an ember catching a drop of paraffin, flaring bright for a moment, then dying. 'Thank you, Baker,' she said.

'Ta ta, love.' I turned my back on her and made my way along the dingy passage. 'Keep your legs crossed and your hand on your ha'penny,' I called.

'Don't do anything I wouldn't do.'

'Don't give me much scope, does it.'

She was still standing at the door after I'd dropped a large sliced on next door's window sill, run over to the van, slung the basket in the back, and jumped into the driver's seat. I gave her a wave as I pulled away and began to work out if I'd got everything I needed for the customers on the end of the round.

Saturday morning was foggy, and the fog went on getting thicker all day. Saturday was a long day because I had to collect money, do the books and cash in. And of course Saturday was a day I wanted to get home quickly so I could get ready to go out in the evening. The fog caused me to fall behind schedule. I didn't stop for tea breaks or lunch. Before I turned into Dolly's street I put on the woolly hat to please her.

Dolly's curtains were closed. There was no answer when I knocked. No note. I stuck a loaf on the window sill, stuffed the hat in my pocket and ran next door.

'Hello, Baker.' Mrs Koslowski was a fat, middle-aged woman with the slightest trace of a Mid-European accent, who worked in a pork pie factory all week. 'Funny weather still.'

'Yeah. We've been having plenty lately, haven't we.'

'Plenty of what?'

'Weather.'

'Oh. Yes,' she said uncertainly. 'I suppose we have really.'

'Did she want one next door, do you know?'

'Ooh, no. Haven't you heard?' Her voice dropped to a dramatic whisper. She made round eyes and puckered her lips. She'd obviously got a choice bit of gossip, and wanted to make the most of it. 'Here, do you know what? She done herself in, that one.'

'What d'you mean?'

'Ooh, everyone's talking about it.'

'You mean Dolly?'

'Ay?'

'Who?'

'That Mrs Marshall next door. Her hubby came home from work Thursday and found her in the bath with her wrists slashed. He said he can't think why she done it.'

I added a good bit on her bill. Dolly had left me with a bad debt.

A CRY FOR HELP

'I'll set fire to the house!' she was screaming from the top bedroom window. 'I'll murder the kids! I'll burn the damn place to the ground!'

The disturbance brought several people to their windows and a couple of women into their front gardens. Mrs Bryce at number twenty pulled a face to communicate how shocking she thought it was to Mrs Green, two doors away.

'Do you think you ought to phone the police?' Mrs Green mouthed.

Mrs Bryce nodded and hurried indoors. She informed the police, and the police notified the mental hospital. When Mrs Bryce came out into the garden again, Margaret was no longer at the window, no longer screaming hysterical threats. Number twenty-two was once again as quiet as usual with nothing to distinguish it from the rest of the houses in the row.

Margaret had gone downstairs and was making calls from her own telephone. She sat at the little hall table, her address book open in front of her. She worked her way through the book, dialling the numbers of friends and relations. Sometimes she got an engaged signal. Sometimes the phone rang for two minutes unanswered. Sometimes a recorded voice informed her that all lines were in use and advised her to try the call again later. Sometimes she would hear a human voice and her hopes would rise.

'Hello, Jane...This is Margaret...Can you come over?...No, now, I mean...I need someone with me. I'm here alone and I'm frightened I might hurt the children...No. He's away working still...I can't take any more, Jane. I'm going out of my mind, I really am...Can't you come?'

But Jane had her own children to see to. And anyway it was an hour and a half's drive — even when the traffic wasn't too bad.

Jennifer was getting ready to go out and she just couldn't let Jimmy down.

Pearl would have come except that the car was being serviced and she didn't have any transport.

Peggy was in the middle of cooking and she couldn't leave everybody to starve.

And so on.

No, no, no, no, no...each no was a funeral bell tolling inside Margaret's head. U, V, W, X, Y, and Z were all blank pages. Margaret closed the book and sat staring at its black cover. She felt the scream building up inside her again. Her body began to tremble uncontrollably. Her teeth started to rattle behind the pallid mask of her face. The objects around her in the dingy hall became fuzzy, and then deteriorated into unrec-·ognisable shapes of dark and shade. The scream came burbling out of her, growing and growing, until it filled the hall, and then the house itself.

Police constables Diane Smith and Peter Cook froze just outside the back door as they heard the scream mushrooming like an explosion. They searched each other's faces for a look of confidence that would boost their own failing courage. 'I'd rather deal with a firm of armed villains any day,' PC Cook said, 'than a nutcase. I hope the bin people get here soon.'

Margaret didn't see them come in. She felt the policewoman's hands on her, imitating concern, and the screams subsided gradually into sobbing. Their voices penetrated her consciousness then, although she couldn't understand what they were saying. Nevertheless the soothing sounds were like a tranquilliser. The first words she managed were: 'The children.'

PC Smith found four little ones between the ages of eighteen months and five years huddled fearfully in a corner of one of the bedrooms. Apart from being, understandably, very frightened, they seemed healthy and well cared for. As soon as Margaret had been carted off in an ambulance the policewoman arranged for the children to be taken into care.

During the ambulance ride Margaret continued to come down slowly. She felt like a glider coming gently in to land. A man and woman sat either side of her, holding her hands and stroking her forearms, and voices continued to soothe her. At the hospital she allowed herself to be led across scrunching gravel and along smooth, gliding corridors. She was taken into a room and seated. She sat quietly and breathed deeply. The man on the other side of the desk asked her how she was feeling.

Staring at him she found she was able to focus once more. The shrink was silky and smooth and elegantly grey. He wore a gold-braceleted watch, and a large, gold wedding ring, and a delicate diamond tie-pin. Margaret had never seen anyone wearing a tie-pin before — except in old-fashioned films. Behind the doctor there was a window, and through the window she could see trees trembling a little, and above the trees fluffy white and grey clouds hurrying past, and high above them a layer of unmoving, thin grey cloud.

The doctor questioned her with gentle, professional concern. She felt guilty of betrayal, but she was too exhausted to resist his sinuous probing. She told him about her loneliness. About how they'd moved two years before, while she was still pregnant with Jason. About how wonderful it had seemed at first: a house of their own after the overcrowding and dirt of the city. About her depression after Jason was born, a depression that just seemed to go on and on. About Doug's new job back in the city they'd so recently escaped from, where, he said, he could earn more money.

She felt so overwhelmed with gratitude for the tissues the consultant slid across the desk that she could have hugged him, but she contented herself with an attempted smile.

'He's supposed to come home weekends,' she said, 'but every week he's on the phone with some story about why he can't get back. He's had a puncture. Or the clutch has gone. Or there's been a burglary at work and he has to stay to give a statement to the police. There's always a story. And each week I think, *this* weekend it'll be all right. But it never is. I think he's got another woman. I wouldn't mind him being with her during the week if only I had him at the weekends. But I'm left alone with four kids day in and day out, giving, giving, giving. But nobody's giving anything to me. I'm not a bottomless pit, Doctor!'

'Of course you're not,' he assured her. 'It must be very difficult for you on your own. Do any of the neighbours help with the children?'

'Neighbours! I might as well be living on a desert island. I don't know any neighbours. The people on one side of me are never there, and the only time the woman on the other side opens her mouth is to shout at my children for climbing on her rotten fence. I've lived in that house nearly two years and I don't know a living soul. Nobody speaks. They come home from work and go into their houses and slam their rotten doors. All the kids seem to come to play in my house because none of the other mothers will even let the children in. All my family and friends live in the city and that's three hours on the coach and I can't manage it with four little ones and Jason still in nappies and everything. And anyway I can't afford it. Doug doesn't even bother to send any money half the time. I just wish we'd never come here. I thought it was going to be so good. A new house. Open spaces for the children to play. But I'd go back to those rotten little rooms like a shot if it could all be like it was before.'

'Well, Margaret, I think you need and deserve a rest. I don't want you to worry about the children. They're being looked after by some lovely people, and they're very happy. I want you to have a period of quiet and calm. I'm going to keep you here for a while for observation. Your husband will be notified that you're here, and perhaps that will bring him to his senses.'

A nurse came and said her name was Betty. Margaret allowed herself to be taken along more corridors with bare walls and polished floors and into another room. The room had a bed in it. Betty gave Margaret a nightdress and told her to take off her own clothes and put it on. As soon as Margaret was undressed Betty went away with her clothes. She returned with a glass of water and two tablets. 'I want you to take these,' she said.

'What are they?' Margaret asked.

'Just something to calm you down, dear,' Betty said.

'I've calmed down now, thank you.'

'Come along, dear,' Betty insisted. She was a plump, powdered woman with bleached hair who was fighting a losing battle against middle age. She put an arm comfortingly around Margaret's shoulders. 'They're only mild tranquillisers.'

'I've stopped all that now,' Margaret told her. 'Last year my doctor had me on uppers to get me going, tranks to calm me down, sleepers 'cos I couldn't sleep. It was ridiculous. In the end I threw the lot out. I don't take anything now — not even aspirin.'

Betty was losing her patience. 'Well, I'm afraid you'll have to take these, just like everybody else. We can't have one or two making things difficult, can we.'

'But I'll be all right now. I've been through this before. It's just the loneliness sometimes becomes unbearable and I crack. I suppose I'm just crying out for attention. Then afterwards everything's all right again for a while. You've no idea how good it was to be able to pour it all out to the doctor. I'm all right now. I really am.'

'I'm glad, dear, but I want you to get these down you now, and be quick about it. There are a lot of other patients on this ward besides you, you know.'

'You're not listening to me. I don't need them.'

Without saying anything more, Betty turned abruptly and left the room. Margaret sat anxiously on the edge of the bed, feeling vulnerable, and conscious of her nakedness under the hospital nightdress. After a couple of minutes she heard a posse of footsteps returning. Betty entered carrying a hypodermic needle, swabs, a bottle, followed by a younger female nurse and two male nurses. 'I'll put her in a pad for the night,' Margaret heard Betty say.

'You can't do that!' Margaret protested. 'I don't want to be on my own! I can't bear it on my own!'

Margaret tried to stand, but with an expertise that could only have come from experience, the three newcomers swept her off her feet and pinned her helplessly to the bed. She tried to resist but was unable to move her limbs. She could do no more than arch her back, as Betty turned away to prepare the syringe, and she felt the scream begin to take possession of her once again.

THE SIREN

It was only when Adam picked up one of her swimming trophies that she decided to kill him. He had never hit her before with anything other than his hands, but now she realised that his disturbance was on the verge of changing up into another gear. Shaking with rage he made as if to hurl the heavy statuette at her head, but controlled himself. He slammed it down among the others in the bookcase, making the shelf bounce, and various of the trophies fall and clatter. What followed was the usual. He took hold of a handful of her hair and marched her up to the bedroom. Once the tension had drained out of him, he became again his usual pleasant self, remorseful and concerned, as eager to please as a faithful mongrel.

She'd lived with this Jekyll and Hyde figure for seven years. For the most part he was kind, gentle, caring, considerate. Only in bed did he want to dominate, to master her. And on occasions when he was angry with her he would punish her with rough sex. At first she'd found these sexual games exciting. It was this dangerous, untamed side of him that had made him so attractive to her (despite her feelings of shame and guilt — a sort of betrayal of her 'sisters' that this should be so). But as time had passed, his need for power had become greater. It seemed like a drug to him; it seemed that as he became addicted he needed to increase the dose to get his fix. He was more aggressive, more violent, more often.

For a period, in their early days together, she'd experienced the delicious excitement of being scared, like a child whose father was playing monsters, but this had changed to the insidious bad taste of real fear. It had got to the stage where she began to be apprehensive as bedtime approached; where she began to tread warily each day lest she gave him some excuse to feign anger towards her.

He had warned her often during these rough games that if she ever left him, or was unfaithful in that old-fashioned sexual sense, he would kill her. And he always said this with such intensity that she believed him. In the early days she had enjoyed the awareness of his strength, of her vulnerability. But now, she had come to feel totally powerless, at his mercy, and she had grown to hate him for it.

Too scared to leave him, she felt she needed to find another way of freeing herself from his tyranny, and when he threatened her with her trophy the decision was made. From that moment, whenever she suffered under his oppression, she began to plan. To be sent to prison would be too great a price to pay. It would have to be a perfect murder. And there was the problem of his superior strength. Although she'd been a swimming champion in her teens, she had always been petite. She was beautiful in the water, as graceful as a dolphin, but she had never been well-muscled, and not having swum or indeed exercised in any way for all the years of her marriage, she had lost much of the muscle she had once had.

It was a Saturday morning — the first really pleasant day of spring. Adam was a probation officer, and a good one, committed and involved, though he wasn't sure for how long he'd be able to continue. He found it impossible to keep a professional distance from the unfortunates he had to deal with. His concern tangled him up in the web of their pain and their impossible problems. Often he would have liked to have brought one of them home to offer real support and friendship, and indeed on one disastrous occasion had done so. His anger was often triggered by his rage or frustration on their behalf against the injustices of their lives. On Saturday mornings he used to go unpaid into the office to try hopelessly to catch up with the paperwork of his caseload.

'Will you stay home today?' she asked him.

He shook his head sorrowfully. 'I'm so far behind. The week's taken up with people. Saturday's the only time I get for paper. You know how it is.'

'Please,' she begged.

He smiled, warmed by being wanted by her, and relented. 'If you really want me to,' he said.

'We could go to the French Patisserie and sit outside and have croissants and hot chocolate.'

'Good idea,' he said. Away from the bedroom there was nothing he would not give her or do for her. Sometimes, after he'd been especially rough with her, he would apologise and say, 'It's a small price to pay — isn't it?'

Perhaps, she sometimes thought, it was.

Breakfast was romantic. The croissants fresh. The chocolate hot and sweet. The spring sunshine warm. He smiled at her, his eyes brimming with love, and leaned forward to kiss her. She cleaned up the flakes of dark pastry from around his mouth, nibbling gently with her soft lips like a horse eating from a loved one's hand. 'It's like being on holiday,' he said.

'Let's go,' she said. 'Let's have a holiday now.'

'Chance'd be a fine thing,' he said. 'I've got Albert up in court again next week. And Linton. And I've got to try and do something about Craigie. And Jonjo's hitting the bottle again. And I think Kofi's probably back into dealing, although he won't admit it. And Charlene's walked out on him again. And who can blame her.'

'But Adam, you've been working so hard. You look absolutely wiped out. You need a break from it. I just want to have you to myself for a little while.'

'Really?' he said. His smile broadened and he shook his head slightly. 'It's a long time since you said anything like that.'

She put a hand under the table and touched him. 'Please,' she said. 'I want to take you to that place in Spain where I went with Jill and Angela just after we met, remember? It was so beautiful there, and I missed you so much. I always promised myself I'd take you there one day.'

'Well, I couldn't make it during the next three weeks at least.'

'All right. In four weeks. I'll go to the travel agent on Monday and try to book up. It should be easy enough this early in the year.'

The ocean on the west coast of Spain is cold all year round, and in spring more so than in autumn. But May in Spain is wonderful. There is still the freshness that follows winter, but already the sun blazes down day after day from strong blue skies. It is still the invigorating, youthful sun of romance, rather than the elderly, slightly seedy, over-ripe sun of retirement. The cold winds that often blow off the Atlantic are quickening and full of promise; and exciting and alarming breakers batter ceaselessly against the shore.

She brought Adam to a fishing village that boasted a single hotel, but she chose instead that they would stay in a self-catering villa a hundred metres up a dusty track at the south end of the bay. The days were idyllic. When they rose at last from their bed and went out onto their balcony with its view of the bay, the sun would already be high. They would shower together and go out for breakfast to one of the little cafes in the town. Late mornings they strolled in the surrounding countryside, stopping to chat whenever possible in their broken Spanish to people they met. Sometimes an old man or woman would insist on taking them home, and they would be given green olives and a glass of red wine. They would swim briefly from the town beach, take a light lunch, retire for a steamy siesta. In the afternoons they would drive in their hired jeep along the coast, discovering deserted bays or rocky headlands where they would wander hand in hand, explore the myriad nooks and crannies, swim, sunbathe, read, make small talk, and cuddle and fool around like unseasoned lovers. On their return they would shower and change and go out to dinner, lingering over a bottle of punchy local wine and endless cups of bitter black coffee till late into the evening.

Ironically, Adam, released from the pressures of work and routine, was as loving and attentive as any woman's dream honeymoon husband. And the romance of the place acted on her like an aphrodisiac, which kept him as satisfied and relaxed as a pampered cat. Mornings before they rose, during afternoon siestas, and sometimes where lonely headlands of stone thrust into the apparent softness of the sea, they played and pleasured and loved. And it was better than it had ever been. And she began to doubt. Her purpose wavered. Her man, she realised, was one in a million. She was perhaps as fortunate as her friends thought her to be. And she knew she could not kill him.

There was one moment of the day when Adam showed signs of agitation. As they walked along the beach from the town to take their late morning swim on their way back to the villa, they passed close to the fishermen who would be mending their nets after the previous evening's work. And there was one among them, a big, bold and striking man, who would watch her with undisguised desire. He was a mature man, in the mould of the working-class hero, mahogany-skinned, and hard-muscled, and handsome in a coarse and angular way. The leers of boys and young men would annoy her like persistent flies, but his gaze thrilled her with a current that buzzed from her throat to her womb. Adam was merely irritated at first by the stares, but, being intuitive, was soon aware of her response, and it angered him. But the hot flush of his jealousy could be soon cooled by her loving words and their frolics in the cold ocean, where Adam would labour along like a land creature that had fallen into the water while she darted all around him like a porpoise, or shark.

The ten days of their stay were coming to an end. It was late, at an hour when every previous evening they had been inside the restaurant because of the chill sea wind. But now a dry desert breeze was sweeping across Spain from North Africa, leaving a fine layer of sand in its wake. They had eaten at a table outside. Adam had gone to the toilet, leaving her briefly alone with her thoughts. She realised that her plan was fanciful and ridiculous. She was an ordinary, well-raised English woman. Everyone had their fantasies of course, but they were never acted out. She and Adam would return home and fall back into their old habits both good and bad. She sighed a huge sigh of both defeat and relief.

A man's shadow fell across her. It was Gabriel. She had learned his name from the calls of his comrades on the beach. Was she enjoying her holiday, he asked in Spanish. How long would she be staying. Only two more nights, she told him. He looked crestfallen. She should stay longer, he said. Wasn't their village beautiful. Yes, she said, it was. The sun, he said, the sea. The fruits, the fish. Why would she want to return to the cold and rain and grey skies and fog. Stay longer, he urged, staring into her face with an intense and unwavering directness. She blushed like a school girl and continually lowered her eyes, but each time she glanced up, his look still devoured her. And his eyes, she realised with surprise, were a startling grey, not the dark brown she would have expected. Why wasn't he out on his boat, she tried to ask. And he shrugged and opened his hands in resignation and gave an explanation she couldn't understand, her Spanish being only fluent in the superficialities of weather and introductions. Adam returned to witness her blushing confusion. You are a lucky man, Gabriel told him. The lady is lovely. Good night. And with the arrogance of his manhood, he sauntered away.

'Let's go,' Adam said without sitting down, and she could hear the trembling hoarseness in his voice.

Afterwards, as usual, he was full of remorse. It was just, he said, that he was frightened of losing her. He couldn't live without her, and so on. The following morning he was loving and undemanding. They enjoyed a pleasant walk, a good lunch. At siesta time she told him she didn't want sex, and for once he didn't override her. 'Later,' she said. And they slept for an hour in each other's arms.

'Let's not take the jeep,' she said, as they prepared to go out. 'If we climb over the rocks out the back here we can get down to a tiny horseshoe bay that's completely secluded. It takes about an hour. We found it last time I was here. You can't get to it by road, so there's never anybody there.'

'So why haven't we been before?' he asked.

'I've been saving it,' she said. 'It's just beautiful. It's completely private. And the rocks come right round and over the beach like the mouth of a great cave, and there's no wind, and the afternoon sun shines right in to warm you after you've swum.'

'Okay,' he shouted with shining eyes, as gleeful as an excited child. 'You've made a sale. What are we waiting for?'

'No one ever goes near,' she said coquettishly. 'You can do what you like with me there.'

A broad smile of delight lit up his handsome, sensitive face. 'It sounds too good to be true,' he said.

They spread their towels in the shade of a great boulder at one end of the little beach. There she gave him as much pleasure as she was able, using all the skills their seven years together had taught her. In response he was loving, gentle, considerate. He tried to bring her to orgasm, but something was dead in her. And all the time she could hear the ocean hurling itself apparently self-destructively against the hardness of the rock, but she knew that in fact it was the rock that would be worn down, shaped and ultimately broken by the sea. And finally, weary after the exertions of the scramble over difficult terrain, tired by the long session of love-making in the little corner of Paradise they had come to, they wandered down to the water's edge where the coldness brought shocked gasps and laughter to their lips.

'Let's skinny dip,' he said.

'No,' she said.

'Don't be silly,' he said, taking off the bathers he'd only just put on, and throwing them back up the beach. 'Nobody can see us here.'

'*You* can,' she said. 'I don't want to.'

'Come on,' he insisted. 'That's not like you.'

'I don't want to.'

'Why?'

'I just don't.'

He grabbed her. She struggled to no avail, her anger mounting. He threw the two pieces of her bikini after his own costume. 'Please', she pleaded. 'Don't make me.'

'What's the matter with you?' he said, becoming angry himself. 'Don't be stupid.'

She tried to pull back, but he swung her up in his arms and carried her, still protesting, into the awesome, breaking waves. The beach sloped steeply, and soon the water lifted them both, and they were swimming; they had entered *her* element. 'There,' he said, 'doesn't that feel good?'

'Yes,' she admitted. She made a great effort to compose herself, to put honey back into her voice. 'Come,' she said. 'I want to show you something marvellous.'

They rose and fell on the swell as she swam slowly ahead of him, urging him on. Away to the south they could see the ragged coastline, raw in its natural, unspoiled beauty. In front of them the sun was lowering itself down its majestic blue backdrop towards an ocean that stretched away to the end of the world. To the north was the long spur of rocky headland, a crescent with its back to them, that formed one of the arms that enclosed and protected the little town.

'Where are we going?' he asked.

'You'll see.'

'There's nothing out there.'

'You'll see,' she repeated.

Adam had not been able to swim when they had met. It was some time before his pride had allowed him to learn. And he was not a strong swimmer, still. A mistimed breath filled his mouth every so often with choking sea water. She cajoled him, luring him on. 'I'm getting tired,' he told her.

'A bit further,' she said.

He looked back towards land. 'Shit!' he said. 'How did we get so far out.'

'It looks further than it is,' she assured him.

'I'll never make it back.'

'I'm here,' she said. 'Trust me.'

'I'm cold,' he said. His teeth chattered when he tried to speak. 'I'm so cold.'

'Okay,' she said. 'Let's go back.'

It was dark when she crawled like a turtle, exhausted and shaking, up the beach. The fishing fleet was already out. It was Gabriel, still working on the damage to his boat, who saw the movement on the sand. He turned her onto her back and looked down at her helplessness. Her breasts rose and fell and shuddered with her efforts to breathe. He took off his torn and sweat-smelling shirt and covered her with it. 'My husband,' she repeated over and over. 'My husband.' He lifted her in his strong arms and carried her along the beach, staying close to the water, well away from the lights of the town. 'My husband,' she kept saying. 'Si, si,' he said.

At the villa he laid her, still wet and patterned with sand, on the bed.

He took off his torn shorts and underpants and mounted her. She struggled weakly, but she was like a fish in his hands. He emptied himself into her, then lay with the weight of his body crushing her so that she could hardly draw breath. Then he began again. Less urgently this time, talking all the time in a language she could not comprehend. And despite herself, her body was aroused. She put her arms around his large frame, her hands like butterflies on his back and neck. She looked at his face, but saw Adam's eyes staring back at her, wide with terror. She could feel the strong pull of the current still dragging them away from the shore despite their efforts to swim against it. She swam naked on her back and felt her clitoris swell. Adam's face became disfigured with panic. 'I can't make it,' he said.

'Yes,' she called out. 'Yes.'

His cry was submerged by salt water. He was coughing, spluttering, retching. 'Cramp!' he moaned.

She could see nothing but the frothing water, and then there was Adam's face again distorted with panic and pain. 'Help me!' he pleaded. 'Help me!'

And then she knew she could not see it through. The sea lifted her and threw her down and pounded on top of her. Her tears filled the hollows of her face and she tasted again the salt in her mouth. 'I'm coming!' she cried. And all the tension of her body accumulated in her genitalia, and she felt she must burst with the strength of her sensations. 'I'm coming! I'm coming!'

But it was too late.

Gabriel had finished. He pulled out of her and dressed himself. And she was left alone in an icy and tumultuous sea of guilt.

The police arrived later. And a doctor. Eventually an interpreter. The consul was notified; and Adam's parents, who would fly out and make arrangements to have the body taken back if it was found.

She was sitting up in the hospital bed. 'We just swam out too far,' she told them. Carme, the interpreter, relayed this to the civil guards. Carme's breath smelt strongly of garlic. This woman, to whom the civil guards paid scant attention (occupied as they were with ogling *her*), must have been beautiful, she thought, when she was young. She was aware of her own tousled, mousy hair, compared with the shining blackness of Carme's. And realising that Carme was possibly not much more than ten years older than her, a spasm of panic seized her. She was suddenly and for the first time afraid of growing old. And more, afraid of growing old alone. She added, 'It was foolish.'

One of the guards said something. Carme asked her, 'How were you saved?'

'I'm a much stronger swimmer than he was. We couldn't get back against the current. Eventually...when he...I stopped trying to swim against it. I let the current carry me. It took me out and round the headland. Then I was able to swim into the town beach.' Carme relayed all this. There was some discussion among the guards.

'They say there was a similar incident about seven years ago,' Carme told her.

She could scarcely contain herself from blurting out, *I know. I heard about it. I was here.* Instead she said, 'You'll find our clothes at the little bay.'

'They are collected,' Carme informed her. 'You may be charged.'

'Charged?' she said. Her mouth was suddenly dry and her heartbeat thumped against her chest. The civil guards leered.

'Your swimming costumes were collected too. It is against the law in our country to swim without clothes.'

She began to laugh. The laughter came bubbling out. It would not stop. The three Spaniards looked surprised, then alarmed. And the laughter and the crying mingled, and went on, and on, and on.

THE GARDEN

Tommy Armstrong was at work one day in the pit and he had an awful pain, as though he'd been impaled below his heart by a spike that was protruding from his back. After work he went to see a doctor, who told him it was indigestion.

The following day Tommy had to stop work. The same feeling came on him again. He didn't know whether he wanted to be sick or what he wanted to do, he was in such agony. His gaffer said, 'Where am I going to get anyone to replace you now?'

Tommy said, 'Well, you'll just have to fiddle on, Ernie, till you get somebody. I'm ill, man.'

'I'll go and get you a pot of tea,' Ernie said. So he went away and came back with a pot of tea with a drop of rum in it.

When Tommy felt well enough he made his way to the pit head. By the time he got out of the pit the pain had gone off and he felt fine. It was pay day, so he went and collected his wages.

He went in to work again the next day. The under manager said, 'How are you feeling today?'

Tommy said, 'I feel champion now. I've got a new lease of life.'

But after work he was getting ready to go out to the pictures when that feeling came back again. And then, *whoosh!* Blood! What a mess! Tommy's wife rushed to the phone. An ambulance came and took him to hospital. Tommy heard the doctor say, 'I'm sorry. He's too far gone. There's nothing I can do but take him in and give him a bed.'

The next morning when the same doctor came down the ward he was surprised to see Tommy still there.

The next thing Tommy knew, they were putting a screen round his bed, and then the vicar was there praying for him. And Tommy, who hadn't shed tears in years, broke down crying.

Then he just seemed to float up to the ceiling. He was looking back at himself lying on the bed. He could see the vicar, who had a circle of baldness on his crown, kneeling at the bedside. Then Tommy turned away and he was in a corridor. He went a long way down the corridor, and then he heard voices shouting: 'Tommy Armstrong! Tommy Armstrong!' He looked back and saw lights following him, lights like cap lamps. But they were a long way off, and he kept going.

As he went along he could see a light ahead of him. It turned out to be a doorway which led to the most beautiful garden he'd ever seen. There were banks and banks of flowers on both sides. And there was a straight and narrow path. He walked down the path for a long way, till he came to a bend. As he turned the bend he saw a group of people sitting outside some gates. When they saw him they got up and pulled shrouds over their heads. They all passed through the gateway, but as he came up to the gate it closed in front of him. *What funny people,* he thought, *closing the gates when they saw me coming.*

He looked to see if there was any name on the gate, but couldn't see because of a bright light in his eyes, like the sun. He was trying to shield his eyes with his arm when this face appeared. It was a man with untidy fair hair hanging down to his shoulders. He was a young man with a blonde beard, and a big, hooked nose on him, and lovely clear blue eyes — just like the face on the little pictures Tommy used to get for attendance at Sunday School.

Then Tommy was on the bed again. There was a nurse sitting there rubbing his hands. She said, 'You've been away a long time. Wherever have you been?'

When Tommy Armstrong got his deputy's ticket, he was told, 'We want a good man on the Rescue Brigade.' So he joined. Over the years he did a lot of work with them. Then he was called for the last time. He was picked up by the fire tender and taken to the pit head. They couldn't get into the pit at first. The Salvation Army were there. It was dinner time and they were giving out chips and pies and pop.

Young Joey said, 'Have a chip, Tommy. The chips are lovely.'

Fred said, 'You eat that many chips, Joe, you must have a square arsehole.'

'If you've got any sense you'll eat nothing,' Tommy warned. 'You don't know what we'll find in there.'

'Oh, we'll be all right,' Joey said. 'These are for free.'

Tommy said, 'You carry on. But I don't want any. Give me a couple of blankets. I'll be lying over there in the sand. Give me a call when you want me.'

At twelve o'clock at night they came and called him. 'Come on, lad. It's time you were down the pit.' They shook him and got him up. Down, down, down they went: the rescue team, the stretcher bearers, the water-carriers. They each had to carry some gear. And they each had a bottle of liquid oxygen.

When they trooped out of the lift they found a set for them to put the gear in. When they'd got it loaded Tommy said, 'There's room for us, too,' so the men piled into the tub. Away it went, with the men grateful for the ride, until the track suddenly dived steeply downhill like a fairground big dipper. A couple of the lads got the wind up and jumped out. Tommy said, 'It's all right. It's been this way before. It won't be any different this time.' The tub took them to where the ropes had been cut by the explosion. When they got out, the others waited for their mates while Tommy walked on ahead by himself.

He continued until he came to a fall of stone. It was piled up nearly to the roof. There was a tunnel at the top, about a metre in diameter and several metres long. He crawled through and continued on. He'd gone some way when he heard: 'Tommy Armstrong! Tommy Armstrong!' He stopped in his tracks. His mind flew back across the years. To that day in the hospital. And this was it. He looked back and there were the lights. If someone had put a needle in him at that moment, they wouldn't have got a drop of blood out.

When he got over the shock he went on again. He came to another fall of stone, and then another. It was a difficult journey. There were falls at intervals all the way. At last he came to the fresh air base. He waited there till the others joined him, and they got their puffs of oxygen. Tommy looked up at the lamp. 'There's some gas in here, all right,' he said. 'What have we let ourselves in for!' They took their boots off and put on rubber boots and gloves, and they got their breathing apparatuses filled up.

The captain said to Tommy's team, 'There's four bodies along there. Go in and see what you can do. But tread carefully. Keep two paces apart. Don't touch the sides or you'll start another fall. And remember, you're in a dangerous atmosphere.'

So in they went, with Tommy Armstrong shoving on in front. He pushed through a canvas door and came to the face engine, and he saw the first body. It was lying face down, almost naked. All it had on was its short sleeves and its belt. Everything else had been blasted off him. Tommy guessed he was a deputy because there were dozens of caps lying about. They were as clean as if they were straight out of a shop. There was not a mark on them. Tommy was amazed that the detonators and the powder hadn't exploded.

He got the canvas shroud and spread it out. His team arrived as he pulled the body over on to it. It wasn't a pretty sight. Tommy's mates ran off, back towards the fresh air base. *What's the matter with them?* he wondered, and carried on with his work. He wrapped the body in the shroud and wrote the lamp number on the canvas. He rolled it on to the stretcher and strapped it down so that it wouldn't fall off on the journey to the top.

Some of the others came back. They couldn't speak because they were wearing their breathing apparatuses, but they explained to Tommy in sign language why they'd run off. When he'd rolled the dead man over, they'd vomited at the sight. Yes, thought Tommy, it was the free food from the Sally Army that had caused that.

Two of them carried the body away. Tommy peered under the face engine. There was another one under there. He threw the shroud in first, then crawled under, followed by two of his mates. The body was trapped by the belt. Tommy got hold of its hands to try to pull it onto the shroud. *Has he got gloves on?* Tommy wondered. The dead man's fingers came away in Tommy's hands. There was just the bone left. When he did that one of the other fellows vomited again and had to scurry away out of it. Only Joey remained. Tommy signalled to him that he should go as well if he wanted, but Joey indicated that he would stay.

They climbed over the top of the conveyor to the face and discovered two more bodies, but these were in an appalling state. They had burst open with the force of the explosion. Tommy could taste the charnel atmosphere even through his breathing apparatus. They gathered the body parts into two heaps, unable to avoid contaminating themselves as they did so, and got them wrapped up, and wrote the dead men's numbers on the sheets. *I'll have to burn all my clothes when I finish this job,* Tommy thought.

They searched around to see if there was anything else lying about. Tommy squeezed under to the other side of the face, and he saw another body hanging. It had been a stone-stripping shift. When the explosion went off this man must have been standing astride the shaker pan. The ten foot metal pan had shot up and the man was hanging by his ankles. His body was part buried by a fall of stone.

Tommy and Joey cleared the stone away from the upper body. Then, using whatever lengths of metal they could find lying about, they tried to lever him free. But it was no use. Tommy asked Joey if he had a knife, and when the lad shook his head Tommy sent him back to the fresh air base to fetch one. Joey returned with a penknife. It was the best he could do. So Tommy hacked and sawed at the man's ankles. There was no other way to get him down. Joey looked the other way.

When the body fell, they got it wrapped up and onto a stretcher, and strapped it on. Then Tommy took his mask off and shouted for someone to come and fetch the body.

The shout did it. A rumble started. The rumble grew into a growl. The stone fell all around them. Tommy was deafened by the roar, blinded by the dust, paralysed by dread, and then smashed to the floor. He lost consciousness briefly, but was conscious again before the dust had settled. They were in a small cave, the three men, one dead, one dying, one no more than grazed and terrified. Surprisingly, both cap lamps were still working.

'Keep your mask on,' Tommy said. 'Don't panic. They know we're here. They'll get through. Be patient, lad. But don't start shouting or screaming, or you might start another fall.'

Tommy's own mask had disappeared. But it didn't matter any more. His legs were mercifully numb. He twisted his neck to see what had happened down there. The lower half of his body was crushed beyond repair. And there was no way to staunch the blood that was forming a dark pool around him on the pit floor. He could feel his life ebbing. He talked to Joey to calm the boy. He told about the time he'd been ill, years before. About the blood he'd lost then. About the strange experience he'd had.

'So you won't go if it's not time, Joey,' he said. 'You're a brave lad. It'll be even more terrifying when you're on your own. But remember what I told you: resist the urge to shout and scream. Be patient, lad. They won't rest till they get you out.'

Tommy turned out his lamp and rested his cheek on the back of his hand. He looked up at Joey, who sat, hunched, facing him. Tommy couldn't see the young man's features because of the bright light in his eyes.

'I'm just waiting now till I come to that beautiful garden,' Tommy told him. 'I've still got that to come.'

A CRIMINAL OFFENCE

I stopped listening. It was pointless. I remembered the last time I'd stood in that dock. Then, I was innocently hopeful. This time I just felt resentful and defiant. I wanted to shout obscenities at the judge — but I felt too drained. It would have achieved nothing.

The Counsel for the Prosecution wore cold vindictiveness like a stocking mask. Whoever was in the dock, guilty or innocent, abhorrent or admirable — it was all the same to him: he'd want to nail them purely out of self-interest. No wonder Justice was always represented wearing a bandage over its eyes!

At that moment I had a sudden flash of insight. I understood something I'd never understood before. Those people who planted bombs that took life — how they could bring themselves to do it? I'd understood their anger all right — but the children orphaned? — the flesh disfigured or dismembered? From the dock I watched that bastard of a barrister as though he were in an aquarium — I could see his lips sneer and move, but I didn't hear his voice. What I witnessed was a performer who had entered into his role to such an extent that he had discarded his humanity, virtually abandoned his humanness. I understood how a uniform could become part of a person like a new skin; how what was once human, in a uniform, became androidal — and consequently a legitimate target.

Remembering how naive I had once been, flushed me with anger. For the first time during the trial I glanced at my mother. She was dressed tastefully in black, as though at a society funeral. And it occurred to me that, in a sense, this was my funeral, but she was certainly not in mourning for me — she was reminding the world of how *she* had been made to suffer. I couldn't bear to look for long at the composure of her still handsome, melancholy, long-suffering face. Her expression alone was a dishonest but powerful witness for the prosecution, an unspoken denial of the damage she had done to me.

My mother had castrated me while I was too small to defend myself, so that I've grown up impotent and frightened; she'd suffocated me with over-protectiveness and double-binding manipulation, so I've become asthmatic; she'd deformed me into physical and emotional ugliness, so, as an adult I am friendless and confused and full of self-loathing. It was because of all this that I had tried so hard to get psychiatric help. I went repeatedly to our GP, a friend of the family (that is, a friend of my mother), and asked to be allowed to see a shrink, but my request was always refused. He would have spoken to her, and she would have put the kibosh on it because she would have felt it as some sort of stigma on her should *her* son have had to have that sort of treatment. So I was given tranquillisers to calm me down (when I was already too passive), and a good talking to to make me wake myself up (which I'd have thought any fool could see was a contradiction). And each of those refusals left me feeling even more impotent, afraid and confused, and had me reaching for my inhaler.

I made other attempts to get help too, without success. The attitude seemed to be that, if you were aware that you needed help, you weren't sick enough to be given any. Finally, in desperation, but after careful thought, I went onto the common with sulphur, charcoal, and weed killer, ground, mixed, and packed tight in a paint tin. (When I was a child my mother had not approved of other children, but she had approved of educational toys. I had spent many solitary hours with expensive chemistry sets.) I caused a quite spectacular explosion. Then I sat and waited patiently till the police came to take me away. In that very court room I had pleaded guilty. I said, 'I have tried in every way I could think of, to get psychiatric help; without success. I created the explosion in order to attract attention to my need. I hope and believe that this will convince you that I do need help; and that you will see that I get it.'

How could I have been so stupid! In those days I still thought policemen were there to help the elderly and infirm across the road!

Today, when I was asked if I had anything to say, I just told the judge that in view of the fact that he, in his wisdom, had not allowed me to explain fully why I made this latest protest in the way I did, nor to give all of the necessary background information that would have enabled the men and women of the jury to understand my action, I had nothing to add.

The judge was clearly infuriated by my lack of remorse, and I was amused by his anger. He was taking pains to keep up his mask of impartiality, but without much success. In fact, because of his own extreme religious and political sympathies, he was revolted by anything that smacked of radicalism. 'I have been consistent,' he said prissily, 'in attempting to assist you, in every manner possible, in the difficult and complicated procedure of conducting your own defence. But I have said, and I repeat to you now, that I cannot allow you to use this court as a political platform. I remind you once again that you are charged with a criminal offence, and that your defence must be an appropriate one.' Oh, why are they so pompous, long-winded, hypocritical and predictable. I could have written his script for him.

I kept glancing at the shorthand writer in her blue trouser suit and crisp white blouse. Whenever her fingers were able to pause for a moment from their work her fingertips played with the buttons between her breasts or dabbed at her softly waving brown hair. She had a habit of flicking the hair away from her neck with one hand, while giving a simultaneous toss of her head. These little gestures caused a deep pain in my chest and made breathing difficult. You see, I have never made love. I have never even been kissed in a sexual way. I was thinking that now, probably, I never would. I felt myself filling up with self-pity, and hopelessness, and hatred. Yes, hatred. Real hatred. Hatred towards my mother. Towards the Church. Towards the judge — both judges, all judges, and their minions: the police, the screws (who took such delight in humiliating me when I was in prison). Oh, yes, I've begun to understand the so-called terrorists at last. The orphans, after all, are

116

being saved from further corruption at their fathers' hands. The damaged limbs weigh little in the scales of Justice against the damage prevented. And I, I now realise with regret, wasted the one little explosion of my life, there on the common, with no one near.

I began making a mental list of those people I should target, should I ever get the chance again. My mother, of course. Although I must admit to feeling a brief wave of pity for her. The world sees her as someone basking in the sun of righteousness, whereas in fact she is trapped inescapably in the sinking sand of self-denial. She chose religion and death rather than sex and life — and she will never experience joy now. She suffers her brief time on earth in weeds, pretending to have been tragically widowed, rather than admit that her husband was driven to dancing on air in order to escape her ascetic regimen.

Who else? A representative of that death-glorifying international conspiracy which appropriately enough uses a crucifix as its symbol: an archbishop perhaps? I have never met an archbishop, though my mother has.

A judge? Today's judge? That judge at my previous trial? — the one who said: 'It is clear to me that you are indeed in need of some sort of treatment, but your reckless and irresponsible behaviour cannot go unpunished, and therefore I am going to send you to prison for a term of twelve months.' To dismiss him as a buffoon is a mistake. The members of the Klu Klux Klan were buffoons, but thousands of decent people suffered at their hands, were castrated, hung from trees, burnt on the fiery cross (that symbol again!). Hitler was a buffoon. Buffoonery is the carnival cloak of the devil. That particular buffoon, the first judge, was for ever scratching his cheeks and pulling his earlobes. He wore half-spectacles, and a black moustache. Why was it so surprising to find a judge sporting a black moustache? Perhaps I imagined that all judges would appear as shrivelled and senile as this latest one. Or perhaps it was because a black moustache was so incongruous under that little white wig. Oh, yes, the bastards of the world love to dress up, don't they. They adore their uniforms and robes and wigs and coronets and medals and jewels.

That judge, pompous and unimaginably foolish as he was, did me a favour. My mother wanted me to go to Cambridge. I had the necessary academic qualifications, but not the emotional stability. I had stayed at home, doing nothing, for four years. Then that nasty little scorpion unintentionally sent me to the best of all possible educational institutions. It was an unbearable but invaluable stay. In a sense it could not have been more different from my mother's house. In a sense it was so much the same. In both places I was powerless and afraid, and there was no air to breathe. But the contrast in the methods used to achieve the same results threw my world, for the first time, into sharp focus. At home I had been suffocated by chintz and velvet. In the nick the screws favoured a sharp jab to the solar plexus. In either case I was left defenceless and gasping for air. But once away from home, and I would never have been able to leave home if I had not been sent to prison, I was able to tear the swaddling clothes from around my brain. Although I was still impotent I realised that I was not completely powerless; though still afraid, no longer as afraid of my fear; still asthmatic, but the attacks became less frequent and less severe. Above all, I was less confused. Strange that — that having been shut in, I could then see out so much more clearly.

I had known for many years that *I* was a suitable case for treatment, but in the nick I began to see how sick *she* was, how I'd been mindfucked by *her,* how she expressed her neurosis through the Black Death of her religion. Her Church was a blanket that smothered rather than warmed. It was a stone used for grinding down instead of building. It was a knife used for mutilation instead of shaping. I became aware of her pious hypocrisy, her emotional blackmail. Her house was a tomb (no wonder black suited her so well). I remembered with resentment those interminable joyless, airless, Sunday-school afternoons, and the bleak, cold and musty, empty Church-service mornings and evenings. I could see myself as that small animal, harshly scrubbed and laundered, in ironed underclothes, in the vast, vaulted hell of the cathedral, at the mercy of the towering black demons of mother and minister. And I knew then what I had to do.

When I made my way to Westminster Abbey, it was one of those dark, drizzly London evenings that the old B movie film-makers used to be so fond of. Passers-by remained anonymous under black umbrellas.

I'd lost my umbrella, and was using a green one of my mother's. I entered through a side door, and left the brolly on an empty pew. I clenched my fear in tight fists, and bit it back in my throat. I stepped over the rope barrier and strode up the red-carpeted steps towards the high altar. The six-foot gold cross was the first thing I knocked over. Then the two candlesticks, large enough to have graced the table of a giant. I broke the white candles across my knee like kindling. I dragged off the red altar cloth, like a party trick that didn't work, causing candlesticks and candles, the cross and bible, to smack and clatter onto the cold flagstone floor. One of the candlesticks struck my knee, but for once I was immune to pain. I grabbed hold of the weighty bible and ripped out handfuls of pages before throwing it down again. I picked up the gold cross, feeling as strong as Samson, and using it as an axe, splintered a painting on wood of the Last Supper. Before they managed to pin me to the floor I'd assaulted the Virgin, a baby Jesus, and two little angels; and I had bashed in the faces of the Three Wise Men on a picture that hung near to the altar. And even as I was dragged down, leaving my axe embedded in the gold-lacquered picture frame, I hung onto the wall tapestry so that it fell on top of us like a collapsed tent.

I didn't resist when they led me from the court. I went quietly. The uniform guarding me didn't bother to speak. He knew that I was unwilling to fraternise with the enemy. I sat with my knees apart, my hands dangling, staring at my feet. I realised that I always did go quietly. To meals, to bed, to school, to my room for punishment, to Sunday-school, to church, to court, to my cell. Then a vague memory came to me. It was as though, in my mother's house, I was passing a room which had been kept locked and bolted for many years, but which was now not properly secured. I caught a glimpse of what was going on inside. I went back for another look. I peered through the crack, then pushed the door further open. I saw a very small boy having a violent tantrum. My mother, younger then, was hauling this little bundle of fighting fury along the hallway of her house towards the cupboard under the stairs. The tiny boy screamed and screamed, resisting to his utmost. He lashed out with fists and kicked his feet and cried, 'No, no, no! I won't go in there!' Her strength of course was greater than his so he threw himself down, kicking his legs, screaming, 'No, no, no!' 'Stop that!' his mother hissed angrily, slapping at him spitefully. 'What will the neighbours think!'

I realised with a pleased shock that there had been a time when that small boy was continually mutating into a screaming frenzy of raging pain. What happened to him? I wondered. Where was that little boy buried? Along with his father in that dark hole in the churchyard? Or was he still sleeping somewhere like a Sleeping Beauty? Could he still be given the Kiss of Life?

When I was taken back into the courtroom to hear the jury's verdict I went quietly once again, wondering whether I should. The jury foreman was a youthful-looking middle-aged man. He looked fit, strong, healthy and mean, as though he might be an army physical training instructor. He looked the sort who would call his wife and daughters 'stupid' and 'useless', and who would have affairs with other women. (But his wife would see him as 'manly' and 'attractive', and would prefer to suffer under him than have anything to do with someone totally ineffectual and unattractive like me). There was something about his mouth — a permanent suggestion of a sneer — which reminded me of the prison chaplain.

I had no visitors when I was inside. I have no friends. I had no friends as a child. My mother always feared I might be contaminated by other children. Despite her penny-pinching genteel poverty she preferred to buy me books rather than have me bring them home from the public library in case I caught the germs of common children from the pages. Even my mother didn't visit. She said in her letters that I would understand that it was not possible for her to enter such a place. I was kept for part of the time in solitary, 'for my own protection'. I was a natural victim, they said. So I was foolishly grateful when the chaplain came to talk to me. But after the chaplain confessed that he 'chastised' his own children, that he believed 'discipline was an expression of love', I hoped he wouldn't come again. But he did, with the smell of whisky on his breath. He offered me a nip — but I refused. I have never drunk. My mother would not allow alcohol in the house. This time the chaplain volunteered that the prisoners were rotten through and through and that, apart from me, there wasn't an ounce of goodness in a single one of them, and if he had his way a majority of them would go to the gallows.

I said that that was hardly a Christian attitude, and he scoffed and said he'd been doing that wretched job for fifteen years, and he *knew*. I was still unworldly enough to be shocked. I had often met churchmen at my mother's house, and while many of them clearly felt disgust for their fellow men, their repugnance was always covered over with mealy-mouthed hypocrisy, like a mutilated corpse being wrapped up in a spotless sheet.

I told the chaplain to get out of my cell and not come back, and he went, leaving me trembling and wheezing. The next day a screw discovered a dog end under my mattress, even though I don't smoke, and I lost remission. But that was the first time I had ever stood up to anyone, and although it brought me out in a sweat whenever I thought about it, I felt a little better about myself.

While the judge was passing sentence I stared wistfully at the shorthand writer, who lightly touched the buttons of her blouse as though she were about to undo them. I have never seen a living woman's breasts. The judge seemed to be weighed down in his book-lined, wood-panelled habitat as though the black gown was too heavy for his frail old body. I read in the newspaper that judges were among the customers in a South London brothel when it was raided by the police. I began to imagine this judge trying to have sex with the shorthand writer, and I felt overcome by nausea, and had to rummage for my inhaler. The judge had linked his scrawny fingers together and pulled his glasses down his nose. His face was ingrained with contempt, like years of make-up that had never been washed off. He said: 'In view of the fact that this abominable behaviour was so unreasonable and out of keeping with your background and training, it seems to me that your action was that of someone who is severely mentally and emotionally disturbed. I am not going to send you to prison again. I believe that prison could do nothing but exacerbate your problems and that as a free man once more, the probability that you would commit further gross acts of criminal vandalism, with total disregard for property and human life, would be greatly increased. Therefore, in your own best interests, to save you from yourself, as well as to protect society at large from the menace of further manifestations of your inner sickness, I am going to send you to a high security, penal psychiatric institution, where you will be detained at Her Majesty's pleasure.'

I realise now of course that my protest was impotent and childish. I'm beginning to understand so much more. Too late.

LONDON BRIDGE
IS BURNING DOWN

I was a young man then. Bob and Maggie were my closest friends. Bob and I had been mates since we were twelve. We were both in a gang in our school made up of boys who came from broken homes. We used to play hookey together, and we stayed friends after we left school. There'd been times when he was hard up and I was working when I'd been able to help him out. Like when he'd had to get married when he was eighteen. I was Best Man at his wedding. Maggie didn't like me at first. It sounds funny to say it but I think she was jealous of me — of our friendship. But after their little girl was about a year old, Maggie changed. Perhaps it was because I liked Lucy so much. I used to sit with her on my knee, or walk up and down the kitchen with her while Maggie was cooking, or play with her — the sort of games you play with babies, peek-a-boo and all that. I'd bath her, or change her nappies, or anything. If she was crying, and Maggie was busy, she'd always come to me.

From then on Maggie used to mother *me*. Because I was a man living on my own she used to do little things for me, and she liked to feed me up. She said I didn't eat properly and I didn't look after myself. As Lucy grew older Maggie and me became firm friends. Bob was a builder and was always working — long hours, heavy work — trying to develop his little business. He used to come home tired out. He didn't play with Lucy much, but he loved her all the same. She was the apple of his eye. That's why he worked so hard. But I was never too tired for Lucy. If she wanted to go tree-climbing, or someone to play *Snakes and Ladders* with, or someone to be a horse for her to ride on, I was game. I never went to the house without she'd got a picture for me — one she'd drawn herself; or a little treasure she'd found, like a stone with a vein of a different colour running through it, or a bird's egg that had fallen from the eaves. Lucy had Bob's blue eyes and Maggie's dark brown hair (although Maggie's hair was long and Lucy's had been cut short). With that straight hair framing her face she looked like a boy, and yet she was as pretty as a picture.

It was the Christmas when I was twenty-three and Lucy was four. They'd had to go to Bob's mother for Christmas Day and to Maggie's parents for Boxing Day (you know what tyrants parents can be about Christmas; I was lucky like that — I didn't have any), and they'd invited me to stay for a week from the twenty-seventh. I was out of work at the time and I was very glad to go. For one thing, you can feel very lonely at a time like Christmas if you're on your own. And for another it meant getting out of town for a few days. Where I lived you could carve slices of yellow exhaust out of the air with a knife. I had a room overlooking a main road. Trucks used to be going by all night, and there was no danger of oversleeping because of the dawn chorus of cars, buses and juggernauts. On the corner was a pub where they had rock bands every weekend (and even more frequently over the Christmas period). It was a good pub to go to for an evening out — good groups, good atmosphere — but it was deafening. You couldn't hear yourself think. And if I was at home in my room it was like being under siege. The music used to shake my walls. At Bob's there was nothing like that. They lived in a cottage a couple of kilometres from the nearest village. It'd been a farm once, but by then the land was owned by neighbouring farmers. The house had been bought for them by Maggie's parents. It was pretty primitive when they moved in but Bob was gradually doing it up. It was peaceful there and the air was clean. When you lay in bed you could hear the stream that formed the boundary of their little piece of land, and the wind rustling the leaves of the big old sycamore. Of course you still got woken at first light — by the birds. You heard birds all through the day, everything from martins to crows. Sometimes you'd see a skylark or a kestrel, and once me and Lucy saw a heron standing on one leg fishing in the stream.

It was a lovely, cold, dry day, that Tuesday I cycled out. I had two plastic carrier bags on the handlebars bulging with Christmas presents. One bag just had a toy garage in. You see, Lucy liked to play with cars, so I'd bought her a garage and some cars. I knew she'd have more than enough dolls from her grannies. I'd got the garage in one bag and all the small things in the other. After spending Christmas alone in my room, I was looking forward to being at Bob's: looking forward to having a few pints with him; looking forward to being mothered by Maggie; but most of all, looking forward to seeing little Lucy. 'Juicy Lucy' I used to call her. She was like a little ripe fruit.

When I got to the farm, Lucy was standing on the gate at the end of the lane, waiting for me. 'Pete,' she called. 'Pete. What you got in them bags?'

'Never you mind what I've got in my bags,' I said, 'you nosey little parker.' She gave me a big bear hug. I loved that. I hadn't had many hugs in my life. Then I sat her on my shoulders and rode up to the house. Bob and Maggie came to the door. They looked really pleased to see me. It made me feel warm all through. We went inside and while Bob poured me a drink Maggie gave me a kiss under the mistletoe. Then we gave each other presents. And that was the first coincidence. Lucy's present to me was a drawing she'd done with her new felt-tips that she'd got in her stocking. It was a fire engine. Well, I gave her the garage and lots of little cars and trucks to go with it — and one was a bright red fire engine with a ladder on the top. She loved that. She loved the garage and the cars, but most of all she loved that fire engine.

It was one of the best weeks of my life. In the mornings, Lucy used to come and get in my bed. She'd put her icy little hands and feet on me to wake me up. Then she'd jump on me or pull the covers off until I got up. Bob and Maggie were taking advantage of Bob's few days off work and they stayed in bed till late. Lucy and me used to have breakfast together, then we'd play. The weather stayed crisp and bright. Every afternoon we all went for a walk, across the fields, or down the stream, or up the hill. When Lucy got tired I used to give her a piggy-back or a shoulder ride. After tea I played with Lucy again, some game or other, lying on the floor by the fire. She often played with her garage and cars, especially the fire engine. She even took the fire engine to bed with her; I used to read her a story and she'd fall asleep clutching it in her hand.

Some evenings I baby-sat while Bob and Maggie went down the village to the pub. Other evenings I went with Bob to the pub and Maggie would stay home. Me and Bob would have a couple of pints and a game of arrows, then we'd go back. We'd sit with Maggie, huddled around the fire, and have a jar or two before we went to bed. It was cold in that house at night. Bob was in the middle of putting in central heating, but he was working such long hours so he could afford the central heating he never had time to finish the job. They just had the one coal fire in the living-room and a couple of paraffin heaters — one in the kitchen and one on the landing upstairs. We used to sit with our feet in the grate, our legs burning and our backs freezing, supping our beer and singing old pop songs. It felt like they were my family. But it was better than an ordinary family. We weren't family just by accident of birth, but because we'd grown close to one another.

Saturday was New Year's Eve. I put Lucy to bed and read her a story. Then I lay on the bed beside her and we sang nursery rhymes. She sang: 'London Bridge is burning down, burning down, burning down, London Bridge is burning down, my fair lady.'

I said, 'It's not "*burning*" down, Luce; it's "*falling*" down.' But she just went on singing 'burning down' anyway. She had her fire engine with her. She put it under her pillow. When she was asleep I kissed her forehead, and tip-toed out of the room.

The plan for New Year's Eve was this: Me and Bob would go to the pub. Maggie would stay home. About eleven, Bob would come back. He wanted to see the New Year in with Maggie. I'd stay on at the pub — they were having a special New Year 'do' till one in the morning. I'd stay just to see the New Year in, then I'd come home. It was only a couple of kilometres door to door, if that. It only took five minutes on my bike. I could be home by ten past twelve. Bob and Maggie wanted to first-foot their nearest neighbours, Mr and Mrs Anderson, who farmed the fields around Bob's house. Bob and Maggie were going to knock on their door at a minute past midnight with a lump of coal and a bottle of whisky. Then they were going on to the tail-end of a party at Maggie's brother's. They were going by car and didn't need to leave till a couple of minutes before twelve.

Maggie was a bit uneasy. 'Do you think Lucy will be all right?' she said. 'We've never left her on her own before.'

'Of course she'll be all right,' Bob said. 'You worry too much. She'll be snug in bed. It'll only be for ten minutes or so till Pete gets home.'

'You won't be late, will you, Pete?' she said.

'No,' I said, 'I won't be late, I promise.'

'Let the man see the New Year in,' Bob said.

'Yeah, I'll just see it in, then I'll come straight back.'

'You won't forget, will you?' Maggie insisted.

'I won't forget, Maggie. You know I love that little one like my own child. You go and enjoy yourself. I'll see she's all right.'

Well, I did see the New Year in. There was a lot of kissing and hugging and singing after that. I'd had a skinful by then. Even so I was out of the pub by quarter past twelve at the latest. I had a bit of difficulty with my bike. I fell over it twice before I managed to get on. I came a cropper on my way home too when my front wheel got into a ditch. I didn't do the journey as quickly as usual. When I came to the track up to the cottage I tried to look at my watch. There was a bright moon, but I couldn't focus my eyes on the hands. In trying to see the time I rode into the gate and fell off again.

I left the bike there and continued on foot. The next thing I knew, the cottage was in flames. I looked up and saw Lucy at her bedroom window, and then I heard the voice. 'Pete! Pete! Help me!' But what could I do? Call the fire brigade? Bob hadn't got a telephone. The nearest phone was in the village two kilometres away. Or at the Anderson's, nearly two kilometres across the fields. A ladder? Bob didn't have a ladder there. He kept things like that at his yard in town. A blanket to catch her in? All the blankets were upstairs and the whole house seemed to be ablaze. A tablecloth then? But you need someone to hold the other end. And all the time the voice went on, 'Pete! Pete! Help me!' I stood there looking up at the face behind the glass. I couldn't see the features. Just the pale little face framed by the short dark hair. 'Pete! Pete! Help me!' And I thought, I must do something. The only thing was to try to get into the house. Try to get through the flames. Try to get up to the room. But I was afraid. I just stood rooted to the spot. I could see the face even less clearly now. There were tears in my eyes, and the brightness behind the face made it a dark shadow. I pushed my face into my hands. 'Pete!' went the voice. 'Pete! Help me!'

When I looked back at the window, the face had gone.

Bob and Maggie were stunned. Shell-shocked. Bob's eyes were glass. They never found out how the fire started. I said, 'Maybe Lucy was stumbling half asleep along the landing to the lavatory and knocked over the paraffin heater.' Maggie looked at me as though I was a murderer.

I went away. What else could I do? Away from the town where I'd been born, where I'd spent my whole life. I became a seaman. For eight years I sailed the oceans of the world and I carried that burning guilt with me all the time, every minute of the day. I tried hard to leave it behind, but it was the one piece of luggage I carried with me wherever I went. I had to keep moving. Or drinking. Or *doing* something. In spare moments when I was trapped on board ship with nothing to do, I began whittling wood. Then I began to carve pieces of wood into crude shapes. After eight years I left the navy, still carrying a jagged chunk of pain like a boulder on my back. I signed off the boat in Liverpool, so I stayed there. I found work with a carpenter who made door and window frames. It wasn't a satisfying job, but I liked working with wood. In the evenings I went to a woodcarving class. I bought myself a good set of tools, and in my spare time I began making toys.

Then I met a woman. Diane. She was not unlike Maggie to look at, but more 'little girlish', if you know what I mean. She had long dark hair that she usually wore in a thick plait down her back. We were fitting new frames in her father's house. It was a big house — the father was well-heeled. While I was working there Diane came to visit him. She and I got talking. You know how it is. One thing led to another. We started going out together.

Diane had been to art college, but after that she couldn't find any work that she wanted to do. Her grandmother had left her some money, and she'd bought an apartment in a converted warehouse in the old dockland area. She'd had an affair for several years with one of her teachers at the college, but then he'd left her for someone else. She'd been wanting to get away from Liverpool, but couldn't decide where to go. After a few weeks I moved in with her, and it wasn't long before we found she was pregnant. I wasn't sorry, and neither was she. We got married. Diane found several shops that would sell my wooden toys, so I quit my job and stayed home working in the flat. I got quicker and more skilled. I enjoyed my work and I loved my wife, and at last my pain eased. I hoped I might have laid that ghost for good. But whenever I'd completed one toy and was wondering what to make next, the same thought always came into my head: a fire engine. A wooden fire engine. I had to throw my whole weight against that thought. It was a door to all that pain I'd shut away, and if I once allowed it to open the pain would flood out and engulf me.

We called our baby 'Sally'. She was adorable. Diane decided to use the remainder of her money to buy a house. She said Liverpool was no place to bring up a child, and I agreed. We bought an old farm house in Cumbria. It was a strange house. At least, it was strange to me because I came from a different part of the country. It wasn't a big house, but there were two staircases. One went from the kitchen to the bedroom above it. The other led from the sitting-room to the two bedrooms above that. In between was a dining-room downstairs, and over that a room that had been converted into a bathroom. The bathroom had doors at either end, one leading to the big bedroom above the kitchen and the other to the landing and the two smaller bedrooms above the sitting-room. Diane and I slept in the big bedroom. Sally had one of the smaller bedrooms off the landing, and the other was my workshop.

Of course I was worried about fire. I had a fire extinguisher fitted at the bottom of the stairs and another on the landing, and a telephone installed in the sitting-room. It was an old house and when we first moved in it was damp. Diane suggested getting some paraffin heaters. I went berserk. It was the first time I ever shouted at her. She couldn't understand it. 'I only meant for the time being,' she said. The tears rolled down her cheeks and I felt ashamed of myself.

'I don't want you ever to use a paraffin heater,' I said. I didn't explain why. The next thing I bought was an extending ladder — one that would reach every window in the house.

'What have you bought that for?' Diane asked.

'So I can clean the windows,' I said. I put it in the barn.

My toys sold well. I was making enough money for us to survive on. Diane spent a lot of time in the garden. She grew most of the vegetables we needed. After the first winter we had central heating put in. I can't tell you how happy I was. I had clean air, fresh vegetables, a stream running through the garden. I was working at home, which meant that I was my own master. Diane seemed relaxed and content. And Sally was growing into the sweetest little girl you ever saw. She was a happy child. Always into mischief. She had my blue eyes and her mother's thick black hair. We didn't cut her hair and by the time she was three and a half it was way down her back. But just before Christmas, when Sally was four, fed up with the daily torture of having it brushed, she wanted her hair cut. I told her not to, but Diane said she could have it cut if she really wanted. So Sally had her lovely hair cut short. She came with Diane into my workshop to show me.

'Look, Pete,' she said. She always called me 'Pete', like Diane did, never 'Daddy'.

'You look like a boy now,' I said.

'Oh, Pete,' Diane said, 'she doesn't. She looks really pretty.'

We had a lovely Christmas Day. Just the three of us. We had a big Christmas tree in the sitting-room with real candles on. It had been a tradition for Diane when she was a child. Christmas morning Sally came into our room and woke us early. She opened her stocking in our bed. There were just a few small things in it. Then we got up and had breakfast, and after that we lit the candles on the tree and opened our presents. I'd made Sally a dolls' house. It was probably the best thing I'd ever done. I'd made all the furniture to go in it, and Diane had bought a family of dolls of the right size. Sally gave me a picture she'd drawn with felt-tips. It was a clown. The clown was crying. 'It's lovely,' I said, 'but why is he crying?'

She said, 'He's crying because he hasn't got a little girl.'

I felt terrible when she said that. I must have gone pale because Diane said, 'What's the matter, Pete?'

'Nothing,' I said. 'It's all right.'

After Christmas dinner we went for a walk in the woods. I was teaching Sally to climb trees. I promised her that as soon as she could climb well enough I'd build her a tree house. 'If I make it in the big old oak tree in front of the house,' I said, 'you'll be able to see it from your bedroom window.' After tea we lit the candles on the tree again. I lay on the floor with Sally and we played with her dolls' house for ages, right up till bed time. Diane and I took Sally up to bed together. We sat on the bed while Diane read a story. Then we sang carols to her until she slept. She went to sleep clutching the little girl from the family in the dolls' house. Diane and I just stood and looked at her. She was so pretty — even though she'd had her hair cut. I hugged Diane. We kissed. Then I picked her up in my arms and carried her through the bathroom to our bedroom. We undressed and lay on the bed and began to make love. Then I remembered the Christmas tree candles. 'I'd better go down and blow them out,' I said.

'Please don't!' Diane said, holding on to me. 'I've got to go down in a while to clear up. I'll do it then. Don't go now. Please!' I have to confess that sex was the one area of our relationship that wasn't completely satisfactory. I'd lived on my own too long, I suppose. But for whatever reason, Diane wanted more than I could give. There'd been times when I hadn't been able to do the business, when I'd made excuses — and she feared that this is what I might be doing now. I didn't want to spoil our day. So I made love to her, and afterwards we just lay in each other's arms without speaking. And then I must have fallen asleep.

When I woke I felt confused. I was in my bed. Diane was beside me. But something was wrong. Then as my brain cleared I heard the crackling. I smelt the smoke. I felt the heat. I jerked up. Diane woke. 'What's the matter?' she asked.

'Fire!' I shouted. 'Fire!' I ran into the bathroom. The landing was ablaze. I couldn't get through the doorway: intense heat, choking fumes, and scorching flames forced me back. I ran through my bedroom screaming, 'The house is on fire! Sally! Sally!' I pulled on some jeans, raced downstairs and across the kitchen, but the dining-room was a furnace. I dashed outside. Apart from the kitchen and our bedroom above it, the whole house was burning. Diane ran round to the front of the house where Sally's room was. I ran to the barn for the ladder. I dragged it into the garden and had just got it onto my shoulder when I heard the voice. 'Pete!' it cried. 'Pete! Help me!' I stopped and looked about to see where the voice was coming from. I thought I caught sight of Sally's face at my work room window. 'Pete! Pete!' the voice called. 'Help me!' I threw the ladder to the ground, extended it, and manhandled it up against the wall below the window. I started up the ladder, but the face had disappeared. Then I saw it at the bathroom window. I scrambled down and lugged the ladder further along. The fire on the ground floor had spread now into the kitchen. The smoke and heat were terrible. My skin was parched and cracking. My lips were blistering. My body hair was being scorched off. The roar of the fire, and the crackling of the wood as it was being consumed were increasing. Every so often there would be a great crash as part of the roof collapsed, or sections of floor fell through. Before I started up the ladder I looked up at the window. I was shaking from head to foot, in a state of total panic. The face had disappeared. Then I caught a glimpse of something at my bedroom window. I dragged the ladder along to there, but by then there was nothing to be seen. And then the face appeared at the work room window again. And then my bedroom. And then the bathroom. I couldn't see clearly because of the smoke, and the tears in my eyes. The little pale face framed by its short dark hair stared down from one window after another. I stood helplessly, immobilised by memory, and cried, while the voice called, over and over, 'Pete! Pete! Help me!'

I remembered, going unsteadily into that other house, all those years before. I remembered the agony of loneliness, the ache of longing I used to suffer. I remembered creeping into Lucy's room. I remembered getting undressed and sliding into her bed. I'd had too much to drink — but I know that's not enough of an excuse. I just wanted, desperately, someone to cuddle. And afterwards I tried to stop her tears, and told her she must get back to sleep, and never tell anybody. And then, of course, the enormity of what I'd done hit me. The fear that she would say something to her mother, and of what would happen then gripped me so tightly I could hardly breathe. I was still unsteady as I lurched along the landing, clutching my clothes in my arms. I stumbled against the paraffin heater and looked aghast as fire instantly spread across the runner of the landing and caught the bannisters. I ran downstairs to fetch water. I don't know when it was that the thought first came to me that this might be the answer to the problem my folly had created. By the time my alcohol befuddled brain had rejected that idea, the stairs were ablaze, and I didn't know what to do. Soon the heat forced me outside, where I stood helplessly, staring up at the little face at the window, listening to that heartbreaking plea for help.

The house was an inferno. All that was left of the roof suddenly caved in sending a shower of sparks thirty metres into the air. Diane was at my side, slapping me, punching me, tearing at my face like a wild cat. 'Pete!' she was screaming. 'Pete! What are you doing! Didn't you hear me? She was at her window! She was calling us, Pete! Why didn't you come? Why didn't you come?'

I couldn't bear to look at Diane after the fire. I couldn't bear the emptiness in her eyes. I left. I came south. I don't know where to go. I don't know what to do. I don't want to live any more. But I'm frightened of burning for ever. I'm frightened of fire.

GETTING THE BIRD

Redundant.

Chucked on the scrap heap.

Early retirement — at nineteen!

I'd had several jobs in the four years since I'd left school, each one harder to find than the one before — and I'd got the sack from all of them. I stood outside the factory with Steve among the grim landscape of the industrial estate, wondering where to go — what to do.

'We can go to my place and have a cup of tea,' he suggested. Steve and I had met while labouring on a building site the previous year, but the firm we'd worked for went bankrupt before the development was half built. We'd been friends (and partners in crime) ever since. It was a good partnership, based on my daft ideas which got us into deep water, and Steve's practicality which got us out.

In the time I'd known Steve I'd never been invited to his home. I'd often wondered whether he had some guilty secret there — like a demented aunty they kept locked in the cellar, or a backyard full of 'pot' plants. All I knew was he lived in a cramped council house with his mum and dad, his granny, a younger brother and an older sister.

Neither of us had wheels just then, so having time to kill, we went on Shanks's pony, scrunching over the broken glass and trying to avoid the dog shit. Steve never had much to say for himself, and I was trying to make up a rock song lyric that would make me rich, so neither of us spoke. I'd got the title, and I'd got a chorus. All I needed was a couple of verses, a tune, and a rock 'n' roll star who wanted to sing it.

I pulled out my packet of *Gauloises* (they tasted terrible but, being French, my hope was they'd impress the birds). Steve glanced at me. 'My mum was a heavy smoker,' he said. 'She's dying. Of lung cancer.' I put the coffin nails back in my pocket in case the smell of the smoke upset him. 'She was in hospital,' he went on, 'but she's back home now. They send them home when there's no hope.'

This was the first I'd heard of his mum being ill. 'Sure you want me to come back then?'

'We've got to carry on, haven't we.'

'Here, look!' In the car park across the street was an old Royal Enfield motorbike with a heavy old sidecar attached. We sauntered over.

I started it up on the kick start, Steve climbed onto the pillion, and we roared off. Round in a circle! I'd never ridden a bike with a sidecar before. The weight of the sidecar kept pulling me to the left. Round and round we went, like kids on a roundabout.

'What're you playing at?' Steve yelled.

'Just going for a spin,' I yelled back.

Then two big blokes in boiler suits, waving jumbo-size spanners, came running across the car park, barking like huskies that haven't been fed for a week. We jumped off, leaving the bike to go round on its own, and legged it.

I sat by their living-room fire with a mug of tea while Steve went up to look at his mum. I flicked the bottom of my packet and took a fag with my mouth. I heard footsteps on the stairs and a man entered the room. I presumed, correctly, that it was Steve's dad. All I knew about Steve's old man was that he'd been a wharfie — till they'd rationalised his job out of existence. The man was small and strong-looking, like a pit pony. But his face was haggard and he looked as though he'd been crying.

'So you're the famous Darkey,' he said.

'Yeah. Dark by name — dark by nature.'

'I've heard about some of your escapades.'

I was surprised. I took the fag out of my mouth. 'You never want to believe half what you hear.'

To carry on being sociable was too much of an effort for him, and he went through to the kitchen.

Steve came down looking drawn. He took his mug of tea off the mantelpiece and sat in the other armchair.

'How's your...?' I nodded towards the stairs.

'Can't be long now. She's in terrible pain, but she's so doped up she don't know what day it is. If it was me I'd double the dose and put her out of her misery.' He nodded at the cigarette packet in my hand. 'That's lung cancer for you. She ain't thirty-nine yet. Ain't likely to be, neither. Them firms ought to be locked up.'

I fidgeted. 'You can't lock up a firm, can you.'

'Well, whoever owns them. Whoever's getting the profit off them.'

On impulse I flicked the unlit fag into the fire, then threw the half-filled packet after it. The blue paper shrivelled in the flames. 'I've been meaning to pack up for a long time,' I mumbled lamely. There was an awkward silence. We both sipped at our tea. 'Where's your gran?'

'Shopping.'

They obviously weren't used to being hard up. There was unnecessary nick-nacks of china and glass in every nook and cranny. His gran looked after the house, his mum and dad had both worked, also the sister. Steve worked when he could get it. Only his brother had never had a job. He'd been on the dole ever since he left school.

Steve suddenly stood up. 'Come up to my bedroom. I'll show you something.'

'You're not turning funny, are you?'

'I'm doing the bride and groom.'

'What — both of them?'

'I do painting.'

'Pictures, d'you mean?'

'I'll show you. Bring your tea. Do you want a top up?'

'No thanks. It's horrible.'

'Is it? My mum used to make a nice cup of tea.'

I wasn't all that keen on passing his mother's bedroom to be honest, knowing she was about to snuff it in there, but I didn't like to admit it, so I followed him up.

Steve shared a room and a double bed with his younger brother. It was the biggest bedroom in the house. It needed to be. It was stacked with painted canvases: in piles on the floor like goods in a warehouse; leaning, like drunks in a packed bar, against the walls; and even in untidy heaps under the bed and on top of the wardrobe. There were tubes of oil paint, and paint-stained plates, and brushes, and rolls of canvas, and wooden stretchers, and old gilt frames, all over the place. 'Your brother must love *you*,' I said.

'I go up the Smoke sometimes,' Steve confessed. 'See exhibitions and that.'

'You never told me.'

'Nah. People just take the piss. Last one I saw was Modigliani. Just fantastic. Beautiful. But so simple. He was unique, Modigliani was. I got a book of his pictures. I'm doing a series of paintings based on them.'

The book was open at a picture of a bride and groom. I flicked through a few pages, and then put it back how it was. 'They don't look very happy, do they,' I said. 'He should've called it *The Bride and Gloom*.' And on the easel was Steve's picture of the bride and groom, unfinished. It was sort of copied, but not copied exactly. Just the idea was copied — it was the same only different. The picture in the book looked like all the other pictures in the book — they had a sort of delicacy and melancholy that Steve's lacked. The one on the easel looked like all the other paintings in the room: large slabs of bright, basic colours; lots of bright yellow and orange and red. Some of them were just patterns, though most of them were arrangements of fruits and things, and people, but simplified. I stood gazing at the pictures that were hanging on the walls or lying around, looking at pictures for the first time in my life really, sort of letting them soak into me. You sometimes wake on a summer morning, after several days of damp greyness, and you open your eyes and see framed in the window blue sky and the early sunlight golden on the houses opposite, and instead of having to drag yourself up, you think, *Oh great — it's going to be a lovely day*. Well, looking at Steve's pictures gave me a feeling something like that.

Steve sat down on the floor among all his paraphernalia. He seemed more relaxed up there in his own habitat. I still felt a bit shocked. When you've worked in grimy factories with someone, and done taking and driving away with them, and a bit of shop-breaking, you don't expect to discover them doing something you usually think of as being a bit pansified. Steve, I'd discovered, was a sort of Jekyll and Hyde: normal when he was with me, and turning a bit peculiar when he was up in his room on his own. I had to readjust my way of thinking about certain things. The effort made me a bit weak in the knees, so I sat on the unmade bed. Steve looked at me as though he expected me to say something.

'Well it's good stuff, my old mate, but you won't get rich out of doing this, will you.'

'If I keep working at it. If I keep getting better.'

'D'you reckon?'

'Why not?'

I thought about that for a moment, and it brought home to me my own lack of talent, or skill, or potential. Steve thought he had a future. I knew I had none.

'Well, you may become famous one day, but it may not be till after you're dead. What about in the meantime?'

He sighed, and shrugged.

'One thing's for certain, Steve: there's no future in going straight.'

'I know.'

'It's like your mum: what sort of life was that?' I shouldn't have said that. It upset him.

'She was penniless when she was a kid,' he said bitterly. 'Then she left school and spent twenty bloody years assembling electric plugs. And that was it.'

'Fucking futile!'

'So, you got any bright ideas?'

It was a good question. I considered it. But my brain had already been damaged by so many hours of state school and industrial noise that my train of thought went soft and dribbled away into daydream. 'Know what I'd like?' I said.

'No, what?'

'I'd like to meet a girl who was...' I swilled the remains of the tea round and round in my mug and peered into the whirlpool, trying to discover what it was I really wanted. '...who was tender, passionate, generous, courageous. I suppose I'm talking about what I wish I was like, really. But I want her to be like that too. And tolerant.' I laughed. 'Especially of me. She'd have to be to live with me, wouldn't she. I'd like to find a woman like that. Live with her. Have kids...'

'Kids?' He sounded incredulous.

'Yeah. Wife and kids. That's what life's all about, isn't it. But you've got to make some bread. And it's no good earning your crust some way that's going to put you to sleep, because if you're a zombie you won't be able to enjoy what you've got, will you. If you want to feel the joy, you've got to feel the pain.'

Steve was only half listening — half dreaming his own dreams. He waited to see whether I was going to go on. When I didn't he took a sip of his cold tea and said, 'Know what I'd like?' It was his turn now. 'I'd like to do some really great paintings. Like Matisse. Or Klee.'

'Who?'

'Matisse. Klee. They're artists. Or Kokoschka.'

'Cock Oshka?'

'Yeah.'

'Sounds like what the drunk homosexual said to Oscar Wilde: *Would you care for some more cock, Oshka?*'

Steve either didn't get the joke, or ignored it. 'They're all great, but in their own way. I've looked at all of them. And done pictures like them. But I can't seem to find my own style. I can't seem to find a direction. I'd like to make a living out of painting. That's what I'd like more than anything.'

'I could give you the address of that firm I worked for.' I'd done a stint at painting; I'd painted hundreds of miles of dark green institution corridors dark green.

'Don't bother.'

'You'll never get anywhere in life if you're going to be fussy.'

'I'd jump in the river with a pair of concrete boots on first.'

'Well I ain't working in no more factories, Steve — I'll tell you that for nothing.'

'You won't get the chance, mate. My brother'd give his right arm for a factory job, and there's nothing going. Nothing.'

I drank down the cold dregs from my mug. 'Listen, Steve: why don't we stop piddling about with petty thieving, and do it professionally — do some proper jobs.'

'We haven't got the contacts.'

'We can start small and work our way up. Learn the ropes. Get to know the right people. Build up the business. Know what I mean?'

'Got anything in mind?'

'Not really. What about that old water mill they've been converting — has anybody moved into that yet?'

'That's hardly in the big league, is it.'

'It's a start. Whoever had that done up must be loaded.'

'Yeah,' he said enviously. 'I wouldn't mind living in a place like that.'

'I wouldn't mind living in a chateau on the Riviera.'

'Or a villa in Bermuda.'

'We're sure to end up somewhere with a lot of bedrooms.'

'Well at least we'll get free bed and breakfast.'

'And room service. But listen, Steve, seriously, let's get some passports. I mean, you never know. If we get a good haul some time, we might want to scarper for a bit, quick like.'

'Best to be prepared.'

'Boy scouts — girl guides. And another thing: let's get a couple of shooters.'

Steve looked startled. 'What for?'

'What d'you mean, what for? I mean, if we're going into this properly we're going to need the tools of the trade, aren't we. Use your nodle. Supposing someone comes while we're doing a job: a security guard; the old bill. What're we going to do — go quietly, like lambs to the butcher's? I've been in some sort of cage all my life, Steve. I don't want to get banged up in the bleeding zoo.'

'No, but...'

'But what?'

'Guns...'

'Look: they may be stronger than us. More of them. What do we do — carry a cosh or a crow-bar? If you wallop somebody with one of them you could do them an injury. A gun's safest. Know what I mean? You show your hand — no rough stuff.'

Steve looked troubled. He was sitting on the floor, twisting his mug round and round between his legs. 'I don't like it.'

'I don't like it, either. But it's a deterrent.'

'A what?'

'A deterrent. If we're carrying shooters and someone comes along, they're going to be careful what they do, aren't they. I mean, it's like them men who go round exposing theirselves. You never hear of one of them assaulting a woman, do you. He just gives her a quick flash, and she screams and runs away. He doesn't have to threaten her or nothing. See, his dong's a deterrent. Like our shooters. We give them a quick flash — they give us a wide berth.'

Steve smiled for the first time that day. 'I never really wanted to be a flasher.'

'There's worse occupations than that. What about a copper flashing his truncheon? Or a hot dog salesman flashing his sausage? Well, are we in business?' I leaned forward and reached out a hand, and he grasped it, though less than enthusiastically.

'You could get a couple off Bob,' I said. 'You know him better than I do.'

'How're we going to pay?'

'We can trade. Couple of cars. Whatever he wants.'

'Okay,' Steve said. 'But I still don't like it.'

Steve may not have liked it. But he did it all the same. We brought in a couple of motors for Bob in exchange for two second-hand shooters and the plates off a *Cortina* station wagon.

Bob ran a little car-scrap-cum-car-repair business. He used to buy up wrecks, and pay us to get cars of the same make, year and colour. Then he'd swap the number plates and one thing and another, and flog the stolen vehicles for a handsome profit. He was a contact worth cultivating because he also did respray and receiving for bigger villains and bent coppers. He rarely talked about it. 'It's best if my left hand don't know what my right hand's doing,' he used to say. 'Then I can't get myself in trouble.'

Back in my little rented room, Steve and I fondled the guns and enjoyed their heavy cold hardness. They were *Walthers,* made in West Germany. Despite Steve's opposition to carrying one, he clearly enjoyed handling it. Always the practical one, he took them apart and cleaned and oiled and reassembled them. We mucked around for a bit, aiming them at things in the room and pointing them at each other like kids playing cops and robbers.

I took careful aim at Sally's forehead. Sally was in a newspaper cutting pinned on my wall. I used to go out with her, till she chucked me for a Hell's Angel. He pranged his bike in a motorway pile up, and she was paralysed from the waist down. That's why she was in the paper. But it was a photo from before the accident. When she was whole.

'Where's the bullets?' I asked Steve.

'Bullets?'

'Them little things you fire out of that hole in the end of the gun.'

Steve was propped up on one elbow, lying across the double mattress that served as my bed. I was sprawled on the only chair in the room. 'We ain't got any,' he said.

'Didn't Bob have some?'

'Well, if he did, he didn't give them to me.'

'Bloody hell. We'll have to get some off him then.'

'What do we need bullets for?'

'For you to bite on when they're amputating your leg.'

'What?'

'For the guns, dickhead, for the guns.'

'But I thought they was only a deterrent.'

'Yeah, but guns ain't going to do much deterring without any bullets in, are they!'

'But what do we need bullets for if we're not going to use them?'

'What sort of question's that? I mean, what've you got in your head where your brains should be — toad in the bloody hole? A gun without ammunition is like...it's like a car without an engine, it's like...it's like when they used to have eunuchs: they used to cut their balls off but leave their cock.'

'Did they? I didn't know that. What did they leave their cock for?'

'I don't know. For them to piss out of, I suppose. I just think it's a bit stupid having a gun without any bullets in, that's all.'

'But if it's only for a deterrent...'

'Oh, blimey! New word for the day,' I sneered, being nasty to Steve because I wasn't on very firm ground. 'Listen, we'll look a damn sight more like we've got loaded guns if we have. I mean — 'cos we'll know it. It's psychological.'

'Psychological?'

'Yes. That's the new word for tomorrow.'

'Okay,' he said reluctantly. 'I'll see Bob in the morning.'

But he didn't. That same night Bob had been run in. He's inside now, doing a five stretch.

We lifted a station wagon. Steve fixed the plates and gave it a tune-up. We put the back seat down so that it would be grateful for what it was about to receive. Then Steve's mum died, and that put him out of circulation for a while.

I cruised past the mill on several occasions. A couple of nights after the funeral I decided to have a prowl around on foot. I left the car and stumbled across a neglected field, scrambled through a hedge, climbed over a new fence that had been erected parallel with it, and scrunched across the gravel of the drive. It was a cold autumn evening. The day had been rainless but the air was damp. There was a small moon like a fingernail clipping. Stars glittered like frost. There was no barking, so if they had a dog it was either friendly or dead. The massive black bulk of the mill loomed above me like a mediaeval tower. It was all darkness and, apart from the mill race, silence. I ran back to the car to go for Steve.

Steve wasn't enthusiastic.

'Come on,' I said. 'You can't look a gift horse in the mouth.'

'I'm working,' he said. 'I've just got back to the bride and groom. I want to finish it.'

'You can finish that any time. We might not get another opportunity like this: the place is deserted.'

'There might be an invalid granny.'

'There's more likely to be a burglar alarm.'

'I could probably knock that out.'

'What — the invalid granny?'

I cut the engine and we coasted down the hill. The gates stood open invitingly. We rolled across the gravel, right around the building, and came to a standstill beside the rear stairway. Steve brought the bag of tools. The rush of water in the mill-race was loud enough to drown the crunch of our footsteps, except to our own ears. Steve began to mount the new timber steps. He jerked, and gasped.

'What's the matter?' I whispered.

'A bloody bat!' he said indignantly. 'A bloody bat hit my head.'

'Think yourself lucky it didn't hit your balls,' I said. 'Might have knocked them for six.'

'Gave me the creeps.'

I followed him up to the back door. I had one hand in my jacket pocket, gripping the gun. The metal was hard and cold, but the feeling it gave me was as warm and secure as a cup of bedtime cocoa. I heard Steve gasp again. This time in surprise as he turned the handle and the kitchen door swung silently open. 'They've gone out and left the bloody door unlocked.'

'Maybe they weren't expecting us.'

'Maybe there *is* someone in.'

'Someone who can't stand bright lights. If it's the invalid granny, I'll chat her up while you rifle her drawers.'

We stepped quietly into the warm kitchen and I pushed the door to behind me. 'They've left the heating on,' Steve said, 'so they can't have gone far.'

'It might just be consideration,' I said, 'in case they had unexpected guests.'

Steve took a torch out of the tool bag and shone it around. It was a huge, high-ceilinged room, newly plastered and painted. 'They didn't make a very good job of the plastering,' I said. 'It's all lumpy.'

'It's supposed to be like that,' Steve said, 'to give it a farmhouse feel. It's hand-plastered.'

'Looks like the plasterer was plastered.'

There was an antique oak table down the middle of the room which looked as though it might have been looted from a mediaeval monastery, with old benches either side of it, and antique-looking oak armchairs at either end. 'Lovely table,' said Steve, stroking it.

'Yes,' I said. 'It's bigger than our kitchen. If they walled it in they could play five-a-side soccer on it.'

'This is the way to live,' Steve said longingly.

'Well I'll tell you what, mate — they'll need a servant to pass the salt. Maybe you could apply for the job.'

Everything else in the kitchen was new. According to Steve the fitted cupboards were also oak, but the timber had been artificially aged. It was a kitchen out of a telly advert.

'Whoever owns this lot can afford to make a small donation to the poor and needy, no sweat,' I said.

'They probably wouldn't even miss it,' Steve added.

'They probably own one of the factories we used to sweat our guts out in. In which case they owe us something in back pay. So, lead on, MacNab.'

Steve opened a door and moved cautiously through. 'Wrong door,' he said. I looked over his shoulder as he flashed the torch around. There was a washing machine and dryer, and a large freezer. There was also an ironing board set up and, rather incongruously, a single bed. 'That's in case the lady gets tired while she's doing the ironing,' I said, 'and needs a lie down.'

'The lady who lives here wouldn't do ironing,' Steve said. 'This is probably the servant's quarters.'

'I expect they call it the Board Room,' I said.

'Why?'

''Cos it's got the ironing board in it.'

We backed out and tried another door which led to a palatial sitting-room. I stayed close behind Steve who continued to lead with the torch. The old, wide floor boards had been sanded and clear-varnished, and there were expensive looking rugs scattered around. There were settees and easy chairs in soft green leather, a baby grand piano, a wall of books. Despite low radiators on all the walls, there was a generous, newly-built stone fireplace with a careful stack of logs in the nook. Steve came to a standstill and let out a breath. 'Look at that!' he said. He was shining the torch onto a painting on the wall. 'Hey, Darkey. I want to put the light on a minute.'

'Don't be daft.'

'Just for a minute.'

'Are you out of your tree? Sure you wouldn't like me to call the cops for you?'

'There's no one here. There's no neighbours. Who's to see?'

I concentrated, trying to tune my hearing in to the wavelength of sounds we're not usually aware of. There was nothing, apart from the rush of the mill-race muted by the thick stone walls and the double glazing.

I said, 'Well let's make sure the curtains are drawn properly first.' I suppose it was partly caution, partly face-saving.

The windows reached almost from floor to ceiling behind heavy velvet drapes. I checked each curtain edge as fussily as a warden in the blackout, then followed Steve around the other three walls, making sure that each of the four doors was closed. Beside the last door Steve played the torch light on the wall and picked out a row of switches. He pressed one and table lamps in various parts of the room transformed our dark cavern into the set of a romantic movie. He pressed again and three clutches of bulbs along the middle of the ceiling blazed down, spoiling the atmosphere. 'All right,' I snapped. 'We don't need all that. It's not bloody Christmas illuminations.' Steve killed the ceiling lamps and pressed a third switch and we were treated to a moment of theatre: a collection of oil paintings emerged from the walls, glowing in a soft, diffused light which came from concealed fixtures.

'Wow!' Steve said. He moved into the middle of the room as if in a trance. He was Ali Baba in the cave of treasures. He put the tool bag down carefully on an oriental-looking table, the top of which was a chess board made of inlaid wood. He switched off the torch and laid it beside the bag.

'Steve,' I said, 'look at me. How many fingers am I holding up?'

'Just a minute,' he said, without taking his eyes off one of the paintings. He moved towards it as if mesmerised. It was a bird in a cage. Not like photographic. More like shapes and suggestions, all in black and white and brown. The bird was a white dove, and it was being crucified — its broken wings outstretched like arms. The only other colour was the drab green of an olive twig dying on the floor of the cage.

'Look at that!' said Steve.

'I'm looking.'

'But just look at it.'

'I've looked,' I said. 'I've looked already. So come on now.'

'Hang about.' We shuffled along and stopped in front of the next picture. It was all oranges and yellows and greens. There was a hand reaching up to open a door of a cage to set a bird free; or it could have just closed the door, making the bird a prisoner — there was no way of knowing for sure.

The next was in violets and blues and browns. There were two birds in a cage. One was female, soft and round, as if she might be sitting on eggs. The other, the male, was rearing up, fierce and strong, with his wings angrily and powerfully raised. It was as though he was trying to protect her from what was outside the cage, from whoever was looking at the picture — from us. We were the oppressors, the persecutors. At the same time, I felt he was trying to impress his mate. He was saying that he would let nothing hurt her, as well as that there was no way he was going to be kept in a cage, that there was no prison secure enough to hold him. But there was a terrible sadness in it, because he *was* in a cage, and there seemed no way he could get out. You could imagine him battering himself against the cold steel of the bars, fighting to the death against the iron glove of his captor. But although you admired his strength, his spirit, his courage, you knew there was no way he could fulfil his promise, no way he could protect his mate, or liberate himself.

We edged around the room, studying one picture after another. Steve was enthralled, staring at each one for precious minutes in imperturbable silence. And despite myself, I found I was forgetting where I was. It was like my first visit to a public exhibition. It was like going to an evangelical rally and feeling myself in danger of being converted. I stood and gazed at the pictures because Steve was looking at them, and there was nothing else for me to do. But I was starting to see in them what they were about — or at least, what I thought they were about. When Steve moved on, I moved on. At each one he was like a hungry cat at a saucer of cream. I stood beside him because he was my friend, and tried to share his interest and pleasure. But he wasn't in fact like a cat with cream at all, because my involvement didn't take anything away from him, but seemed to add something.

The paintings were all on the same theme, although one on the end wall was slightly different. It was larger and more colourful, and there was no cage. There was a bird though. There was a loaf of bread, and a jug of water or wine, and the bird was flying free.

After worshipping in front of it for some time Steve said, 'Beautiful!' It was the first word he'd uttered since we began going round the pictures.

'Yeah,' I said. 'But it's not as true as the others. It's just wishful thinking.'

'What?' He looked at me, surprised and puzzled. I suddenly realised that we had been seeing different things. Steve was appreciating colours, and shapes, and tones, composition, and mood, and technique. He wasn't sure what I meant, so he dismissed it from his mind. It probably felt to him like an irritating piece of grit to an oyster. He gazed at the picture and shook his head. 'Beautiful!' he said again.

And then another thought came to me. 'Maybe that's why you can't find a direction, Steve.'

'What?'

'A direction. You said you couldn't find a direction. You can do good things but you can't find your own way. I think it's because you're not trying to *say* something.'

'What're you on about?'

'Your painting. You're not trying to tell me anything.'

'Painting's not like making speeches, Darkey.'

'You've got the skills. The techniques. The tools. But you're not *doing* anything with them. You've got to *use* them for something. You've got to know what you want to *tell* me, and then you have to use your skills to say it.'

Steve looked at me as if I were talking a foreign language, as if he understood some of the words but not the sense of the sentences. I felt excited and pleased with this idea which had just been given to me, so to speak, like a little present, by the artist, whoever he was. I tried to find a way to explain what I meant to Steve. 'It's like a bricklayer,' I said. 'A really top class bricklayer. It's no good if, just because he's great at laying bricks, he builds a wall a mile high and ten miles long. It might be a perfect wall, but it's no bloody good to anyone. There's too many fucking walls already. What he needs to do is use his skill to build decent homes for people to live in.' Steve gazed at me perplexed. 'Do you see what I'm getting at?'

148

'I don't know.' His eyes were drawn back to the painting. 'I'll have to think about it.'

I looked at the painting too. I saw the bread, which was what we were doing the job for, and I saw the bird flying free, which is what I wanted to do, and it occurred to me that I wouldn't be able to if I was caught standing like a tailor's dummy in some rich git's living-room.

'Well what's the artist telling me with this one?' Steve asked.

'He's telling us to get on with the job and get the hell out of here, or we're both going to end up in a bloody cage.'

'Listen, Darkey.' Steve put his hand on my arm. 'I want the paintings.'

'Are you losing all your marbles?'

'No. Really, Darkey. Please.'

'We could never sell *them*.'

'I don't want to sell them. They're for myself. To keep.'

'Steve, you've already got so many paintings in your bedroom you have to sleep on the landing.'

'I know, Darkey, but...'.

'Anyway, they're too big. They won't fit in the car. You'll have to come back with an articulated truck.'

'We can put them on the roof rack.'

'Steve, man, you're off the planet. We can't go driving round with stolen goods on top of our car. You might as well walk down Main Street with a sandwich board saying, *I am a tea-leaf. Please arrest me.*'

But his jaw was set. The paintings were important to him in a way I didn't understand. I sighed. 'Okay. But let's make it snappy.'

We had to drag occasional tables up to the walls beneath the pictures and balance chairs on the tables and climb up onto them. I never did like heights. 'If I'd wanted to be a bloody acrobat,' I said, 'I'd have run away and joined the circus.' The framed paintings were cumbersome, heavy and awkward. We'd taken four out to the car and had just come back for another one when I heard a door open and then voices. We didn't hear the car arriving at the front of the house because of the mill-race, I suppose. We looked at each other and froze like scared chickens. The voices were jolly. Someone was feeling good about things. It wasn't me. 'The lights!' I hissed.

149

We ran across the room together to the switches by the end door. It was a stupid thing to do, but when you panic you do stupid things. Obviously there would have been switches by the kitchen door, but we ran back to where we'd switched the lights on. In the first darkness after the brightness we were completely blinded. 'The torch!' I said.

'Oh, shit, I put it down somewhere.'

The voices were coming up the hall.

'Forget it.' We scurried through the darkness banging our shins and thighs against pieces of furniture. I heard a door open and a shaft of light threw itself across the room. I plunged at a door in front of me with Steve treading on my heels. He closed the door behind him as someone entered the sitting-room. As I moved forward in the pitch black I was grabbed and smothered by something furry. After a moment of total immobilising panic I realised I wasn't where I thought I was — not in the kitchen at all.

'Where have the paintings gone, Daddy?' a girl's voice asked.

'We're in a bloody cupboard,' I whispered to Steve.

'What are we going to do?'

'What the hell's been going on here?' said a man's voice.

'We'll just have to use the shooters,' I said.

'We can't.'

'Well we can't stay in this bloody cupboard till they call the police, can we.'

'What's this bag doing here?' It was the girl again.

'Come on, Sundance,' I said. I pushed past Steve pulling the gun from my pocket and threw open the door.

'NOBODY MOVE!' I screamed. I couldn't see for a moment in the brightness after the dark of the cupboard so I held my gun at arm's length waving it from side to side. I shouted, 'NOBODY MOVE!' again.

There was a man in the centre of the room, a stocky, bull-necked man in middle age, with untidy, shoulder-length hair and a bushy moustache and sideburns. A slim, attractive woman of about the same age stood behind him, taller than him, wearing glasses. There were two girls, of about eighteen and twenty. One was beside the chess table where we'd left our bag and torch. The younger one was still in the hall doorway.

'Come away from that door!' I ordered. 'And you — get away from that table!' The younger girl was plainly terrified and hastened obediently to her mother, but the older girl stared at me defiantly without moving.

'What the dickens were you doing in our cupboard?' the man said.

'Shut up!' I shouted. 'Pete, close that door.'

Steve stood at my elbow, unmoving.

'Pete,' I said, 'for Chrissake close that door.'

Still no one moved.

'Steve,' I growled through clenched teeth, 'you fucking banana-brain. I'm talking to you!'

'But you said, "Pete". I thought...'

'Well I didn't want them to know our names, did I, you jerk. For God's sake close that door.'

Steve closed the door of the cupboard he'd just come out of.

'Not that door, you clown, the hall door.'

'What d'you want the hall door closed for?'

'Because it's causing a draught,' I said sarcastically. In fact I didn't have a good reason for wanting it closed. It would make me feel less insecure, that was all. Steve slouched around the perimeter of the room, almost hugging the wall as though the people in the centre had some highly infectious disease. I realised we weren't putting on a very impressive performance. The older girl was almost smiling now.

'Listen.' I waved my hand-gun at the family in a manner I hoped looked menacing. 'People like you always think, *It can't happen to me.* Well, let me tell you about two guys I was in the nick with. They were house-breaking, and the people came back while they were there — mother, father, three kids. They only got about twenty quid, but they shot or stabbed to death every member of the family. Those villains were a couple of pea-brains like us, and the people in that family thought it couldn't happen to them.' I paused for effect. 'Think about it.' I was trying to sound reasonable and persuasive, like a salesman with a foot in the door. 'Now, you, over there by the bag, I told you already and I don't want to have to tell you again. MOVE!' I bellowed like a deranged sergeant-major in the US marines, stamping my foot and thrusting the gun towards her. She started, and the blood drained from her face. She was quite tall, almost as tall as me, and slim, with long dark hair. She stayed where she was.

'Please, Alice,' her father said. He didn't sound as posh as I expected him to. 'Come over here with us.' So, with a contemptuous look at me, but with some relief too, she joined the others.

My vocal sheepdog having done its job, I began to feel guilty, and sorry for them. 'Listen,' I said gently. 'I don't want to cause any distress. Do what I ask, and I promise no one'll get hurt. I don't like to use a gun; neither does my friend, who I've called Steve, though you understand that's not his real name. But we don't want to go back inside. I've used a gun before to stay out of the nick, and I'll use it again if I have to. Please don't make it necessary. Nothing can be more important to you than your safety, and the safety of your loved ones. I used to have a girlfriend once — I've got her photo on my bedroom wall — she's paralysed from the waist down now. She's not out of her teens yet, and she'll be in a wheelchair for the rest of her life. That was caused by a shooting. Another life ruined, wasted. That beautiful girl is one cripple too many already. It's not worth it. So let's keep everybody safe, okay?'

The man said, 'Take whatever you want. But clearly it won't be in your interests to shoot anyone. So why don't you put those toys away.'

I felt angry, but I pretended to be more angry that I actually was. I exploded like an hysterical Hitler. 'I'm the one who gives the orders round here! So don't play the smart-arse with me. You just do as you're told!' I took a deep breath and added more quietly, 'I only kill when I'm excited or scared — so cool it.' I let that sink in. Then I said firmly, 'Sit down on that settee. All of you.' I was surprised to find I was enjoying my new role. I hadn't done any amateur dramatics before.

The older girl looked at me in her rebellious way again, but her father said, 'Let's all do as he says, my dears.' And they all sat down.

'Is there anyone else in the house?'

'No.' The father seemed to have appointed himself spokesperson for his side. But then so had I for mine.

'A nice place you've got here.'

'Yes. We liked it.'

I let that go. I wasn't sure what to do next. The four of them sat in a row, like wise monkeys, looking at me. The father was at one end with an arm around Alice, then the younger girl, and the mother at the other end, holding her daughter's hand. They made a nice little grouping, posed as if for a family portrait. I couldn't make the dad out. He looked more wary than afraid. He was rich, but not upper class. The females had breeding, but from his looks you might have guessed he was their gardener. Only his manner made it clear that he was the husband and father. He was wearing a greyish-green casual suède jacket over a grey check shirt, with an olive-green choker around his bull neck. His moustache and his long hair were greying and his eyes were green. He looked smart, but not quite respectable somehow. I hardly noticed the younger girl, but her big sister was striking — not at all English-looking: a strong, suntanned face, with her father's green eyes. But despite the eyes she was her mother's daughter, although the older woman's warmth had become, or was as yet, fire. The mother had a sympathetic face. There seemed to be no anger marking it. Only concern, as though she felt anxious for all of us. I felt drawn to her. I was aware of a vague feeling of longing. I wanted her to like me.

I glanced at Steve. He was looking at me too, expecting me to give a lead. At first I thought we should just call it a day and scarper, but I had to think of some way of preventing them from getting on the blower to the law before we got out of the gate. Then it occurred to me that if we got picked up we'd get done for armed robbery anyway, so we might as well be hung for a sheep as well as a lamb. The five people in the room waited in silence while I stood worrying at the problem, trying not to look worried. 'You're sure there's no one else in the house?' I said lamely at last.

'There's nobody,' the man said.

'Is there any chance of anyone coming?'

'No.'

'You sure of that? Because if I hear a footstep, or a car, or a door opening, I'll assume it's the pigs and I'll have to start shooting. Understand?'

They looked as though they understood.

'Okay, Steve, I'll take care of these. You go on loading the pictures.'

Steve seemed grateful — both to be able to put his gun away, which he'd had dangling limply in his hand in a most unthreatening manner, and also to have something to do. Especially as that something was to get the rest of the pictures he so much coveted. He moved a table, and then a chair, and climbed up to liberate another of the caged birds from the wall.

The man cleared his throat. 'Excuse me, lads,' he said. 'I'd rather you didn't take the paintings.'

Steve stopped what he was doing and looked at me with raised eyebrows.

'Yes,' I said, 'and the shop keeper would rather we kept our fingers out of his till. Steve, for Chrissake get on with it. We haven't got all night.'

Alice sat forward on the settee, her face a fury of indignation. 'What right have you...'

'SHUTTUP!' I cut her short in apparent rage. Everybody jumped, including Steve who nearly dropped the painting on the floor. I thought feigned fury would be the most effective method of keeping things under control. I figured that if they thought I was some sort of unstable lunatic they would be less likely to risk anything silly. Also I was getting a real buzz out of having them scared of me. It made a change because, as a rule, I was always scared of everybody else. 'I have to tell you, Alice,' I said pleasantly, 'you've got a lot of bottle. I respect that. I really do.' Alice tried to mask her feelings with scorn, but I could see she felt flattered. 'But even so,' I went on reasonably, 'do me a favour and don't cause trouble,' and I let my voice rise to a shout, 'or I'LL BLOW YOUR FUCKING HEAD OFF!'

In the silence that followed, Steve clambered off his chair, tipping it over so that it fell off the table and crashed onto the floor. It pleased me to see the terrified reactions of our victims to the sudden banging from behind. They thought the shooting had started.

'Sorry,' Steve said.

He waltzed past me, his arms full of painting, like a lover. 'Stay away from the bats,' I said.

The roar of the mill-race increased as he opened the back door. He seemed gone an age. I found the silences difficult. My costume seemed to become invisible, my mask transparent. I glanced down to make sure my fly was zipped up. I tried to think of something to say, and when I did, my voice reassured me. 'I'd like to apologise for causing you all this discomfort,' I said. 'I mean, we just wanted to lift a few valuables while you were out. We didn't want to threaten anybody, or scare anybody, or hurt anybody. You could've collected the insurance and bought replacements. It would've just been a little inconvenience for you, and it would've helped us a lot. I'm sorry you came back before we could clear off, but my friend, the culture vulture, became ensnared so to speak. I'm especially sorry to you, Missus,' I said to the lady. 'You've got a nice face.' She smiled a surprised, sad smile at me.

Steve came back and moved his table and chair to the next bird.

'Look here,' the man said. 'I'll give you all the cash that's in the house, but I'd be very grateful if you'd leave the paintings.'

'And I'd be very grateful if you'd keep your bloody trap shut!' I shouted.

'But they're of no use to you. You won't be able to sell them, so they'll just end up being damaged, or thrown away.'

'Listen, you fat philistine. It so happens we don't want to sell them. We leave the buying and selling of works of beauty to the men who smoke the big cigars. They're not just investments to us. I mean, I know why your sort buys works of art. Not because you've got any under-standing of them. They're just property to you. A hedge against inflation. Just a way of using the money you stole from your workers to make even more for yourself. It's nothing but lust and greed. You might as well put frames round your stocks and shares and hang *them* on the wall.'

The man looked more and more astonished as this tirade continued. 'Well what do *you* want them for?' he asked.

'Because,' I said proudly, gesturing towards Steve, 'my friend, here, happens to be an artist. And he doesn't look at these paintings and see profit staring him in the face. He sees beauty. Ain't that right, Steve. And beauty's not for sale,' I said self-righteously. 'And, as a matter of fact,' I added, 'although I'm no artist myself, and although I don't know nothing about art, because I'm working-class and ignorant, we spent a long time here this evening looking at these pictures, and let me tell you, that artist who painted them spoke to me. He communicated something to me like I've never got from paintings before. Ever in my life.'

The effect of this speech on the people on the settee was astonishing. It was almost as if my words had disappeared the gun out of my hand.

They began to fidget with an agitation that seemed to be a mixture of wanting to laugh, to share a secret among themselves, to shout with indignation, to welcome us into their home. I was shaken and didn't understand what I'd said that could account for it, and didn't know what to say next to restore calm.

'And I'll tell you what,' I stumbled on. 'That man, I know from looking at his work, and from the communication I received from him through his work, would be more than delighted to know that those paintings were going to be kept by someone who appreciated them for their real value, rather than having them hanging, like framed money orders, on the walls of some insensitive fat capitalist pig like you.'

'Well!' the mother said. It was the first sound she'd uttered. The four of them continued to fidget, and then, first Alice, and then her father, and then the mother, and finally the little sister, began laughing. They were trying to stop themselves but the laughter kept bubbling out. Laughter kept cackling like machine-gun bursts from one or other of them, up and down the settee. I looked helplessly at Steve who was standing on his perch like a caged bird himsel, gazing in bewilderment from them to me and back.

I felt embarrassment flood through me, reddening my face, followed by rage. 'What's so fucking funny?' I screamed.

The laughter stopped. The man sighed. 'Well,' he said, 'I think I should know something about where the artist would like those pictures to hang.'

'Why's that, clever dick?'

'Because,' he said, 'I'm a professional artist, and, as a matter of fact, it was me who painted them.'

Well, I felt a right Charlie after that little bombshell, standing there holding my little gun without any bullets in. The next thing, Steve and the man get into a rap about painting. And before I know what's happening, the lady's asking us if we want a cup of tea.

I could see everything was getting out of control. It felt like belting down a highway in a fast car and having the steering wheel come off in my hands. It seemed like only histrionics could save the day. On the sideboard behind me there was a table lamp, a bird made out of scrap metal, a carved wooden box, and a miniature tree in an earthenware bowl. I sent the whole lot crashing to the floor. 'What the hell's going on here?' I yelled. 'What is this — some sort of nuthouse? It's like a pantomime. I come here to do a job and what happens? First I find myself at a preview in a public bleeding art gallery, then at a discussion group about painting, and now you're trying to turn it into a mad hatter's tea party.'

Silence. That had deposited a turd on the mat. Silence that is, except for the rush of the water outside. There wasn't so much as the ticking of a clock. After a while Steve said, 'What're we going to do now, then?'

'Get the bloody paintings on the car. Then we'll see what else they've got worth having.'

'But we can't take the paintings. Not if he's the artist.'

'Look, Steve, if you don't want the whelks, don't muck 'em about. It's up to you.' And with that he went out. After a while he came staggering back in with one of the pictures. He put it down while he reorganised the table and chair. Then he climbed up and began hanging it back on the wall. 'Steve,' I said. 'What the fuck are you doing?'

'Just putting it back.'

'When you've done that, perhaps you'd like to redecorate the living-room. And you could hoover the carpet while you're at it because we must've trod a lot of dirt in, what with all this coming and going.'

Steve leaned away from the wall looking at the picture. 'Is this one hanging straight?'

'Have a look in the tool bag. Maybe we brought a spirit level. Yes, Steve, it's lovely and straight. Now will you come down from there and leave them bloody pictures alone.' I turned to the man. 'Where's your car?'

'By the front door.'

'What is it?'

'A *Volvo*.'

'Station wagon?'

'Yes.'

'Leave them on the car,' I said to Steve. 'He can put them back himself.' And then to the man: 'Car keys!' He slid forward on the settee to dig them out of his trouser pocket. 'Chuck them to Steve.' He threw them onto a rug at Steve's feet. 'Have a look round, Steve. See what you can get. Stick the stuff in the *Volvo*.'

Steve came over to me and said quietly, 'Why don't we just forget it and make ourselves scarce?'

'*We* might want to forget it, mate,' I whispered, 'but they won't. We're going to do time for this, Steve. The only chance we've got is to get out the country for a bit. And to do that we're going to need some bread. I don't like this any more than you do, but we've got to take all the small valuables we can. What else can we do?'

Steve sighed. 'I guess so,' he said. 'I should have stayed home and done the bride and groom.'

'All right,' I said. 'No need to rub it in.'

After Steve had gone reluctantly about his business the family sat without speaking for some time until Alice suddenly blurted out, 'I suppose this makes you feel big.'

'Alice!' said her mother reprovingly.

'What's your other daughter's name?' I asked the mother. 'The mousy one.'

'Marianne.'

'Don't be rude about my sister,' Alice said.

'Alice, just you go right on being a pain in the arse, and don't worry, because I like you a lot and I wouldn't hurt you. But one more word out of you before I ask you to speak and I'm going to put a bullet right through poor Marianne Mouse's little paw.' And I took careful aim at Marianne's foot, which she drew back against the settee. Her parents sat forward protectively.

'Alice, dear, please,' her mother said. I felt quite chuffed with myself. Then the woman turned to me. 'Why do you do it?' she said. 'Why are you doing this?' She had a deep voice for a woman, a sexy voice, with a trace of a foreign accent.

'Have *you* ever done factory work?' I said. 'Have you ever been on the dole?'

She looked me in the eyes for a long time before she answered. She'd got the message already, but she resigned herself to it. 'No,' she said.

'What about the old man?'

'No.'

'Enjoys his work, does he?'

'Yes.'

'What's wrong with that?' Alice put in. 'If he's good at it and can make a good living, why shouldn't he enjoy his work?'

'No reason.'

'Wouldn't you like to do something you enjoyed?'

'I am. I like standing here talking to you.'

'Wouldn't your friend like to be a successful artist?'

'That's just the point, Alice. That's why your old man isn't out this evening nicking things from some other bugger's house. He can get rich without working.'

'As a matter of fact he works extremely hard.'

'All right. He can get rich doing what he wants. I can't even get rich doing what I don't want. I mean, I want to work at a plastics press about as much as I want to saw my own little finger off with a blunt penknife. But most of the time, market forces won't even let me do that.'

'Perhaps you don't have anything to offer the world.'

That was like a boot in the balls. It must have showed on my face, too, because the mother said, 'Alice! That was unkind and unnecessary.'

But I knew it was true. Searching through the dingy cellar of my self, I could lay hands on nothing that seemed to be of value. 'Okay, so I've got nothing to offer. Was I born like that? Or was it stamped out of me? And if so, who by? And why? And what about Steve? He's got talent. But after a lifetime chained to a hod or a lathe the only thing he'll be able to paint is the inside of his own prison door. And the only colour left in his life will be black.'

The four of them sat with their eyes on my face, but no one spoke. Every silence seemed to transform my clothes into the costume of a clown. I couldn't bear it, so I snarled, 'And anyway, Tiger, I wasn't talking to you. I told you already to keep your trap shut.'

Alice's eyes flared in anger. I turned my attention back to her mother. 'I've been shovelling shit for people like you for too long. And you haven't settled the account. The bill's yet to be paid. Lady, you've been doing me wrong.' I was surprised and amused at my little rhyme which had spontaneously given birth to itself, so to speak, and, wondering whether I might be able to adapt it for use in my song, I smiled at her.

She didn't smile back, so I added quietly, 'And I don't want to do it any more.'

'I hear what you're saying,' she said. 'But is this the only alternative?'

'If you've got a better idea, you tell me. Listen: There's nothing I'd've liked better than to have a home like this and a mum like you. Maybe I could've been something. But I'm nothing. Look at me. See this scar? My old lady hit me in the face with a bottle when I was four years old because she was drunk and I wouldn't stop crying. That's a logical way to stop a kid from crying, ain't it. That's the sort of logic I grew up with. I never had stitches because she didn't want anybody to know what she did. She was frightened and ashamed. I'm scarred down my left side here where she poured scalding water over me as a punishment because I got out of bed and came into the other room when she was entertaining a man there. A mother's love is a blessing, ain't it. That's the sort of mothering that formed me. Now listen, don't get me wrong. I'm not giving you a hard luck story. I'm just trying to learn you something because it's outside your experience. It's another world down there. Listen: You know why my mother was like that? Because when she was a kid, in the slums and in approved schools, she was given a beating almost every day. She was physically abused. She was sexually abused. She was treated like a little heap of shit. And that's gone on all her life. It's still going on. She's worked for the last ten years in a factory. It's not actually under the ground, but it might as well be because there's no windows. They don't want the women to get distracted from the belt. Frightened they might look outside and see a butterfly perhaps fluttering against the pane, or see a kid playing with a ball, or see a bird flying free on the wind. There's no glass in the sides of the building, only in the roof. And then it's the sort of glass you can't see through, so they can't even look up and see the sun or the clouds. They're like moles, those women. They go into that dingy hell every day like vermin crawling into a hole in the ground. They freeze in winter because it's like the South Pole. They have to wear coats, and scarves, and gloves with the fingers cut out. And in the summer, the sun coming through that glass roof turns the place into an oven, and the women faint and fall off their stools onto the floor or the belt. There's a couple of hundred women working there and last week they all got a little surprise in their wage packet. No, not a bonus for all those years of faithful service. Not a letter of appreciation. No. Just a little note saying the factory's closing down and they ain't needed any more so they can go and fuck theirselves. The people who own that factory live in places like this and they treat their workers like shit, like compost, so they can live off the fat of the land. And because my mother's been treated like shit from the cradle to the grave, she always treated me the same. And that's why I am who I am. It's why I'm ugly, damaged, and deformed, why I've got nothing to offer. It's what they do to you. It's like a person's a jug. You can only pour out what's been poured in. There's no magic that can change piss into milk.'

I was suddenly conscious that, for the time being, I had a power over them that was nothing to do with the gun in my hand. For the first time in my life, people were *listening* to what I said. And the words had been coming out of me like stamps from a machine that's suddenly gone haywire and continues to spew them out in a long line, one after the other, even though nobody is putting any money in. But then I realised with a sort of panic that the machine had stopped. It had emptied itself. No more stamps. No more words. I scrabbled around in my brain like a man afraid of the dark, feeling for a light switch in an empty house. The only thing I could think of was what I'd been saying to Steve in his room that day we'd decided to do this damn job.

'I want to find a woman,' I said, 'a loving, warm sort of woman, like you Missus. And I want to have kids. Steve finds that strange. He wants to produce great paintings. I don't have any talent — like you told me, Tiger. My kids'll be my paintings. But I want to give them all the time and attention and affection they need, so they grow up to be people I can be proud of. I don't want to treat them like shit. And that means I mustn't go on letting people treat me like shit, doesn't it. I owe that to my children — if I have any. I owe it to them to be somebody. And if I can't be somebody like you can, then I've got to make somebody of myself the best way I can.'

Steve had come in and was gawping at me. I felt exhausted. Sweat was running down my face and body and going cold. I was making a fool of myself again. My mouth was becoming a smiling, rubbery wound, and a large tear was forming on the white pancake disguising my face.

I felt as though my trousers were about to fall down. I was hyper-conscious of the fact that the gun had no bullets, that it was in reality no more than a toy. And I felt ashamed, like a child that has just had a tantrum. I felt trapped. As though *I* was the one who couldn't leave the room—or speak without leave. I needed someone to rescue me, to break the spell I seemed accidentally to have cast over myself as well as over them. The mother looked as if she was struggling to speak but couldn't. I wanted to run to her and fall on my knees and be held in her arms. I was on the verge of tears. So I screamed at Steve: 'What's the matter with you? You're standing there like a spent prick at an orgy!'

He jumped. He looked as scared of me as any of the others. 'I've put some stuff in the car,' he said. He picked up his bag of tools and moved towards the hall. I could see relief beginning to relax the faces of the family. I didn't move. Steve waited in the doorway looking at me inquiringly. Sometimes he made me feel like his father.

'Steve,' I said, 'aren't you going to thank these nice people for their hospitality before you get into their car and drive off with all their most treasured possessions? Didn't your mum teach you that after the party you should always say thank you for having me?' He looked puzzled. I saw his Adam's apple bob as he swallowed. 'They can describe us to the filth, Steve. And Peter-the-painter here could draw our portraits to a T. And it's possible he may even know the registration number of his own car. Do you think we'd make it to the main road?' Anxiety began to creep back into faces and lodge there.

'Well what're we going to do?'

'We could shoot them.'

An expression of terror leapt into his eyes as he glanced at my gun. Had I got hold of some ammunition without telling him, he was wondering.

'Or you could find something to tie them up with.'

'Where from?'

'Don't ask *me*. Ask *them*. They live here. I don't.'

Steve cleared his throat and addressed the settee. 'Excuse me...'

There must be easier ways of earning a living, I thought. 'Hang about,' I said. 'I've got a better idea.'

'This is a lovely motor,' I said. There was a radio and cassette player, but I didn't put any music on. I needed to think. The engine hummed softly, as soporific as a lullaby.

Steve was talking soothingly to Marianne, behind me. 'Darkey wouldn't hurt a fly,' I heard him say. 'He's just putting you on.'

I glanced at Alice. She didn't seem nervous. She was sitting up very snooty and straight, peering into the tunnel of light made by our main beam in the darkness ahead. 'Where are you taking us?' she wanted to know.

It was a good question. I didn't answer. I didn't know the answer. I was driving aimlessly around a tangle of country lanes, failing to find any signposts in my mind, more often thinking about Alice than concentrating on the problem of what to do next. As the car rounded a bend we surprised a young rabbit on the crown of the road. He stared at us, like an irascible landlord at trespassers. I had to brake sharply, then he turned and began to bound down the road. I cruised along behind him singing:

> 'Run, rabbit, run rabbit, run, run, run,
> Don't give the farmer his fun, fun, fun,
> He'll get by without his rabbit pie,
> So run rabbit, run rabbit, run, run, run.'

He bobbed and zigzagged, but he kept right on down the road. I put the car into neutral and switched the ignition off plunging us into blindness. I heard Alice's sharp intake of breath. 'Now you see him...' I said. I counted slowly towards ten under my breath, trying to remember the curves of the road but my nerve broke at seven and I switched on again. 'Now you don't.' Rabbit had done a bunk. Some of the rigidity sighed out of Alice's body and she began to breathe again.

'I don't want to be a rabbit any more, Alice,' I said. 'I've been running scared too long already; running but not getting anywhere. Trapped — but there ain't no one going to flick a switch and disappear the walls imprisoning me. But what I've realised is, it's all a confidence trick. There ain't no walls there. They get us to forgo our freedom by making us afraid of the dark.'

I was really thinking aloud, pursuing the rabbit in a flight of fancy. I thought Alice might say admiringly, *I never thought of it like that before*. But after a moment's pause she just said, 'Thank you for not hitting the rabbit.'

I realised I'd shown myself up as a pretentious idiot. I was glad of the dark as I flushed with shame, and I suppose the anger was to disguise it. 'What do you think we are, Alice — fucking barbarians — just because we don't have smart accents and good educations? You think because we grew up on council estates we don't have feelings?'

'I'm sorry. I didn't mean that.'

I was flustered by her apology, but didn't know how to accept it. 'What would I want to splatter a rabbit for? I've got nothing against rabbits. Rabbits never did me no harm. No rabbit ever insulted me.'

'I'm sorry. It's just that once, for a very short time, I had a boyfriend who used to deliberately run over anything in the road. He thought it was funny.'

To my surprise a plague of rats began savaging the walls of my stomach. I told myself that jealousy was inappropriate, for all sorts of reasons, but that didn't put an end to it. 'I expect he was one of them public school boys, was he. That's what you'd expect from them.'

'He was actually. But you're wrong about us. We're not what you think we are. My father's not a capitalist. He's not a pig.'

'I know.'

'And he's not even rich.'

'Well it don't look to me as if he's having a nervous breakdown over how he's going to pay the milk bill.'

'No. We're lucky. He sometimes earns a lot of money these days. When he does, he spends it. To make up for all the times we've gone without, he says, so that he could do the thing he wanted to do. And of course, he's got into terrible debt over the house. He hasn't got any money invested. No stocks and shares or anything like that. He thinks it's immoral. Grandad was a shop steward. My parents have always been socialists. He was a working-class boy who went to art college. He's very talented...'

'I'll say he is,' Steve threw in from the back.

'He often sells paintings or gets commissions. His work has become very popular in the last few years. But he's got no security. He could be penniless next year.'

'He's a good man,' I said. 'I can see that from his work. I respect him. I'm sorry about how I had to behave.'

'You didn't *have* to behave like that.'

'What else could I do?'

'We could have sorted it out reasonably.'

'I wasn't to know, was I. It was a chance in a million.'

'It's not too late.'

'Too much shit's flowed down the sewer now.'

'You've got a lovely turn of phrase, vicar,' Steve said.

'It's a pity though,' I said. 'I'm sorry I upset your mum.'

'She's lovely,' Alice said.

'Tell us about her.'

'She's French. She's a cellist. She used to play professionally. She's a wonderful mother. Warm. Loving. She never gets angry. Though Daddy says she was more tempestuous before we were born.'

'You ought to meet *my* mum. That would be an education for you. The sort of education you missed out on in them finishing schools.'

'We didn't go to finishing schools.'

'Well your education can't be finished without meeting my old lady. She's a real laugh. Take the way we got our council house. We used to live in two grotty rooms up the Smoke. Then she meets this priest with dirty habits. Or is it only monks who have dirty habits? Anyway, this priest starts getting up to some monkey business with my old girl. But she can't resist bragging about it all round the congregation. He tries to ditch her, so she starts borrowing money. He could hardly say no, could he. I remember coming home from school one day and finding her standing fuming beside the phone. *Here,* she says, *When someone answers, ask to speak to Father O'Malley.* So she dials, then hands me the phone. When the housekeeper answers I ask for the priest, and soon his voice comes on. She snatches the receiver out of my hand and starts screeching down the phone: *I knew you were there. You ought to be ashamed of yourself. You a priest, and telling lies to a poor widow!* Next thing, he wangles her this council house miles away. It shows how these things work, don' it. We weren't even on the housing list.

'She's always chatting up blokes, my old girl. She'll try it on with anything in trousers. Tally man. Milk man. Insurance man. The man who collects the rent. That's how she pays half her bills. She's a sad case really. She makes advances to every man she meets, but she don't like sex. She can't get a bloke without it, but when she's got a bloke she don't want it. That's why no one will stay with her. She went to this marriage bureau once. I don't know what she put on the form but she got herself a geezer with a Rolls Royce. She made him pick her up from work. She'd get in the Roller outside the factory and sit there till the forewoman drove out in her Mini. Then the geezer had to overtake the Mini so my old one could wave at the forewoman, like Lady Muck, out the window. She's a real laugh at times. Ain't that right, Steve?'

'She's nutty as a fruit cake.'

'She'd put on a right performance if she met you. She'd think you were the sort of girls I ought to go out with. Well, so do I — but for different reasons. Anyway, she'd put on her telephone voice. That's pathetic, that is, hearing a poor person trying to talk posh. She used to keep a scrap book of the queen. Used to cut pictures of the Royals out of the paper and paste them in. She's still got it somewhere. But she don't do it any more. She ain't really got anything now.'

I'd wanted to put them at ease, to be the entertainer. But it wasn't coming out right. Nobody was laughing. Yet I couldn't seem to leave it out, or even change gear. I was like a wound-up talking doll. 'You want to meet her and see how the other half lives. Her house is the furthest extreme of ugly bad taste you could imagine. Everything in it is cheap and nasty. But it's funny, sometimes she surprises you. One time she got a piano. A Freeman's. She must've come the "poor widow" bit at work. She'd never been near an instrument in her life — at least not a musical one. Reminds me of that joke: newly married couple go to the quack for advice on contraception. He gives them a packet of johnnies and tells them to put one on the organ every time they have it off. A few weeks later they're back in tears 'cos the bride's up the spout. *Didn't you do what I told you?* he says. *Yes,* the man said, *except we haven't got an organ so we put one on the piano.*'

Steve guffawed, but the girls didn't seem to be amused, so I hurried on. 'Well, anyway, the day the piano was delivered she sits down and starts playing tunes. By ear. Terrible stuff, mind. Hymns, and all that sort of crap. Next thing she's off on some melodies I've never heard before. *What's that?* I say. *Oh, nothing,* she says. *I just made it up.* She used to love that piano. I took the front off to see how it worked. I used to like watching the old hammers going. Then one day she had this flaming row with her boyfriend. Ron was his name. He was a truck driver. He used to take me with him in the cab sometimes, and give me a few bob for helping with the deliveries. They had this terrific row in the kitchen and she comes storming in. I was sitting on the floor in the living-room, trying to mend a puncture in my bike. She plonks herself down and starts taking it out on the old joanna. Ron comes after her, hopping mad, and gives her a right hander which knocks her off the stool. Then he picks up the stool and starts smashing the piano works with it. Well, my old one goes bananas. She runs out the room and comes back with a carving knife and tells him to get out. *You come at me with that and I'll slit your throat with it,* he says. *I'm not that much of a fool,* she says, *but I'll tell you what, Ron. If you don't get out of my house right now, this minute, the next time you fall asleep I'll cut your balls off, so help me God. I've suffered enough from your tool, and your temper, and enough's enough. So if I were you I'd get out now while you've still got something to hold on to.*

'Blimey, that was a long time ago. But I can remember it as vivid as anything. A perfect summer day. The window was open and the net curtain was billowing in. It didn't seem the right weather somehow for all of that. He called her all the names under the sun, but he went. She never did get another piano. She was a fighter all right. My problem was, whenever she didn't have a bloke it was me she was fighting. When I was a kid I used to lay awake at night and pray for her to die before morning so I wouldn't have to live with her any more. Steve's mum died last week, didn't she, Steve. Another wasted bloody life.'

Alice turned towards Steve. 'I'm sorry.'

'Do you miss her?' Marianne asked him.

'Yes,' he said. 'We never got on very well, but I do.'

'Somehow,' I said, 'I don't feel so bitter towards mine any more. More sort of sorry for her, angry about what happened to her. Know what I mean?'

'What happened to your father?' Alice asked.

'I didn't have a father. My mother caught me off a toilet seat.'

'You must have had one.'

'All I know about him is he was Irish.'

'That's why Darkey's got the gift of the gab,' Steve said.

'He was on shore leave from the merchant navy. The old lady says the two weeks she spent with him were the best two weeks of her life.'

'He must have been a nice man.'

'I don't know. I sort of hope he was. Though it doesn't matter really, does it.'

It was quiet in the car. Just the hum of the engine, and my voice droning on. 'I'm sorry,' I said. 'I didn't mean to go on like this. I just meant to tell you some funny stories.'

We motored on. A T-junction. A hump back bridge. A double bend. And then, there in the lights, with the arrogance of a star in the spotlight on stage, was a tawny owl. I stamped on the brakes and we stopped with a bounce. He, or she, was standing on the grass verge at the side of the road, like a hitchhiker waiting for a lift. There's always an intense thrill when you meet nature unexpectedly. 'Oh, wow!' I said as I pulled up.

'He's *so* beautiful,' Alice said. 'Can you see him, Mari?'

'Yes, he's lovely.'

'Do you think he's saying his prayers, Steve?' I asked.

'Why?'

'He's a bird of prey, isn't he?'

Steve groaned.

'He really is impressive,' Alice said. As she leaned forward into the moonlight I was able to see her face, for the first time unmarked by anger, fear or scorn. Her looks were still bland with youthful inexperience and innocence but you could see that if life treated her well she would grow into a beautiful woman. She caught me gazing at her and held my eyes with hers.

'He's going,' Steve said. 'There he goes.' But I couldn't look, until Alice had released me by turning away, and by then the owl had been swallowed by the night.

'So proud,' Marianne said.

'He wouldn't look so good in a zoo,' I said. I twisted in my seat to look at Marianne. 'Well that was something, little mouse, wasn't it.' She lowered her eyes. 'Aren't you glad you came now? I mean, if you'd stayed home you'd have just done something boring like watch television, or play monopoly, or wash your hair and go to bed. But first we've seen the bunny and then the owl. Who knows what we'll find standing in the middle of the road next.'

'A policeman probably,' Steve said.

'Well if we do, that's one I will hit. I'll mow the bastard down.'

The temperature in the car dropped ten degrees. I could feel that Alice was brittle again, like ice. 'I wish I could stop running off at the mouth,' I said. I slipped the car into gear and we slid smoothly forward into the unknown.

'Where are you taking us?' Alice asked for the second time.

This was the question occupying us all, but Marianne was too timid to ask; Steve didn't want to look foolish by revealing he was as much in the dark as they were; and I still didn't know the answer. 'You'll find out when we get there,' I said, trying to sound as if I did.

'You're still running,' Alice said quietly. 'And you're still scared. And you're still trapped,' and then, mimicking the way I spoke to Marianne, she added, 'little rabbit.'

Checkmate. But I'm a good loser. I've had plenty of practice. 'You're right,' I said at last. We looked into each other's eyes. I sighed and said, 'You're right,' again. 'You know something, Alice?' I said, staring back at the road. 'You're a really fantastic person.'

'I'd still like to know where we're going.'

I thought for a while, and then I said, 'Alice, Marianne, this whole thing got a bit out of hand. But the trouble is, once you get into the mire so far you can't get out again. The truth is, we're up shit creek, Steve and I. I mean, there was no malice intended, but for what we did tonight we could really get the royal shaft. I don't want to sound melodramatic, but if we get sent down for this, we'll really be fucked, you know, in every way. I know how you must feel about us after tonight and everything, but I wonder whether you could be forgiving enough, generous enough, to help us. We actually need your help pretty bad.'

'Let's go back and talk it over with my parents,' Alice said.

'No way. However good they are, relatively speaking, they're a different generation. They've probably called the cops already. I wouldn't trust them. I'd trust you.'

'What do you want us to do?'

'I'm not sure yet,' I said.

We came into a small village: a green just about big enough for a cricket match, as long as you didn't hit the ball too hard and didn't mind triangular boundaries; a well-preserved church; a face-lifted pub; half a dozen residences oozing wealth. 'We should've done one of them instead of your old man's mill,' I said to Alice. 'Except, then I wouldn't have met you, would I.' I pulled up beside a telephone box. 'You'd better give your folks a bulletin,' I said. 'They'll be worried stiff.'

We all four crowded into the box. I was in bodily contact with Alice. I could feel her warmth, and I could smell the smell of her skin and the sweat of her recent fear. I closed my eyes. I wanted to stop running. I wanted to stay where I was. It felt like a good place to be. Alice spoke into the phone. 'Hello, Daddy...Yes. You needn't worry any more. Everything's all right now...They're being very nice to us...We don't know...Tell her not to worry...We're fine, honestly...' She looked at me. 'He's asking where we are.' I shook my head. 'I'd better not say...No, they're not. Everything is fine, really. Please don't set the police onto us or anything.'

Then the receiver was passed to Marianne. She told them everything was all right, that we were being nicer to them now. That she wasn't scared any more. 'Tell them about the owl,' I whispered. Marianne looked at me as though I was off my rocker. I felt like a seven-year-old. 'Well,' I whispered to Alice, '*I* thought it was exciting.'

'It was,' she said.

'Perhaps he was waiting for a pussy cat.'

'Owls don't eat cats,' Steve said.

'Not to eat, dozey — to run away with.'

'Ay?'

'To sea.'

'To see what?'

'To elope in a boat, you dope.'

'The owl and the pussy cat went to sea,' Alice quoted for Steve's benefit, 'In a beautiful pea-green boat.'

'They stole some money,' I added.

'Took,' she corrected.

170

'Well where did they take it from? It doesn't say they took it out of their savings. Taking, lifting — same thing. They stole some money, and plenty of honey, wrapped up in a five pound note.'

'Honey in a five pound note?' Steve said.

'That's where the expression *sticky lolly* comes from.'

The three of us laughed at this silliness, brought on, no doubt, by relief and tiredness.

'No,' Marianne said into the phone, 'not a drop.'

When we got back in the car the atmosphere was quite different — a lot of tension had been siphoned off. 'Our first problem,' I said, 'is where to spend the night. We'll freeze to death if we sleep in the car. The best thing would be to go back to my place.'

Alice turned to look at Marianne. Then she said, 'All right.'

'I'm afraid I won't be able to keep you in a style to which you're accustomed,' I said. 'It'll be a bit cramped.'

'Then perhaps,' Alice suggested, 'you should come home with us.'

'We've already talked about that,' I said. 'We couldn't risk it. I'm sorry about how we behaved earlier. I'm sorry we upset you. And sorry we're upsetting your old ones. In fact I'm sorry we did your place at all, except...well, you'd never have spoke to yobbos like us otherwise.'

'It's a rather extreme way of making friends.'

Friends? She'd said, *friends*. I felt I must be glowing, like someone who's swallowed a fuel rod out of a nuclear reactor.

We were coming into the town by then. It wasn't so much a town as a sprawl of towns that had spread and joined like ink splotches on a blotter, leaving little oases of countryside here and there, like the area where Alice's mill stood. We drove around till we found a phone that hadn't been vandalised so the girls could tell their parents that everything was still all right and that they wouldn't call again till morning. I parked a couple of blocks from my place and we continued on foot. The streets were dark and deserted. I looked for the moon but couldn't see it. I couldn't even see any stars. It was cold enough for our breath to be visible in the light from the street lamps. Our footsteps sounded thunderous on the echoey pavement. I kept looking anxiously over my shoulder. It occurred to me that if the cops were on to us, and had been told we were armed and dangerous, their marksmen might pick me and

Steve off, thinking to save the girls. I kept expecting the sudden pain — the impact — the noise. I wondered which would come first. I walked with my arm around Alice. 'You have to understand,' I'd said, 'that we need to hold you just in case you decided to make a run for it; and so we look natural to anyone passing us in the street.' We walked like lovers, my cheek resting on her hair. Her hair was soft and smelled of apples. My feelings were a hotchpotch of fear and delight, of apprehension and desire. I was a court jester dressed partly in warm red, partly in ice-blue. I was a fool. In a fool's paradise.

As we turned into the street in which I lived I heard, then saw, the man walking towards us. I couldn't breathe. My rib cage had become iron and was winched tighter with each step. Thoughts, like unarmed fugitives fleeing tracker dogs, raced through my mind. Was this the filth? Were there snipers on roof tops? Would one of the girls appeal for help? Then I thought that if I was going to be shot, or put away, the thing I wanted more than anything (the condemned man's last wish) was to kiss Alice. I stopped abruptly in the shadow mid way between two street lamps and turned her to me. I slid my hand inside her collar onto the back of her neck, my fingers splayed and reaching up into her hair. 'Pretend you like me,' I whispered, and kissed her on the mouth. It was so sudden Steve and Marianne stumbled into us. Alice was taken by surprise and froze momentarily, and then softened and melted into the kiss. It was like nothing I'd ever experienced before. It had the softness of a baby's hands and the intensity of a forest fire; the gentleness of a nursing mother and the passion of a terrorist explosion. It was a kiss of life that seemed to spiral up and up into the night sky as the approaching footsteps grew deafeningly louder in my ears; but the steps passed without hesitation and began to fade and we came floating back to earth as gently as down on a windless day.

Alice's lips parted from mine and she turned her face away. I held on to her for support, trembling like a spin dryer. 'I've never been kissed like that before,' I whispered, my voice unsteady and slurred as if over-oiled with alcohol.

'Neither have I,' she said, and we continued on our way like shell-shocked lovers to the chill house and my bleak room. Once the curtains had been drawn, veiling our strange intimacy, I switched on the light and put a coin in the meter for the fire.

'Is this...?' Alice said.

'Yeah. Sorry it's so small. A little rabbit see — a little rabbit hutch. It's all I need.' I had to sit down on the mattress. My knees were still weak.

Marianne and Steve took turns in the bathroom, which was the one used by all the occupants of the house, and I felt ashamed suddenly. Alice sat beside me on the edge of the bed. 'Where are we going to sleep?' she asked.

'Well, I thought, the bed. A lot of people use them. You tend to get a better sleep than you do standing up and leaning on the door.'

'But there's four of us.'

'That's true. I guess we'll have to agree to all turn over at the same time. Steve can squeeze over there by the wall, with Marianne next to him, then you, and I'll lay on the edge till I drop off. Then I'll clamber back on again. Think of yourselves as the cheese and tomato filling in a sandwich. You can choose whether you want to be the cheese or the tomato. See, we have to be in contact with you, otherwise we wouldn't know if you did a bunk in the night, would we.'

'What will you do, once I've locked the bathroom door, if I open the window and scream for help?'

'Oh, they're used to that sort of thing round here. No one would take any notice.'

'What will you do?' Her eyes were serious, big, and brown as chestnuts. And the whites were unmarked and perfect.

'What could I do, Alice? My life is in your hands.'

'Have you ever shot anyone?'

I studied her mouth as she spoke. Her lips were shapely and sensuous, and her small teeth perfectly white and regular. 'You've got a lovely set of gnashers, girl,' I said.

'Have you?' she insisted.

'No. Mine are all crooked. And I've got fillings in my fillings.'

'Have you ever shot anyone?'

I sighed in defeat. 'No,' I said. 'I've never fired a gun in my life.'

'And Steve?'

'He wouldn't know which end the bullet came out of. He's the gentlest person you could meet. Oh, Jesus!' I said. 'Why do I get myself into these crazy situations? Look, Alice, it all seems like a game now. But, believe me, it's no game. I've been lucky with the courts so far, but with the charges they could hang on me for tonight, armed robbery and kidnapping, I could spend the next twenty-five years of my life locked away. I couldn't cope with that — with being caged. You know what battery hens do, don't you. They peck each other raw. They're bald and bleeding and too old to lay when free-range hens are just coming into their prime.' I laid my hand tentatively on hers, expecting hers to be pulled away, but she didn't move. 'I heard about this fox once,' I went on. 'He got caught in a trap. The trap clamped on his foot and held him, and the fox couldn't tear himself free. So he gnawed through his own leg. Through the fur, the skin, the flesh, the bone, the nerves, the tendons. He chewed his own bloody leg right off to get out of the trap. I guess that's what men do in prisons. They peck at each other like hens in batteries and they eat away at themselves like trapped animals.' I insinuated my hand into hers. 'After twenty-five years of that, what would be left of me? I'd be an old man. The kids I could've had would've grown up and gone away. They would've been older by then than I am now. And I'd never have seen them being born, or watched them grow, or played with them. I'd never have spent a single night with someone I loved. And if you scraped all the left-over bits and pieces of me into a heap, you still wouldn't have enough to put together to make a person anyone could love.'

All was quiet, inside the house and out. Then the toilet flushed and I felt the strength drain out of me. I felt exhausted suddenly. I wanted Alice to take me in her arms and cuddle me to sleep. Marianne came in. I patted the bed beside me. 'Come and sit down with us, Mari.'

She came, but sat on the other side of her sister. Alice extricated her hand from mine, and they put their arms around each other. I felt a pain inside like a white-hot burn, but the causes of it were too complex to analyse.

Steve came back. And then Alice, and then I, used the bathroom. I washed, and brushed my teeth, slowly and carefully, thinking about Alice, dreading a sleepless night, wondering what to do in the morning.

When I returned to my room I found Steve sitting on the chair humming *Can't Buy Me Love,* and drumming the rhythm on his thighs with his fingers. The girls were cuddling each other, and Alice was stroking her sister's hair. 'I don't know about you lot,' I said, 'but I'm just about wiped out. I'm going to bed.' I turned off the electric fire and the light. A street lamp showed orange through the thin curtains as we sardined ourselves onto the mattress.

'This must be what it's like to be married to siamese twins,' Steve said.

I lay on my side, rigid as a broom handle, facing Alice, who was lying on her back. 'At least we won't be cold,' she said.

I felt like a starving prisoner who had been sat at a table groaning under the weight of a feast and forbidden to eat. I moved my face into Alice's hair. It felt like cool water on a hot day. I could smell her smell of apples again. 'Tell us about yous,' I said.

'What do you mean?'

'Tell us the story of your life in five one-minute chapters.'

'It wouldn't take that long. There's nothing much to tell. We've just been very lucky, very privileged.'

'Daddy wasn't,' Marianne put in.

'They had times when they were penniless when we were small, but we've mostly been well-off as long as I can remember, or at least we were only hard-up for comparatively short periods, so it didn't matter. Being poor was a sort of game.'

'Daddy would say, *Sorry, girls: pocket money, new clothes, school trips, and treats have been abolished until further notice—piggy bank's empty.* Remember, Ali?'

'Yes. Then after a few months he'd sell something, or get a commission, or Mummy would do a tour leaving us at the mercy of Daddy's cooking, and then we'd go on a shopping spree or have a holiday, and all would be well again.'

I lay in the dark listening to the cosy sounds of their breathing, and the hostile noises of the world outside: tom cats somewhere were threatening each other, a dustbin lid fell and clattered, in the far distance a couple of drunks were shouting or singing, a motorbike's barbarity slashed the sleeping face of the night.

'Go on,' I said.

'There's isn't anything else to say really. Mummy and Daddy were always very loving to us. I get on well with my sister.'

'Most of the time,' Marianne mumbled sleepily.

'Except when I go to find something and she's borrowed it without asking.'

'But she doesn't draw the line at borrowing my things without asking me.'

'What work do you do?' Steve asked.

'I'm studying classical guitar. And Marianne's just started at the Guildhall.'

'Violin.'

'Daddy's parents are super. They lived in a council house till they retired. Grandad worked on the railways. Then Daddy bought them a little cottage, and their garden is a dream.'

'They work really hard.'

'They never stop. Nanny grows flowers and Grandad grows fruit trees from seed. He plants apple pips and carefully nurtures them, and talks about the sort of fruit he will get from the trees as though he believes he's never going to die.'

'He's got lots of old varieties that have almost died out.'

'Our French grandparents were totally different, but lovely too. They were both university teachers. Very formal, and so... civilised. But not at all old-fashioned.'

'They never treated us like children,' Marianne said sleepily, 'even when we were very small. Just like equals really, always discussing politics and philosophy and art.'

'I can't imagine that,' Steve said. 'A home with music and paintings and that.'

'It's like a different species, Steve,' I said. 'Like butterflies and moths. They flit about among the flowers in the sunshine, while we crawl around in heaps of old clothes in the back of a cupboard.'

'You wouldn't criticise him for doing the best for us that he could, would you?'

'Of course not. I wouldn't want to drag you down to our level. It's just envy that's all, and regret.'

'We were just lucky,' Alice said.

'I'm glad.'

'Even when we get kidnapped we get nice kidnappers.'

I moved my face slightly so that it touched hers. I shifted slowly, one part of my body at a time, tense and trembling like the plucked string of a guitar, alert for any sign of anger or displeasure, ready to recoil at once like a woodlouse closing into an armoured ball, but she remained relaxed and unmoving as I snuggled up to her in the slowest of slow motion — a film projected frame by frame.

'The thing I remember best from when I was small,' Alice said dreamily, 'is that Daddy used to put us to bed every night, and he always used to lie down on the bed and sing to us till we fell asleep.'

'I'd sing to you,' I said, 'except I can't sing in tune.'

She laughed. 'Neither could he. But that didn't matter at all.'

'Steve's a good singer,' I said. But I knew he'd be too shy. So I began quietly, tunelessly, singing. And when I ran out of songs, I sang the words of *The Owl and the Pussy Cat* to a tune I made up as I went along. By then they were breathing so evenly I assumed they were all asleep. 'Why don't we go to sea, Alice?' I whispered, not thinking she would hear me.

'Have you become an owl now,' she murmured, 'instead of a rabbit?'

'You've become a pussy cat,' I said, 'instead of a tiger.'

She turned her face to me and we were kissing, mouth to mouth, tongue to tongue. Then I heard myself say something I'd never ever said before in my life. 'I love you,' I said.

'That's a funny thing to say to a hostage,' she replied.

Early next morning Steve and I took the girls out to phone, then returned to my room for breakfast. Three of us squatted on the mattress and Steve sat facing us on the chair. 'What now?' he asked, his mouth full of bread and honey.

'First thing, fence the loot, then wrap up the takings in a five franc note and go to sea in a boat.'

'What you on about?'

'Going to France.'

'France,' he said, taking another bite. 'Oh, wow! We can go to the Opera.'

'What?'

'We can go to the Opera.'

'The what?' I thought that, because he was eating, I'd misheard. 'Listen, don't eat with your mouth full.'

'The Opera. The Opera House in Paris.'

'The opera is very good in Paris,' Marianne said.

I stared at Steve in amazement. 'Since when are you interested in opera?'

'I'm not interested in opera.'

'Oh, I see. You're not interested in opera, so you want to go to the opera.'

'I want to see the Chagall.'

'The what?'

'The Chagall. The ceiling.'

'I didn't know you could speak French.'

'I can't.'

'You can't speak French, so you were speaking French.'

'I wasn't speaking French.'

'Didn't I understand you to say that "shag-all" is French for "ceiling"?' Alice burst out laughing, and Marianne nearly came to grief choking on a mouthful of tea.

'No,' Steve said. 'No, listen. Chagall is a painter. A Russian painter. He painted the ceiling in the Paris Opera.'

I blushed with shame now for my ignorance. 'What colour did he paint it?' I said sarcastically. 'Public lavatory green?'

'I've only ever seen it in books,' Steve said.

'Maybe instead of selling us seats they'd let us lie on the floor all through the show so's we can get a good butcher's at it. Anyway, once those crooks have finished cheating us we won't be able to afford luxuries like the opera.'

The girls weren't laughing any more. 'You don't have to sell our things,' Alice said.

'I'm sorry, Alice, but we've got no choice. We need the bread. It's our ticket to freedom. What else can we do?'

'I've got money,' she said.

'Enough for four of us to get to Paris?'

'Four?'

'Yes.'

'Don't be silly.'

I could feel anger rising in me, fuelled by hurt and fear. 'Alice. Last night. What happened last night?'

'What did happen last night?' Steve asked.

'I can't just run away like that,' Alice said.

I got on my knees so I could face her. 'They sailed away for a year and a day,' I yelled. 'Hand in hand they danced on the sand!'

'Shuttup, Darkey!' Steve hissed. 'Bloody nutcase.'

'Look, Alice, I don't want to be rich. I don't want to be famous. I just don't want to keep getting fucked in the eye for the rest of my life. I don't know what happened last night, Alice, but I do know that I want you. You're the best thing that ever happened to me, and I don't want to lose you. I can't go away from you, but if I don't go away they'll put me away. I need you Alice. I want you. I love you. Please, come with me.'

She hesitated. I was standing naked in the dock, waiting for the jury foreman to pronounce.

She moved forward so that she was on her knees too, and put her arms round me. 'I'll tell you what, Darkey,' she said. It sounded strange and beautiful, my name on her lips. 'We'll drive down to Dover and take the hovercraft across to France. We've got an apartment in Paris because Daddy sells most of his paintings there. If we leave now we can be at the flat this afternoon. We could even go to the opera this evening. I'll stay with you tonight, but I'll come home tomorrow. You and Steve can stay at the apartment. No one will be going there till Christmas at the earliest. I'll leave you money for food. I'll talk to my parents tomorrow when I get home. Then I'll phone you. I'll let you know if it's safe to come back. Otherwise I'll come over to see you soon.'

'You've got enough for that?'

'I've got credit cards. Money's not a problem.'

I felt like a child. 'Okay,' I said. 'Sounds great.' I looked at Marianne who was sitting on the bed. 'You could go back home if you wanted,' I said.

'Thanks a million,' Steve said.

'No,' Marianne said. 'I'll stay with Ali.'

The girls phoned home from Dover. They were as reassuring as possible without giving anything away, but the parents sounded more edgy — the waiting between calls was getting them down. Steve and I were excited, like kids being taken to the fair, but trying not to show it. Neither of us had been abroad before — or on a hovercraft. It was a long haul to Paris, but I insisted on driving. Alice directed me through the city, and we crossed the Seine. My senses were greedy; everything was strange and new. The apartment was on a wide, tree-lined avenue. We had to go on a couple of hundred metres to find a space to park. It was good to leave the car and use our legs. It was sunny, and several degrees warmer than it had been in England.

It was an expensive street. Antiques. Modern and reproduction furniture. A delicatessen. Chic clothes. Jewellery. Patisseries brazenly flaunting cakes brimming with cream, and tarts bulging with feasts of fruit. A shop that sold nothing but glass paperweights: multi-faceted like diamonds, crystal clear, shivered rainbow. And of course on every corner a café, with potted palms on the pavement and penguin waiters.

We halted outside huge wooden double doors. Alice pressed numbered buttons on a panel inset into the stone wall and in response to a 'buzz' opened a small door in one of the larger ones. We passed through a dim passageway into a small courtyard. After the concrete din of the city streets it was breathtaking in its unexpected green beauty: a carpet of ground cover; a medley of shrubs; two tall, elegant trees, still with their autumn foliage; and a backdrop of ivy covering its three stone walls. Alice spoke cheerily to an elderly woman who appeared in a doorway at the foot of the stairs. 'She's telling the concierge you're friends who will be staying awhile,' Marianne said. I could see by the way the old dragon was eyeing us that she wasn't thrilled at the prospect.

We walked up to the fourth floor. 'Who's this "Fairy Anne", then?' I asked Alice.

'Fairy Anne?'

'Yeah. You and the old dear kept going on about Fairy Anne.'

Alice's laughter filled the stairway. 'Ça ne fait rien,' she said. 'It means, "It doesn't matter".'

The apartment, which had been inherited from the grandparents, had three bedrooms, a living-room, kitchen and bathroom. The rooms were large, the ceilings high, and the cornices elaborate. In contrast to the modern style of the converted mill, the furniture was antique, or at least old. It was stuffy in there because the whole block was centrally heated. Marianne went round opening windows and shutters. 'Look,' she said. 'You can see the Eiffel Tower.' We crowded onto a tiny balcony with a black wrought iron railing, above the busy street, and there it was, looming over the muddle of roof tops like a giant prick a kid had made with a rusty meccano set.

Alice tried to call home, but there were no lines free and she was told to try again later. She then phoned to arrange seats at the opera. 'It's Puccini's *La Bohème*,' she told Steve. But it was all the same to him. 'I'm exhausted,' she said. 'Let's have a rest, then go out for a meal.'

She took my hand and led me to her room. Without needing to speak we undressed and climbed into the single bed. We lay holding each other for a long time. I let my hand settle like a fallen leaf on her belly, and then on her breast, and we began to kiss. Slowly, so slowly, gently, wonderfully, we made love. I was a boat on a soft undulating sea. I was the earth and above me a slender tree swayed and moaned in a tropical wind. I was steel drilling through earth to reach clear water. I was a sea gull lifted by invisible currents to heights I'd never known, and carried this way and that, up and down on an ever changing wind. I was weightless and warm and secure. I had been lost for a lifetime and at last, for the first time, I had come home. I had been an aching prisoner serving a life sentence, but the bars of my cage had dissolved and I had found freedom. For a moment which seemed to be outside time the tension of my nineteen years evaporated from my body and I was safe.

We lay, wet with sweat, pressed so close our bodies, moulded into one another, felt as if they had merged. 'Why are you crying?' she asked. And she wiped tears from my skin with the hands of a sculptor shaping the face of a lover in clay.

'I'm not.' I said. In reply she kissed the new tears forming in my eyes. 'I thought there was just fucking,' I said. 'I've never made love before.'

We showered. I washed her. Her hair. Her body. Arms. Hands. Breasts. Arse. Cunt. Legs. I washed her feet. I was worshipping my Goddess. And then she washed me, her hands strong and gentle. We stood entwined under the waterfall of our momentary Eden. The gushing water seemed to be washing away the dirt of all my years. I felt, for the first time in my life, clean. I felt tall. I was conscious of myself, and I liked myself. I was a Greek athlete. A God. I felt that we must be the most beautiful man and woman in the world.

I put on a clean white T-shirt, jeans, and my black leather jacket. I still had the shooter in my pocket. I'd grown used to the good secure feeling the weight of it gave me. I put my hand in my pocket so I could hold it and looked at myself in the mirror.

'You'd better put something else on,' Alice said.

'Why?'

'For the opera.'

'What's wrong with this?'

'They're funny about things like that here. They're very formal and old-fashioned.'

'If we've got tickets there's nothing they can do about it.'

Steve appeared. Marianne had dressed him in a jacket several sizes too large and a shirt and tie from her father's wardrobe.

'You look very smart,' I said derisively.

'That's more than I could say for you,' he said.

We went out to eat. Dim wall-lights flanking oval mirrors. Fresh flowers in a vase on the dazzling white cloth. The table in a tiny cubicle, so that we had to squeeze close to our partner. Steve was glowing. Marianne looked happy at last. We drank wine with our meal. A lot of wine. Too much. Before we had finished, the world was slightly out of focus and its soundtrack not quite in synch. I felt spongy. When I stood up I found that I was still on the hovercraft. We walked through strange streets that smelled of excitement. We were laughing and singing. I felt overflowing with love, for Marianne and Steve as well as for Alice.

We went into a café to use the phone. 'We're in France...Yes...It's all right, Mummy. They just wanted to get out of the country. They're being very good to us. We'll be home tomorrow and I'll tell you the whole story then...No, Mummy. Better not...Yes, Mummy, really...No, we're free now...Well, yes, Mummy. Please don't worry. We'll be coming home tomorrow. We'll be home tomorrow evening...They will, Mummy, honestly. We're safe. Don't worry, Mummy, love. Please don't worry...'

Mummy, Mummy, Mummy! I hated that word. I hated the fond way she said it. I slammed my hand down on the telephone cradle. She turned on me in anger. 'What did you do that for?' She was a tiger again. A wild cat. Ready to spring at me. To claw my face.

'Mummy!' I sneered. 'Mummy, Mummy, Mummy, Mummy!' And I was suddenly and inexplicably on the verge of tears. I put my face in my hands. 'I'm sorry,' I said.

'That was a stupid thing to do.'

'I know. I know. I'm sorry. Phone her again.'

'I've got no more change. I'll phone her later from home. Come on or we'll be late.'

The opera house was a huge tomb of greyish-white, like a mouldering square wedding cake, with groups of green-winged angels on the top, and besmirched white statues guarding the doorways. Pigeons and people flocked outside among the litter and broken wine bottles on the vast terrace of stone steps. The foyer was all marble and archways, statues and staircases, hustle and bustle, hubbub and light. I took the tickets from Alice. A uniform barred the way. 'What's he on about?' I asked.

'He says you can't come in without a tie.'

'A tie? What's a tie got to do with anything?' I spoke directly to the uniform. 'Fairy Anne,' I said. 'Fairy Anne.' I tried to push past but two more uniforms joined him and wouldn't let me through. 'I paid good money for this ticket,' I shouted. 'I've bought the bloody seat so I've got a right to sit in it. What's a tie got to do with it? You don't listen to singing through your bloody tie. Unless that's where you keep your deaf-aid. I listen through my bloody ear'oles. Look! Look! Look!' I yelled, showing the uniforms my ears. 'And anyway, I don't even want to listen to the flaming music. All I want to do is look at the sodding ceiling.'

'Darkey! Darkey! Please! Please!' Alice was saying. 'Come away!' She was pulling my arm.

'Okay, okay.' We all four walked out onto the grey steps in the chilly autumn night. 'Okay. I've got to have a tie. Alrighty-tighty. I'll have a tie. Steve, give us your tie.'

'What's the use of that?' he said. 'Then I won't have one.'

'Yes, you will. Yes, you will. You don't think I'd go in the bleeding opera without you, do you. This is for you. Especially for you. Just give us your tie, will you.'

'It doesn't matter,' Alice said. 'We can come another time.'

'If the Vietnamese had all been like you,' I said, 'they'd never've beat the bleeding Yanks. We paid our money. Your dad worked hard to earn that. We've got a right to go in.'

Steve took off his tie and handed it to me. I pulled it out to its full length, then bit into the material about half way along. I made a tear with my teeth, then ripped the tie in half. 'Here y'are, mate.' I handed one half to Steve who put it on, while I tied the other half round my neck above my T-shirt. 'How does that look?' I asked. We were laughing helplessly at the little ragged ties. 'There. That's a tie, isn't it? Come on, then. In we go. They can't stop us now.'

Steve and I marched shoulder to shoulder back to the barrier. The girls followed. I proffered our tickets, but massed uniforms blocked our passage. 'I've got a bloody tie on,' I protested. 'You said I had to have a tie to come in and now I've got a tie so I'm bloody coming in. My mate wants to see the ceiling for Christ's sake. Come on, Stevey!' We dodged and weaved through the over-dressed ruck of posh night-outers. There was shouting and running feet and rough hands yanking my clothes and pulling my hair. 'You're like the little men who drove the trains for Hitler!' I screamed. And though I struggled, I had the sensation of being caught by the undertow of a strong tide on a stony beach, the water dragging me, the stones battering me, and then I was flying — a human cannonball, and then the jarring shock as my body slammed into granite, its unyielding ridges biting and bruising me as I bumped and bounced down the steps.

When I ceased rolling I was hurting in so many places I didn't know which pain to be concerned about most. It was almost impossible to breathe, to move, to get up. Someone was helping me. It was Alice. Her hands were like soothing cream on burns. She was kissing me. Her face was wet with tears. 'Are you all right?' she was asking, over and over.

'Sure,' I said. 'Never felt better in my life. Aaaahh!' It was agony to stand straight but I was laughing and Marianne was helping Steve limp towards me like a wounded comrade. The laughter came bubbling up out of me like water out of a spring and we were all laughing again in a confused jumble of four bodies, each leaning on and clinging to the others. 'Well,' I asked. 'Are we going to give it another try?'

'Certainly not,' Alice said.

'But Steve wants to see the shag-all,' I said. 'Shag-all — that's French for ceiling.' And we laughed again hysterically.

'He can see it another time.' Alice insisted through her laughter, 'After I've bought you a jacket and tie.'

'Another time?' I argued. 'He might be dead by tomorrow. He might go to his grave and never've seen it.' And we all laughed.

'Don't worry,' she said. 'It's going to be there for a long time.'

I didn't like giving up so easily. On the other hand I was too sore to be keen on getting thrown out again. 'Okay,' I said. 'Fairy Anne. Fairy Anne.'

'Fairy Nuff,' added Steve.

We set off home. We decided to walk rather than take the metro. We'd got into the frame of mind of having a night out.

We strolled or hobbled along, gazing in shop windows, and staring at squares, and statues, and churches. We had a rest by the river for a while, stopped often to kiss, and twice went into a bar for a drink. We played several rowdy games of table football. Alice couldn't stop scoring goals. The girls had never played before. 'Beginner's luck,' Alice said.

It was quite late when we got back to the avenue where they lived. I was tired. My feet ached. My body was bruised and sore. But I was happier than I'd ever been in my life. We were hungry again, so we went into a café and gorged chocolate cake and drank strong, bitter coffee. I held hands with Alice. She began wiping chocolate from her lips with a serviette. I pushed the serviette away from her mouth and licked her lips clean, and kissed her. 'I love you,' I said. 'That sounds corny, but I mean it. I really mean it. What's "I love you" in French?'

'Je t'aime.'

'Je tem.'

'Je t'aime aussi,' she said.

'In a few moments,' I said, 'we'll be in bed together. We'll be naked. Our bodies will be warm and our skin soft, and we'll make love gently, and savagely, and we'll laugh and shout and go to another land.'

'Shush! You're talking too loud. Everyone's staring.'

'Who cares? Paris is for lovers. Let the world hear. You know what.

That land we go to — that's what they mean by Paradise. I never thought Paradise existed before. But now I know. It's the place where everything is beautiful. Where you escape from all the sad and hurting things that fill this world. You know something? I never realised before this afternoon, but I hurt all the time. I mean I really hurt. But this afternoon the hurt went away.'

'And this evening at the opera house it came back again,' Steve said.

'Right,' I said. 'But this afternoon the hurt went away for a while — and that was Paradise. And that's where we can go again.'

Alice stroked my cheek and I looked deep into the warmth of her eyes. Eyes as brown as rich earth. 'You are a lovely man,' she said. 'Your eyes are the same colour as your hair. And you look as mischievous as a devil.'

'I doubt whether they allow devils into Paradise,' Marianne said.

'They certainly don't allow them into the opera house,' Steve said.

'Don't remind me,' I said. 'I hope the shag-all falls on their stupid heads.'

'Not before I've seen it,' Steve said.

'Hey! Got a pen?' I asked. 'Somebody give me a pen.'

Marianne rummaged in her bag and handed me a biro.

'I,' I said, 'am going to write a poem. For Alice.' I took a paper serviette from the dispenser and smoothed it out on the table, and began to write. Three heads crowded round, merging their shadows on the paper. 'Get out,' I said. 'You can't look till it's finished. It might not work. It's just an idea.'

And, trying to shield my writing from them with my arm, I wrote: *For Alice.* I had to write very gently so that the pen didn't tear the soft paper.

> *There is no reason*
> *why it should be me*
> *who sleeps with you*
> *(the men in chains and cells —*
> *their flesh is crying too)*
> *but I want to kiss your mouth and skin*
> *I want to be at home*
> *in you.*

I read it through a couple of times, then let the others see it. Tears came into Alice's eyes, and she kissed me.

'It's beautiful,' Marianne said.

'You're a poet and don't know it,' Steve said.

'Well you're an artist,' I said, 'so draw something.'

Steve took the pen and a serviette and with just a few lines drew two hands holding each other. That amazes me when somebody can do that. Just draw something that looks like what it's supposed to be. One was a man's hand and the other a woman's. He wrote: *For Marianne. Love Steve*. And handed it to her shyly. I looked at them and suddenly realised how beautiful they both were. There was a mousiness about them both: they were pretty and soft and harmless. And in both their faces was a gentle eagerness for life, a quiet enthusiasm, an undemanding optimism. And I thought that if Alice and I lived together, and that if Steve and Marianne did too, they'd be my family. And Alice's mother and father would be like parents to me also. And behind me the days of greyness, of ugliness, of cold squalor, were dying and being laid to rest. While in front of me there was morning, there was springtime, there was sunshine. 'Come,' I said to Alice. 'Let's go. I want to make love with you.'

Alice left money on the table, and we strolled along the glitzy avenue to the apartment building. I had one arm round Alice's waist. My other hand was in my pocket holding the pistol. I felt invulnerable. Alice pressed the magic numbered buttons and the small door buzzed and she pushed it open. We all four stepped through into the dark passage. The door clicked closed behind us. As my eyes grew accustomed to the dimness I realised there were four men in front of us standing in a semi circle, and they were uniformed. Maybe it was the drink. Maybe it was my stupidity. Maybe it was too many Hollywood movies. As if by reflex, with my left arm I pulled Alice in front of me as a shield and my right hand pulled the shooter out of my pocket and thrust it forward. And as if my arm controlled theirs the snouts of four guns lunged towards us. Steve cried, 'No!' and pushed Marianne behind him and the dim light reflecting on one of the barrels burst into vivid brightness and I felt tiny particles of something wet and warm splatter onto my face. There were screams. Steve was lying now on the cobbles at my feet. Part of his face wasn't where it should have been. It was Marianne who was screaming.

'Throw down the gun!' someone was shouting in English. The voice had a French accent. 'Throw down the gun!'

Its clatter as it landed echoed in the entry. I just stared at what should have been Steve's face. There was part of a face there. There was skin. and blood. And bone. White bone and white teeth. Scattered. Messed up.

Then Alice wasn't next to me any more. I was alone. Someone was ordering me to do something. I couldn't take my eyes off Steve. A blow in the face spun me round, tore my eyes away like tearing my arm free from a factory machine that had taken and chewed up my hand. They put my hands against the wall, above my head, kicked my feet apart, and frisked me. Then I was being dragged away.

'Alice!' I cried.

There was no reply.

So many *if only*s. I sit here in this cell in an English prison, torturing myself with *if only* this and *if only* that.

Since I was sentenced I've had only two visits. My mother came once. At first we had nothing to say. Then she got on to, 'How could you do such a thing?' 'You've disgraced me.' 'To think that a son of mine.' And so on.

I said, 'Don't give me that. Do you think I'd be here if it wasn't for you? I'm doing time for me, and I'm doing time for you, and for my father, whoever he was, and for all the other pricks who passed through you.'

The row got worse. She left saying she would never come again.

The only person who I wanted to see, who I want to see, came just once. She sat, and her eyes were tears which she hadn't meant to shed, and her face was a blur because of mine. The notice said: *VISITORS ARE NOT ALLOWED TO TOUCH THE PRISONERS. ANYONE INFRINGING THIS REGULATION WILL BE REMOVED.* Yet all I wanted in the world was to be touched by her, to be held. And the space between us, I thought, was twenty years wide. But it was more than twenty years in fact. It was a lifetime. The width of death itself.

'How's Marianne?'

'She's much better now.'

'Your parents?'

'They're well.'

'You?'

She didn't answer. She bit her lip cruelly. Her hands tore a tissue to shreds. 'How are *you*,' she said.

'Don't ask.'

The silences were filled with our choked attempts to speak. We tried to hold back the tears, lest once they began to flow, the pain trying to thunder out of the body like an express out of a blocked tunnel might literally tear the frame apart.

'I love you, Alice.'

'Don't.'

'Je tem.'

'I can't wait for you.'

I wondered if a screw had knocked me off the chair. They were attacking me again. They were sitting on my chest. I couldn't breathe. Gradually I resurfaced. I was still in the visiting room.

'We'd be old,' I said.

'And the baby would be grown up.'

'Baby?'

'Our baby.'

Time was a white hot laser of pain. I don't know for how long.

'I'm pregnant,' she said.

'Mine?'

'Yes.'

'It's what I wanted more than anything.'

'I know.'

'But not like this.'

No more words would come. The letters on the notice were steel bars. Were leather straps holding me in the chair.

'I won't visit again.'

'You must.'

'I shan't write.'

'You're all that's keeping me alive.'

'I'll never see you again, Darkey. I don't want our child to grow up without a father like you did. We're selling the house. Moving away. I'll start a new life. When I meet a man who I think will be a good father for your child, I'll marry him. It'll be the best thing for the baby, Darkey. You must want that, don't you?'

I had to summon every ounce of strength from my twenty years to break the straps that held me. I took hold of the bars like a latter day Samson and tore them apart. The building was falling in on me, crushing me. Bricks and mortar. Stone and timber. But I had to go to her. I had to hold her. But it was like trying to run on the bottom of the sea. I could hear her cries. Fading away. Receding down that long tunnel that led to life. I fought to go after her. But the prison fell on me and trapped me and paralysed me. I was smashed by the rubble, choked by the dust, crippled for life.

I have no visitors. I receive no letters. I still have more than nineteen years in which to share this cell with Steve who is with me with half his face shot away. Steve who never finished his painting of the bride and groom. Steve who I realised I loved like a brother. Steve whose flesh was splattered onto my face by stupidity — mine and theirs. And I don't know how we can survive, Steve and I. I don't know how we can survive the humiliations and the indignities, the brutalities and the rapes. It wasn't like the prosecution made out at the trial. I have written down this story of what it was really like. This is what has helped me to survive so far. But now it is finished? What now?